THE FAVORITE CHILD

CATHRYN GRANT

INKUBATOR
BOOKS

Published by Inkubator Books
www.inkubatorbooks.com

ISBN (eBook): 978-1-915275-88-2
ISBN (Paperback): 978-1-915275-89-9
ISBN (Hardback): 978-1-915275-90-5

PROLOGUE

Flames ripped across the night sky. They seemed driven to consume the surrounding atmosphere as completely as the pale green three-story home they were devouring. The sound was like ten thousand insects gnawing on wood and plaster. Teeth and jaws crunching through rooms imagined and brought to life in the Victorian era, restored to their original beauty forty years ago, and meticulously maintained every year since. Gone with the lick of a one-thousand-degree Fahrenheit tongue of fire.

The odor of smoke suggested a pleasant bonfire, not the death raging through the house, filling pale pink lungs, asphyxiating peacefully sleeping bodies.

It burned freely for an hour before the shriek of fire trucks pierced the chilly night air of the northern California coast. Far too much time had passed before the emergency call was placed, but there were other things that had to be taken care of first. The story needed to be believable and airtight for the police.

1

The moonlight poured through the bedroom window. It woke me from a dream that was already slipping through my fingers as my eyes opened. I was glad to escape it, but something about the way the light filled our bedroom gave me the feeling I might have stepped into another dream.

It was always this way when Michael and I stayed at my parents' home. The bed was familiar but not; the room was our own, but not ... and the house where I'd grown up was such a part of me that it appeared frequently in my dreams whether I was sleeping under its eaves or at our home in Mountain View.

I got out of bed. My throat was dry, my tongue tacky against the roof of my mouth. I placed my hand on my round belly. I passed a soundless word of comfort to our baby girl curled inside my womb, her sleep undisturbed at the moment. My bare feet brushed the cool wood floor as I walked to the door and opened it. I moved along the silent hallway and down the curving staircase to the first floor.

In the kitchen, I filled a glass with water and took a small sip, hoping that would tell me whether I was awake or dreaming, even now. My body was moving, my thoughts were coherent, but the feelings from the dream gave me the sense I was still in another place. Wind seemed to be cutting through the thin fabric of my nightgown. Strands of hair had plastered themselves across my face, clinging to my skin for dear life. I was scared. But I had no idea why.

Dreams in my parents' home often featured my older brother and sisters, probably because when I was sleeping there, they were also home visiting. It was as if we all reverted to our former selves when we came home, and that childhood world recreated itself in my dreams. Jake telling us girls how life worked, the shifting alliances among us, the jealousy that ate at our roots but was never to be talked about. Never. The Ledger family didn't indulge in petty emotions like jealousy. Shunning that kind of self-pity kept our family strong.

I carried my glass of water to the living room, taking small sips as I passed through the cold rooms. Everything was so quiet. Even my breath was difficult to hear. Was I walking in my sleep? But if I was, would I be having that thought? Would I be aware of cool water running across my tongue and down my throat?

I went to the bay window that looked out across the flower garden, then to the wild growth of beach grasses and junipers and Monterey pines that stood between the house and the edge of the cliff, with the dark waves of the seemingly endless Pacific Ocean beyond.

Perched near the edge of the cliff was a gazebo. Inside, clearly visible in the moonlight, was a woman wearing a white dress with straps crisscrossing the back. My sister, Sunday, had worn a dress like that to dinner the evening before. As I watched, she rushed out of the small, round structure. Another figure stumbled after her, grasping at the back of her dress, but she broke free and ran. The other one wore dark clothing and a jacket with a hood, impossible to tell if it was male or female. They chased after her, caught the skirt of her dress, and pulled her close. The two began wrestling with each other.

The glass of water started to slide out of my hand as I realized the one wearing the dress was dangerously close to the edge of the cliff.

I cried out, hardly realizing I was shouting, forgetting they couldn't possibly hear me. "No! Stop!" I slammed the glass on the windowsill, splashing water on my hand. Were they trying to hurt Sunday or the opposite? Then Sunday seemed to collapse, or disappear completely, as if she'd gone over the edge of the cliff.

I turned and raced out of the living room, through the foyer, and out the front door. I ran along the path that wound through the garden and began thrashing through the wild grasses and across rough ground, trying to get to the cliff. There was a path, but the moonlight didn't touch the ground enough for me to see where it was with all the wild growth. Small stones cut my feet, and long, waving beach grass grabbed at my legs and the hem of my nightgown, slowing my progress.

Finally, after what seemed like half an hour, but was only a few minutes, I reached the open space around the gazebo. The building was empty. Sunday and the other person were nowhere in sight.

I moved carefully, stepping closer to the edge of the cliff. The cold was more intense now that I'd stopped moving. The wind was stronger, coming right off the open ocean. It tugged at me as if to pull me closer, pushing me to lose my balance.

Looking over the edge made my stomach collapse into a thick liquid that felt like raw egg. One moment, I wanted to jump off, to know what it felt like; the next, I was certain someone would shove me over, and I would be crushed on the rocks below.

As I looked down, I shivered. I felt my body sway. I expected to see a white dress fanned across the rocks around Sunday's broken body. There was nothing but darkness and a streak of moonlight across boulders dark with water. Could she have fallen where the moonlight wasn't touching the rocks? Should I climb down the narrow trail that led to the strip of sand and rocks? Should I get Michael?

There was no longer any doubt I was awake, but had I been walking in my sleep when I saw Sunday and the other person? Still dreaming a dream that seemed so familiar? In that half-awake state where the mind creates nonsense stories? No one was here now. The other figure had disappeared as cleanly as Sunday. I continued staring down at the rocks, willing my eyes to see through the darkness, straining to find anything that told me she'd fallen, half-sobbing in fear that she had.

Why, when I looked over these sharp-edged cliffs, did I always expect to see a body on the rocks below? There was always a compulsion to look down, and always that expectation. Where did it come from? I hated it, and I couldn't get rid of it. I moved back.

It was a dream. I was sure of it. The violent struggle, Sunday's disappearance as if she'd been pushed over. I was alone out here. Hadn't I dreamed something like this before? Many times? I hated the edge of that cliff. Hated the sheer drop. Hated how we'd grown up with that threat of sudden death just a few hundred yards from our play yard.

I made my way back to the house and up the front steps. Inside, I climbed the stairs to the second floor and went to Sunday's bedroom. Slowly, I turned the knob and opened the door a few inches. Sunday's body was clearly visible, curled up under the comforter. I opened the door wider and saw her blonde- and brown-streaked hair spread across the pillow. I whispered her name, but she didn't move. Her white dress was on the floor. I considered tiptoeing inside and touching it to feel if it was cold from the night air. Was she truly asleep? If she was, I didn't want to wake her from a pleasant dream. I closed the door carefully and walked down the hall to my room.

As I pulled my own comforter over my shoulders, I was sure I'd been awake the entire time. But at the same time, it still felt like the kind of vivid dream that clings to your brain long after you wake. Sunday was not lying dead at the base of the cliff. She was sleeping peacefully in her bed. I wondered how long I'd stood at the edge, looking down at the rocks and the crashing surf.

2

The way my parents treated Sunday was like something out of a gothic novel. It wasn't normal, in modern times, for parents to give most of their attention, lavish gifts, and more privileges to one child, was it? Other families we knew weren't like this. It made my parents seem like monsters in some ways, although in every other part of our lives, and the way they treated us individually, they were relatively normal parents. They didn't neglect the rest of us. They were warm and interested in our lives. We had more than most children. We were loved and cared for— we just existed in the shadowy edges of the spotlight that surrounded Sunday.

Sunday was showered with privileges and gifts and attention that were so blatantly beyond what the rest of us were offered, what choice did we have but to envy her? But envy was a quality that did not reflect well on a person's character, so my parents directed us to find ways to keep it from taking possession of our hearts.

My father, Dave Ledger, was a family wellness guru. At his insistence, everyone called him Dave instead of David. He assured them he wasn't a guru. Instead, they should think of him as a wiser older brother. He'd made a fortune writing books, giving speaking tours, and hosting weeklong retreats where he helped families follow the same principles that shaped our family. Principles that he believed were critical to keeping a family solid and strong, resulting in lifelong love and commitment. Solid families valued the family unit above the individual, so they avoided breeding selfishness. They kept their emotions under control, eliminating destructive drama, and they didn't allow jealousy to poison their relationships. Above all, they were loyal to one another.

His principles were the foundation for productive, happy children and produced marriages that lasted until death. The family was the primary building block of society. Without strong families, the entire culture would fracture and crumble. Humanity would descend into chaos. My father was going to change the world, one family at a time.

I didn't feel the same uncontrolled jealousy of Sunday that Jake and Collette did. Maybe it was because I was younger, and I never knew life without Sunday. Maybe I'm just not a jealous person. Maybe I could see that Sunday didn't have everything they thought she did. There was no doubt she had a much larger bedroom, private horseback riding lessons, and trips alone with our parents, and that she went to a more expensive college. But she didn't have the fierce loyalty of siblings that the three of us had. I could see how much that hurt her.

Like my other two siblings, I did grow up craving attention from our parents. It was almost a sickness with us at times, how much we wanted them to notice us, at least, more than they did. It wasn't that they failed to pay attention. But the imbalance with Sunday made us desire it unnaturally.

All of it bothered me even less now that I was pregnant, partially because my parents acted as if I were carrying the next Dalai Lama in my womb. My father wanted me seated beside him at the dinner table now, and when the meal was over, he placed his hand on my belly, feeling my baby's presence there, waiting for the small flutter of her feet as she shifted gently inside me. My mother, Paula, looked at me with happy tears in her eyes whenever she caught my gaze, as if we shared a secret my sisters and sister-in-law weren't privy to.

After years of longing for just a little more from them, the extra love felt nice. It softened the edges of what had gone before, and made me glad to be home for our annual summer holiday.

THE MORNING after my waking dream—or my sleepwalking, or whatever it had been—I didn't mention the experience to Michael right away. He was so protective of me now that I was pregnant. He wouldn't have liked it that I'd been wandering around barefoot in the dark, especially outside, risking tripping and falling, possibly hurting the baby or myself. I would tell him eventually, but I was still trying to figure out which part had been a dream and which part was real.

After we'd all had breakfast, Sunday pushed her chair away from the table and stood while the rest of us were still finishing our cups of coffee or tea. "Why don't we go for a ride, Dad?"

"Don't beg," my mother said. "It's off-putting."

"I'm trying to talk to Dad." She turned her back to my mother, deliberately straightening her shoulders, taking my father's hand. "I'd like to have a father-daughter chat. It's a perfect day, not a wisp of fog. I'll ask Quinn to—"

"Your father has to work on his next podcast episode," my mother said. "He doesn't have time."

"Dad can speak for himself." Sunday didn't even look at

my mother. It seemed as if she couldn't care less what my mother was complaining about, which was strange.

"He's put it off for three days. It needs to get done today," my mother said.

"Maybe for an hour ..." my father said.

"No." My mother stood and walked around the table to stand near Sunday. "He can't go. Don't pressure him like this."

Sunday dropped my father's hand and whirled around to face my mother. "I'm not pressuring him. I asked him to go horseback riding for one hour."

"He can't go."

"Dad?"

"I probably should get—"

"It's one hour. I haven't had time alone with you all week."

"There's plenty of time," my mother said. "No rush. Let him get his work done."

"Why are you talking for him?"

"Because you're being needy."

"I'm not."

I didn't think she was being needy at all. I didn't understand my mother. She never tried to stop Sunday from doing anything she wanted. Never. Her strange, sharp attitude added to the distorted feelings I'd had in the middle of the night. Why was my mother so determined to stop Sunday from going riding with my father? What was the big deal? She acted as if it was the worst thing she could imagine.

Sunday pulled her phone out of her pocket. She entered her passcode and pressed a number. "Quinn, will you saddle Evergreen and Nobility? My dad and I are—"

My mother reached for the phone, trying to pry it out of Sunday's hand.

Sunday lifted it above her head. My mother jumped slightly, batting at her arm. What was wrong with her?

"I can go for an hour," my father said.

"No. You keep putting this off, and it needs to get done."

"Back off, Mom!" Sunday put the phone to her ear. "Are you still there, Quinn? Can you get them ready?" She nodded once. "Thanks." She returned the phone to her pocket.

My father was already halfway out of his chair. He came around the table and put his arm around my mother's waist. "Don't ever speak to your mother like that."

"She's acting crazy. I just want to go for a ride and talk to my father. You have all day to do the podcast."

"I told you to watch your tongue, Sunday. That's not how you speak to your mother, and you know it." He pulled my mother close as if he was comforting her, although she didn't look like she needed comfort. "It's better if you go riding alone right now. You need to calm down. I'd rather not be with you when you can't control your emotions."

Sometimes—and I knew my siblings were with me on this—I got so sick of hearing about the family principles. It made me feel like I didn't get to be a normal person. Speaking your mind, getting a little emotional about it, should not be considered a failure that results in time out, which was what he was telling her.

"I just wanted to go for a ride with you!" Sunday was crying now.

"You need to settle yourself," my father said.

Crying harder, as shocked by this sudden rejection as I expected we all were, Sunday bent her head forward to hide her wet, splotchy cheeks and hurried out of the breakfast room. The rest of us sat in confused silence.

All but Jake. Seated next to his wife, Bella, he leaned back in his chair, his broad shoulders and muscular arms giving him a slightly intimidating look, even though he wasn't standing, wasn't towering over anyone. He had a smug look on his face. More than Collette or me, he resented Sunday with a passion that was sometimes terrifying. The years of bitterness seemed to have carved hard lines in his face. Maybe because he was the oldest, the resentment had more time to put down roots. As far back as my memory went, Jake was jealous of Sunday's place at the center of my parents' hearts.

None of us understood why they acted as if they loved her more. And because of it, despite the love our parents did show to the rest of us, Jake, Collette, and I had tiny holes in our hearts. Because Sunday was treasured in a way we were not.

I turned to my father. "Why won't you go with her?"

"She's out of control."

"She just wants to go riding. To have some time alone with you." I heard the wobble in my voice, as if even mentioning this basic desire was a shocking breach. But it was.

Everything about the past few minutes was shocking. I felt like I was in another sort of dream world. Sunday never cried. None of us did, because my father believed that indulging emotions magnified minor problems out of proportion. What was more frightening was this was the first time I could recall my father denying Sunday anything she'd asked for. It was the first time I'd heard a sharp edge to their voices, and it pierced me, leaving in its wake the childish fear of helplessness. It felt as if my whole world was shifting sideways.

They stared at me, silencing my questions with steady, practiced gazes. I went to the breakfast table and took a sip of orange juice that was too warm now. I left the room and climbed the main staircase quietly. I went to Sunday's bedroom, which looked out over the front garden, and knocked.

"Go away."

"It's Annie."

"What do you want?"

"Are you okay?"

"Leave me alone."

"Do you want to—"

"Annie, I said leave me alone." Her voice was muffled, as if she'd pressed her face into the pillow.

I went to my room and lay down for a while. When I finally got up, it was to look out the window and see Sunday and Quinn riding Evergreen and one of the other mares, Sugar, toward the trail that ran along the top of the cliffs for miles, offering spectacular views of the ocean. I watched them until they disappeared from view.

No matter how much my parents' favoritism toward Sunday had given me endless cravings for affection and attention from them, watching them turn on her so suddenly was deeply unsettling.

3

THEN: SUNDAY

It's not my fault that Mommy and Daddy love me more than Jake and Collette and Annie. I don't even know if it's true, but Jake says they do. He hates me. So does Collette. They said it's my fault because I'm fake. I don't think I know what that means. Not real, he said. But I'm real. I cried when he said that, and he laughed.

Jake and Collette, or one of them, put earthworms in my bed. I screamed and cried so hard when I felt all those slimy things wiggling around my toes. Then Collette snuck into my room and put her hand over my mouth and said I'd better not let Mommy or Daddy hear me crying like a baby. She put her mouth right up to my ear, so her hot breath was on my face. She whispered that if I told, they would do something worse. She left the worms in my bed. I had to sleep on the floor. I cried for a long time.

I don't want them to hate me. But sometimes I think I hate them.

The only one who loves me, except Mommy and Daddy, is Annie.

But Jake and Collette hate that, too. They tell Annie I'm a

bad person. They tell her I tricked Mommy and Daddy into liking me better. They tell her I'm a liar. I don't think Annie knows what that means, because she's only four. She just giggles when they say that, which makes me happy. But I don't think she'll giggle for very long. I can see her little mouth looks worried when they say bad things about me.

I want them to love me. I try to be nice. I told them I can't help it, but they don't believe me. I asked Mommy if Collette could have my horse because it's prettier, but she said no, because I'm a better rider. That made Collette so mad she pinched me all over the back of my arm. She said it wasn't true, because I'm a little brat and she's been riding for eight years and there's no way in hell I'm as good as her. We're supposed to tell when someone says a bad word, but I knew Jake would do something worse to me if I told, so I didn't.

When I went out to the playhouse to look for Annie today, I knew Collette or Jake had said something really bad to her. They were always saying I couldn't play with her. They said I was tempting her to like me. They told me I was trying to steal her from them. They said she belonged to them, not me.

Annie was sitting on the steps of the playhouse. She was holding her stuffed rabbit that she takes everywhere. It has overalls with buckles, and she likes to buckle them herself. When I said *hi*, she looked like she was going to cry. Then she looked scared. Really scared. She told me to go away.

"Let's pretend we're princesses with magical powers," I said.

"Go away."

"Why?"

"I can't play with you."

"Why not?" I walked closer to where she was sitting.

She squeezed her rabbit and hid her face behind his ears. "Jake will push you off the cliff. He'll tell Daddy I did it. And you'll be dead." She didn't cry. She stared at me as if I were already dead.

I started crying. "I love you, Annie."

She stood up. She hugged her rabbit and walked away. When I turned to watch her, she didn't look back at me. After she was gone, I went into the playhouse and sat on the floor in the corner. I stayed there all day. I didn't cry tears, but I cried inside. It was almost dark when I came out.

4

After the coldness from both my parents caused my sister to rush out of the breakfast room, sobbing like a little girl, I didn't see much of my family for the rest of the day.

During these long family holidays, which Michael was starting to complain were a little *too* long, all of us tried to make sure there was some space built in for alone time. None of us wanted to spend three solid weeks, every hour of daylight and long into the evening with the people we'd grown up with. Breathing room was necessary if we were to enjoy each other the rest of the time.

In the evenings, it was like we were young children again, as we played board games or did jigsaw puzzles in front of a roaring fire in the enormous stone fireplace that dominated the living room. On the Northern California coast, fires were a regular feature in the evenings and early mornings when the fog came in. During the day, we tossed a Frisbee or played softball. We went hiking, climbed along the rocky shore below the property, exploring tide pools and collecting shells, or drove a few miles south to a sandy beach. And of course, everyone spent plenty of time riding the horses. We'd grown up riding, and it was the reason my father had bought the beautiful old Victorian house surrounded by twenty acres of relatively level ground, where our horses had created their own trails over the years.

Deeply disturbed that Sunday had been so upset, especially while I was still unsettled from my dreamlike experience the night before, I needed to get away from my family. I needed to reorient myself to the lives Michael and I had created, to put my childhood back in the corners of my memory, where it belonged.

I put on leggings and a top that showed off my bump, and Michael and I drove to the nearby town of Mendocino. We wandered in and out of the shops, spending more than necessary on baby clothes. My friends back home had planned a shower, and the employees at the nursery I owned and managed were also planning something. The next time we came to visit, it was likely my mother would invite over a few people whom I'd known growing up, who would also shower me with more infant clothes than a child could possibly wear in twelve short months. Despite all of that, it was thrilling to stroke the unbearably soft fabric of all the tiny shirts and pants, dresses and hats. I put both hands on my bump while the store owner wrapped them in tissue paper to bring back to my parents' house, where I could place them in a drawer and look at them every day.

We ate lunch at a bistro and spent an hour in a bookstore before heading back to the house. That evening, Sunday went out for dinner, which seemed to be a relief to my mother.

I never heard her come in. Our house was old, and it had the creaks and groans you expect with a large house that's been settling into its foundation for over one hundred years, but the sound of the front door was distinct. Footsteps on the wide, uncarpeted oak stairs were difficult to conceal, and walking up and down those smooth wood steps in stocking feet, even bare feet, could be treacherous, so we rarely did it without shoes.

At breakfast, Sunday's chair was empty. Because we'd been raised that way, all of us were used to getting up at sunrise and rarely lingered under the covers once the sky was fully light. None of us stayed in our rooms after eight in the morning.

"Isn't Sunday having breakfast?" I asked.

No one responded.

"Did you tell her we're eating?" I directed this at my mother.

She laughed. "It's not a surprise, what time we eat breakfast. Habits are what give life its shape and make it comfortable and satisfying. Isn't that right, Dave?"

My father nodded sharply and took a long swallow of orange juice. Since his hair had started thinning at the top, he'd begun shaving his head, and I still wasn't used to it. Every time I looked at him, I startled slightly, more aware of his deep-set hazel eyes and his eyebrows, which were now entirely gray.

I pushed my chair away from the table and stood. I dropped my napkin onto the seat. I left the room and hurried up the curving staircase and around the corner to Sunday's bedroom. I knocked. There was no answer. I knocked again, my knuckles a dull thud on solid wood. "Sunday?"

Knowing my uninvited presence might not be welcome, but unable to stop myself, I opened the door. The bed was made, the pillows arranged at the top. The dresser was empty of anything but a pale blue glass bowl of seashells and a ceramic sculpture of a seagull. I opened the closet. The hangers were empty, and her yellow suitcase was not standing at the back as I'd expected. In the bathroom, all her makeup and hair products were gone.

When I returned to the dining table, the rest of my family members were buttering their toast and refilling their glasses of juice. "She's not there. All her things are gone."

"I guess she left," Collette said.

"Why would she do that?"

"She's still in a snit about not being able to go riding with Dad," Jake said.

I sat down, but I didn't feel like eating the egg dish I smelled cooking in the kitchen. "I don't think she'd leave without saying goodbye." I thought of what I'd seen on the cliff. Obviously, nothing had happened to her that night, since I'd seen and talked to her since, but it had left me feeling worried about her safety. "She wouldn't just leave."

"She absolutely would do that," Collette said. "Do you want me to carry in the eggs, Mom?"

"Thanks," my mother said. "I'll get the bacon and sausage." My mother and Collette left the table. Bella began collecting empty juice glasses.

I turned my attention to my father. "Did she say anything to you about where she was going?"

He took his phone out of his pocket and looked at it for a few seconds before answering, a gross violation of the family rule that no phones were allowed at the table. "I don't know where she is."

"I don't understand. She's just ... gone."

"Because she didn't get her way," Jake said. "You saw how she exploded when Dad couldn't go riding yesterday."

Since my father had already broken the rule, I pulled out my phone and sent a text message to Sunday. There was no response, which wasn't completely surprising. She and I didn't exchange messages often, and when we did, both of us were slow to reply.

My mother and Collette returned with the food, Bella close behind them.

"Why is your phone out?" my mother asked.

"I was checking on Sunday."

"You know the rule."

No one mentioned Sunday again as they got busy serving the egg casserole, strings of cheese stretching and tugging from the spatula with each serving. The aroma made my mouth water. At the same time, my stomach felt uneasy as I wondered how concerned we should be. Watching Sunday struggle with that hooded figure at the edge of the cliff couldn't possibly mean anything now, but the memory clung to the back of my mind. I felt as if I'd had that dream before, and each time, I forgot that it was recurring. Or I'd seen something similar. Trying to sort the dream from memory was giving me a headache. It wasn't that I thought I'd had a premonition. I didn't believe in that sort of thing. But it wouldn't leave me alone.

While we ate, Jake started talking about the curriculum for his junior high school history classes. Summer had just started, but his head was in the big class project that would take all of October and November. I couldn't listen. I couldn't do anything but wonder what was going on with my sister. She and I weren't close, but I cared about her. And something wasn't right.

When Jake finally paused for air, I spoke. "She didn't say anything to anyone?"

"Who?" Bella asked.

"Sunday. She's missing."

Jake laughed, a loud, threatening sound, like a barking dog. "She's not missing. Don't be so dramatic."

"She disappeared into thin air. She sure seems missing to me. She was planning to stay three weeks just like the rest of us, and after five days, she's suddenly gone, and no one knows where she is, and she didn't answer her phone. That sounds like something's wrong."

"Do you answer your phone every time it rings?" Jake asked.

"It's been twenty minutes."

Michael put his hand on my leg and squeezed it gently.

"Don't worry so much," Collette said. "She decided to leave. You said her things are gone. So she's not *missing*. She's always been impulsive."

My mother nodded eagerly. I stared at her. Had Sunday always been impulsive? I didn't think so, but even if she had, it wasn't like my mother to agree with Collette when she criticized her.

"Especially since she got divorced," Bella said.

My parents stood and began clearing the table. They seemed utterly disinterested in where Sunday had gone. Normally, they would consider one of us leaving as an act of treason meant to sabotage the family vacation, but in this case, they acted as if they hardly noticed. At the same time, they seemed to be ignoring each other. They disappeared into the kitchen, my father carrying a stack of plates and my mother clutching the handles of the fruit tray.

The minute the door closed behind them, Jake slurped his coffee for dramatic effect. "Besides, who cares if she's gone? She sucks up all the energy."

Bella scooped her hair away from her eyes, showing a shadow of dark hair beneath the soft blonde. She leaned toward Jake and kissed him full on the lips, not stopping when my parents returned. Neither of my parents commented on Bella's public display of affection as they took their seats and picked up their coffee cups. She finally moved away from Jake. I sent another text message to Sunday:

I'm a little worried about you. Let me know you're okay.

I left my phone on my lap so I would feel it vibrate if she

responded. *When* she responded. I looked at my father. "Did Sunday ever talk to you yesterday, Dad?"

"Annie, give it a rest," Jake said.

My father pushed his chair away from the table. "Delicious as always, Paula." He stood and plucked a toothpick out of the crystal container in the center of the table. I felt Michael's arms tense beside me. He hated my family's crystal glass of toothpicks, hated how they used them at the table. He hated the whole idea of toothpicks. He said it was like spitting into your mouth and swallowing it, right in front of other people. Still working the toothpick around the spaces between his teeth, my father walked out of the room. A moment later, I heard the front door open.

I shoved my chair away from the table and followed my father to the front porch. He was standing at the railing, resting his hip against it. He was tall so that I still looked up to him as I had when I was a little girl. He was gazing out across the garden that stretched from the porch, twenty yards to the gravel area where the freestanding garage and the parking area were. On the right, it reached all the way to the open area, wild with beach grasses and trees, where I'd run two nights ago, desperate to reach Sunday, to be sure she was okay.

I leaned on the railing beside my father. "Aren't you worried about Sunday?"

"I—"

"Did she ever talk to you yesterday? She seemed so anxious about it."

"Where did you get that idea?"

"I've never seen her so upset like that." Maybe once I had, but it was so long ago, I wasn't sure. "She really wanted to talk to you."

"She just wanted to go for a ride on her schedule. She was being selfish."

"It wasn't about going riding. She wanted to talk to you. Alone."

He shrugged. "She went riding with Quinn and seemed happy about it." He broke his toothpick in half, closed his fingers around it, and patted my shoulder with his other hand. "Now that the podcast is done, I can relax. I think I'll take Nobility out. Sorry you can't ride while you're carrying the baby, but the newest little Ledger will be here before you know it."

"She's a Coffey, though." I laughed. "Right?"

"Sure. Maybe she should hyphenate."

"Probably not. Since I don't."

"I suppose not." He looked disappointed. He crossed the porch, opened the door, and went into the house. I sat on the steps and looked at the beautifully designed and maintained garden, complete with a white marble statue of an angel at the center. My mother loved that angel, treating it sometimes like a member of the family, greeting it when she went out to work in the garden. My mother was the one who had inspired me to open a nursery. I loved digging in the dirt and knowing about plants and how to help them thrive as much as she had. I wished I could remember working beside her in the garden as a small child, but all my childhood memories were blurry. She must have, though. Why else would I love gardening so much?

Now, the thought didn't give me much pleasure. I was too disturbed by my father's insistence that all Sunday had wanted was a horseback ride. It had seemed clear to me she wanted to talk to him about something. Was he obtuse, or had I completely misread her desire?

5

My family dispersed for the day, as we usually did after breakfast during these marathon family holidays. We all needed to breathe. As large as the three-story, five-bedroom Victorian house was, complete with library and formal dining room, it could still feel claustrophobic. Partially because my mother liked to collect artwork and antique furniture, and she could never part with any of her cherished possessions to make room for new acquisitions. It wasn't a hoarder's atmosphere by any stretch, but every room was well fleshed out.

My siblings all took their horses out, my mother left to meet friends in her flower arranging group, and my father went into his study to begin work on his next book now that he had one ready for publication in six months' time.

Michael and I sat on the wide front porch to read, both our tablets loaded with books, and we watched the sun ease its way through the clouds. In the emerging sunshine, the image of Sunday struggling near the edge of the cliff felt more like a dream. The whole thing, even coming down the stairs for a glass of water, felt like something I'd dreamed, then had a clear, detailed memory of. I remembered the beach grass grabbing at my legs ... but now, my legs looked smooth and unblemished below the hem of my dress. My dreams were so vivid. I hated that I often couldn't tell if they were memories or dreams. Especially here. I wasn't sure if it was the ancient house, filled with the lingering energy of previous families, or just proximity to my parents and siblings. Maybe it was the wild, crashing waves that could be heard through our partially open bedroom window or the now-unfamiliar food my mother cooked.

"I don't understand why everyone is so unconcerned that Sunday disappeared," I said. "Their reaction is a little creepy."

"It's not the first time your family has exhibited creepy behavior." Michael closed the cover of his tablet and placed it on the table between us.

It wasn't a secret that he thought our family principles were quirky at best, and that my dad was slightly pompous about his phenomenal success, his books and podcasts and seminars. Michael thought my dad was a know-it-all, telling other people the secret to a good marriage and a strong family, as if there were only a single way to achieve that end. He said my dad took credit for happy families, when there were an infinite number of factors that caused families to feel connected to each other. It was impossible to attribute happiness, which could not be quantified anyway, directly to following my father's advice.

He thought my family kept our emotions locked inside to a degree that wasn't healthy, thanks to the belief that being overemotional had a way of feeding on itself and making things worse. I thought my father's view made sense. I'd seen it already in my own marriage after only three years together.

Once, Michael had even said the devotion that some of my father's students showed to him seemed almost cultlike.

We fought about that comment for three entire days. Finally, he backed down and said he shouldn't have used such a loaded word. We made up, and I felt like he was sincere in his apology ... but at the same time, I think he still believed people put my dad on a pedestal, treating him as if he had superhuman insight, which Michael said he absolutely did not.

Michael is a divorce attorney, so he tends to look at relationships from a slightly darker perspective. Maybe that's why he didn't understand when people were so excited with how my father's books and weekly podcasts made their marriages better and helped them resolve issues with their children.

"I'm worried something happened to her. She still hasn't answered my messages."

"It's only been an hour. Give it a day or two."

"What if something happened to her?"

"Like what?"

I shrugged. "It just feels like something isn't right. Don't you think it's strange to take off without telling anyone?"

"It's rude. It's selfish. But it doesn't mean something's happened to her."

"Everything just seems off."

"How so?"

"My parents never talk to Sunday like they did yesterday. Or criticize her."

"True. But that means Jake was right. She's having a tantrum because they called her on it."

"I feel ... it's hard to describe." Dreamlike memories of Sunday struggling on the cliff flickered at the back of my mind.

"Maybe you feel guilty because you and our baby girl have stolen the spotlight." He grinned at me.

"I don't feel guilty."

"You're not used to so much attention."

"You're right, I'm not."

"They are besotted." He laughed. "I can't imagine what they'll be like when she's born. I'm slightly concerned about it, to be honest."

"Grandparents always want to spoil the grandkids."

"They seem very proprietary toward her. I'm more concerned they'll try to brainwash her."

"Don't say that."

"I don't want them teaching that 'family principle' nonsense to her."

"You think I'm *brainwashed*?"

"No."

"Then why did you say it?"

"Poor choice of words. I just want to be sure the boundaries are clear. These vacations are kind of long. We need to think about keeping them to a few days in the future. Three weeks is too much."

"But she'll love it here. She'll learn to ride. She can explore tide pools and play on uncrowded beaches. There's so much land to explore, not like our tiny yard at home."

"Three weeks is a long time."

"Maybe when she's older. But at first ... we'll see."

I picked up my phone to see if Sunday had replied. There was a text from my best friend telling me she was taking a vacation from her phone. She would message me in two weeks. She knew I was with my family, so it seemed like a good time. If I wanted to talk, I could call her husband's phone.

While I'd been looking at her message, Michael had picked up his tablet again.

I closed my eyes and let the sun, fully out now, warm my face. I tipped my head back slightly and let my hair hang down over the back of the chair. Feeling the heat on my throat felt good.

There was nothing unusual about Collette and Jake—and by default, Bella, because she always stood by her man—not caring much that Sunday was missing. They'd hated her for as long as I could remember. They'd always wanted to choose sides, and they wanted me on their side. They played tricks on her and teased her and let her know they didn't like her. They thought she had it made because our parents gave her everything she wanted, because they gave her so much more than we had. But I always thought she would have given up her huge bedroom, her more expensive horse, her trips with them, and her elite college in a heartbeat. She would have traded everything to have the friendship and love of her siblings.

She and I were a little different, although it's difficult to understand why. Maybe I wasn't as mean as Jake and Collette. Maybe because Jake and Collette were born two years apart, followed by a six-year gap, then Sunday and I were two years apart, it created natural alliances. But Jake didn't like that balance and wanted me on their side. I didn't want to take sides. There shouldn't be *sides* among brothers and sisters.

But for some reason, I was almost afraid to be around Sunday, as if my presence might be bad luck for her. I had absolutely no idea why. It was a ridiculous superstition. Superstitious beliefs went against the family principles my father taught, so I never mentioned it.

Opening my eyes, I glanced at Michael. His head was bent over his tablet, and he seemed to have forgotten I was there. His nearly black hair glinted almost metallic in the sunlight. His skin was already lightly tanned from the few days we'd been on the coast, two of them spent on a sandy beach a few miles south, where he had no problem bodysurfing in the fifty-degree water and stretching out directly on the sand to dry and warm himself. I preferred to protect my skin under an umbrella, and I only braved the chilling water up to my knees, even when I wasn't pregnant. He was slender, with the wiry muscles of a runner. I liked looking at his forearms, watching the subtle movement of his muscles as he held his tablet and swept his finger to turn digital pages.

I looked at my phone again, knowing what I would find— still no messages from my missing sister. I went to Instagram and clicked on her profile. Ninety percent of her photos were pictures of her in dance costumes—solo and with groups. She had over a hundred thousand followers because she was a backup dancer for some pretty well-known singers; quite a few of her posts featured photos of her with those big names.

Scrolling through the pictures where she was out with friends—drinking, enjoying spa days, traveling to tropical beaches, I looked for people she'd tagged who might know her well. I tried to decipher from the sometimes-indecipher-able screen names the ones I'd heard her talk about. I followed fifteen of them, hoping for a quick follow back from at least two or three so I would be allowed to message them.

In less than ten minutes, I was rewarded with six new followers. I messaged them and told them I was her sister. I told them I was worried about her, that she'd gone missing, and asked if they'd heard from her recently. Four replied. One had spoken to her about a week ago, but wasn't aware of any major issues. Zero had heard from her in the past two days.

6

Michael and I made sandwiches and went for a leisurely walk along the top of the cliff. After a mile and a half, we stopped and spread out a blanket. We sat looking out at the ocean, not talking much, equally soothed and entertained by the drifting and diving of the gulls over the water. After we ate, we lay down, curled against each other, and took a short nap. I arranged my sun hat so it covered both our faces.

When we woke, Michael put his hands on my belly, and we lay there for a bit longer while he waited to see if the baby would move. She didn't. She usually waited until bedtime to make her small flutters felt. We kissed for several long minutes, then started our walk back.

At the gazebo, I stopped, feeling the images from my dreamlike wandering pierce my mellow feelings. "I think I'll sit out here for a few minutes. Do you mind taking our things back?"

"Extending your time away from the constant belly stroking?"

I laughed. He kissed me and headed back toward the

house, carrying our blanket and basket as well as my sun hat. I stepped inside the gazebo and sat down. Although I'd spent much of the past three hours staring out at the endless blue of the Pacific, I turned my attention to it again. I never got tired of looking at the water—sapphire blue or slate gray or a vicious green, it was always beautiful. From the gazebo, I could see waves crashing on the huge boulders closer to the shoreline, sending spray far into the air, making me think it might blow inland and brush across my face.

I also loved the gazebo because I could enjoy the view without having to battle the weird compulsion I had when I walked along the path. I often found myself looking down at the shore, as if I had to check to see that no one had fallen off the cliff. I had no idea where the compulsion came from. I wasn't sure if it was a distortion of a somewhat normal fear of heights, or something else.

The dream or memory, whatever it was, kept trying to push its way into my thoughts, but I shoved it to the side and tried to assure myself that Sunday was fine. The dream was unrelated to whatever reason she'd left. As my family kept saying, she'd taken the time to pack her clothes. But I still wondered why she hadn't told even my parents. I wondered why no one had heard her leaving. She'd arrived for our family vacation in an Uber, but I hadn't heard a car turning in the parking area or been woken by headlights splashing into the darkness of our bedroom.

I stood and went to the doorway of the gazebo. The ground just outside was worn to bare earth from people going in and out over the years. It was slightly muddy from fog and drizzle that had dampened everything most nights. I looked down to make sure I didn't place my foot in a particularly wet patch. As I did, something glinted at me, half buried in the mud. I bent my knees for a closer look.

A large diamond winked back at me. With a tiny ruby

above the diamond, the stones were set in a platinum teardrop. I knew it was platinum because it was Sunday's necklace. I plucked it out of the mud, ignoring the grit that wedged beneath my fingernails. The chain came with it, the clasp still done, the chain broken. As I lifted the diamond, the broken chain slid out of the loop and fell back into the mud. I picked it up and cradled both pieces in my hand.

My parents had given the necklace to Sunday on her eighteenth birthday. She wore it every day as far as I knew. It was an obscenely large diamond for a girl that age, and far beyond anything Collette or I had ever received. In fact, neither of us had been given any precious stone. Not even our birthstones.

I stepped around the mud and turned to face the house. Jake was standing near one of the trees in the open area between the garden and the cliff. He was staring at me as if he'd been watching me for several minutes, maybe the whole time I'd been sitting there. He didn't wave or smile. He stared for a few more seconds, then turned and walked toward the house.

It was strange that he wasn't curious about what I'd been fishing for in the muddy patch below the gazebo step. I wondered why he wasn't interested. Usually, Jake wanted his finger in everything that happened around our family home. I shook off the thought and hurried back to the house. I went directly to the kitchen, knowing my mother would be starting dinner.

Without saying anything, I opened my hand and held it out to her, showing her the mud-encrusted diamond and chain.

For a moment, I thought I heard her gasp, but when I took my eyes off the muddy necklace and looked at her face, her expression was neutral. She didn't take the necklace from me. "Oh," she said. "Sunday mentioned she'd lost it.

I'm glad you found it. If you don't mind cleaning it, we'll take it to the jeweler to have the chain repaired. They can check the setting to make sure the stones aren't loose." She smiled and returned to dipping chicken pieces in egg, then rolling them in flour and seasoning for her incredible fried chicken.

"I'm shocked she didn't demand we form a search party to look for it," I said.

My mother laughed.

"She loves that necklace. She wears it every day," I said.

"How can you possibly know that?"

"Every time I see her, she's wearing it. She has it on in most of her Instagram photos."

"I don't have an Instagram account."

"I know, Mom. I'm just saying ... I can't believe she didn't say anything, ask us to look for it, ask if we'd seen it."

"She's careless with her things."

"No, she's not."

My mother turned on the faucet to wash her hands and let the rushing water fill the silence. Why was she criticizing her favorite child? I didn't get it. I felt like my head was going to explode. "Mom? Aren't you worried about her?"

She continued scrubbing her hands. "I'm sure she's fine."

"She was so upset. I've never seen her like that."

"Haven't you? She's always had her tantrums." She laughed softly. "I suppose that's why we gave in to her so much."

"Tantrums? I don't remember that."

She turned off the faucet and dried her hands.

It felt as if we were talking about two different people. Had Sunday had tantrums and cried a lot as a child, and I simply didn't remember? Why had no one mentioned this until now? "Why are you saying all these negative things about her?"

"You know the family principle—no hysterics. It makes small problems seem insurmountable."

"But she—"

My mother turned to face me. She smiled as if we'd just had the most heartwarming mother-daughter chat. "How are you feeling? Your color looks good. Did you and Michael have a nice walk?"

I nodded.

"Walking is good. I bet our little girl will be kicking up a storm tonight." She moved closer and placed her hand on my belly.

"She usually does after I walk." I waited until she moved her hand. "I'm getting more worried—"

"This is the best part, your fifth month. No more sickness, you can still move around easily, you're not tired, and you can feel her activity. I loved the fifth month. Every time."

I smiled. "I am feeling pretty good."

"Just make sure you're eating enough. Do you want an apple?" She reached for the large ceramic bowl on the center island. She took an apple and handed it to me. "It's washed."

I knew it was washed. That ceramic bowl had held fruit before I could reach that high. I studied my mother's smiling face and thought about how everyone always marveled over how we looked so much alike. I couldn't see it, but everyone remarked on it when they saw photographs of us together. My father was always talking about it. Even Michael made a big deal out of it, telling me he appreciated knowing what I would look like when I was in my late fifties.

My mother and I had the same narrow face and wide blue eyes. We had the same very straight dark brown hair, my mother's touched with lowlights now, to minimize the gray. She and I were the same height, and we both had narrow hips and small breasts. Even though I could see these indi-vidual features that were technical mirror images, when I looked at photographs or stood facing her, I didn't see myself at all. It was the same when I looked in a mirror.

Gazing at her now, I wondered if my daughter would look as much like me. I wondered if I would be as blind to seeing the resemblance beyond a catalog of features.

I helped my mother cut the cooked potatoes and chop celery and onions and mix the potato salad. I prepared the ingredients for a green salad. When she was ready to fry the chicken, she dismissed me. "Go put your feet up. If I need help serving, I'll ask Collette or Bella." It felt strange to hear her leave Sunday's name off the list. As if she'd ceased to exist.

Instead of going into the living room, where I could hear my father, Jake, and Michael talking about the merits of several superhero characters, I went outside and wandered back to the gazebo. It was one of a few places, outside of going for a long walk or a ride on my horse, where I could almost guarantee being alone, so I liked hiding out there, sometimes for hours. The rest of my family was averse to sitting in that tiny open building that seemed designed to grab the wind as it whipped off the cliff, pulling it through open spaces of the structure. I called Sunday's number. It rang a few times and went to voicemail.

I raised my voice above the sound of the wind. "Hey, it's Annie. I guess you know that." I laughed, my voice shrill and jumpy. "I'm worried about you. We all are. Give me a call. 'K? Or text me. Any time. Just to say you're okay. Bye."

It felt inadequate. I wanted to do more. That broken necklace suggested that watching her struggle with a person I couldn't identify had been very real. It wasn't a dream, no matter how much it felt like one, and even if I'd dreamed something similar many times in the past, this time, it was real.

That night in bed, as I fitted myself against Michael's back, resting my chin on his shoulder, I whispered in his ear, "I saw something the other night that I didn't tell you about."

"Hmm?"

"I went downstairs for a glass of water. When I looked out the living room window, I saw Sunday wrestling with someone right on the edge of the cliff. At first, I thought they threw her over because one minute she was there, looking like she was fighting for her life, and then she just … disappeared."

He turned toward me. "What do you mean, fighting?"

"They were in the gazebo, and she ran out. The other person grabbed at her. I think that might be when her necklace broke. Then they—"

"What person?"

"I couldn't see. She was in that white dress she wore at dinner, so I knew it was her. The other person was in dark pants and a dark coat with a hood, so I couldn't tell. But she just disappeared."

"Obviously she was fine, since we all saw her the next day."

"But they were fighting. And she never looked for her necklace."

"Maybe she did, and she couldn't find it."

"She would have said something about it. She would have begged us to help her look for it. What if the person she was fighting with did something to her?"

"Are you saying you think she's dead?"

My voice shook when I answered, "I don't know. I … I can't believe that. I don't want to believe that. It was just so strange. And when I went out there, they—"

"Out there when?"

"I went out to see if she was okay."

"You went out to the edge of the cliff in the middle of the night? What were you thinking? That's so dangerous."

"She just disappeared. I had to see if she'd been pushed over."

He sat up and turned on the light. "What were you going to do? You should have woken me."

"I needed to get out there as fast as I could. Before it was too late."

"Too late for what? If she fell over that cliff onto the rocks …" He put his arm around me and pulled me close to his chest. "Why did you have to get out there?" he asked. "I don't understand what you thought you were going to do. It sounds like you weren't fully awake."

"You didn't see what it was like. It wasn't just a struggle over the last sale item on a rack. It was violent."

"Maybe you were sleepwalking."

I pulled away from him. "I don't sleepwalk."

"That we know of. I sleep so deeply, I'd never know. You could be having a cocktail party on the landing, and I wouldn't hear a sound. You always have ridiculously vivid dreams when we stay here."

He was right about that. And I always seemed to forget I had them. Why was that? Each time we visited, it was like a new discovery, and then I would remember that it was always the same. Dreams from which I recalled tiny details about the items in a room and the entire sequence of events, not like normal dreams, where you feel as if you're suddenly teleported from one setting to another, or the story playing out in your subconscious changes suddenly.

I resented it that he immediately assumed it had been a dream. I'd finally managed to believe it was real, to be clear in my own mind what had happened that night, and now he'd undermined me without giving me a chance to tell him the whole story. I don't think he intended it that way, but it's how I felt. He didn't believe me. He wasn't worried about Sunday. The disdainful voices of my siblings and the nonchalant tone of my parents had suppressed my voice.

It made me feel foolish. I already struggled with feeling like a child when we returned home for these family holidays. Although my mother had redecorated the room, it remained my childhood bedroom. The sense of myself as a little girl permeated the walls and floorboards.

When I didn't say anything more, he turned out the light, and we slid beneath the covers, holding each other close. After he fell asleep, I slipped out of his encircling arm and out of bed. I left our room and walked to the landing. I dialed Sunday's number again. The call went directly to voicemail. I guessed her battery had died, or she'd turned off her phone.

In the morning, I got up before sunrise and made myself a cup of tea. I started the coffee brewing, hoping the aroma might filter upstairs to the bedrooms and bring my family down more quickly so I could talk to them about Sunday. I'd woken at two in the morning and checked my phone. There were no messages from her. We had to file a missing person report. Waiting any longer was stupid and irresponsible and possibly endangering her further. Maybe the police wouldn't do much, but we couldn't sit around pretending everything was okay.

Within ten minutes, Bella and Jake had arrived in the kitchen. Bella started loading a tray with granola and yogurt. Jake began cutting up fruit to go with it.

"I can't take another meat and potatoes breakfast," Bella said. "This will be nice and healthy for baby." She patted my belly.

I had planned to tackle the members of my family one on one to convince them we needed to be concerned, but the very fact that people needed convincing to be concerned that someone we loved was missing sickened me. Now I couldn't seem to find the words. Bella and Jake talked over me each time I thought I was ready to mention how blind everyone was to an alarming situation. At the same time, I wasn't sure how to be more persuasive. None of them knew what I'd seen, and I didn't want to tell them, especially after Michael's reaction. I shouldn't have to persuade them. The concern should arise naturally. What was wrong with them?

Finally, we were all seated at the table. My father was only pouting slightly over the fact there was no bacon or sausage, and my mother was ignoring the yogurt, which she found disgusting—*Why would anyone eat something that tastes like milk that's gone sour? And you can add fruit flavor all you want, that's still what it tastes like.*

I spooned yogurt into a bowl, sprinkled granola on top, and looked directly at my mother, who should have been sick with worry over Sunday's disappearance. My mother cherished these holidays. She gushed about it every year. She looked forward to them for months. She planned the menus weeks before we arrived. Together, my parents shopped for new board games and puzzles they thought would please us. My mother's family was everything to her, she reminded us every Christmas and Thanksgiving, the two other times of the year we all gathered outside of the summer vacation.

She considered herself blessed that all her children enjoyed each other's company, and that they liked spending time with their parents. It was the reward of a lifetime. The greatest blessing of all. This blessing was attributed to the family principles devised by my father. A family that stayed close when the children were adults was the greatest joy life offered, and following those principles ensured that happened. That was how my mother—how both my parents —saw the world.

Sometimes, I wondered why any of us came home.

Especially Jake and Collette, dragging more psychological baggage than they had suitcases, filled with years of affronts and slights and favoritism toward one child. It was a dysfunctional situation, according to Michael. I hated to agree with him ... but occasionally, when I was feeling brutally honest, I did.

"We need to file a missing person report," I said, keeping my gaze on my mother's face. I tried to keep my tone kind. "I think you're not realizing how serious this is, Mom. I've left voicemail and sent three or four text messages. I didn't pry; I just asked her to let us know she was okay. She hasn't responded. Not even a thumbs-up. I got in touch with a few of her friends, and no one has heard from her."

"That's a little extreme," Bella said.

I kept my attention on my mother. Her face remained relaxed and calm.

"I think you're in a little bit of denial," I said.

"Aren't you the psychologist," Jake said. "Mom's fine because she knows—"

"I can speak for myself, Jake. But he's right. Please don't

get yourself so worked up, Annie." My mother cut a piece of cantaloupe, speared it with her fork, and put it in her mouth. No one spoke while she chewed it as if she were comparing samples. "Sunday took her things. She hasn't disappeared. It's rude that she didn't let us know she was leaving. I'm very upset that she left in the middle of our family get-together, and I think she should have responded to your messages, but I'm not concerned that something's *happened* to her. And we absolutely do not need to go running to the police." She laughed softly, making it sound as if I were a little bit of a lunatic.

"It would make you look alarmist," Bella said.

"In fact, you could get in real trouble for filing a false report," Jake said. "If they came here to check on when we'd seen her, and we told them she took her suitcase and purse and her phone ..." He sipped his coffee, then put down the mug, and leaned back in his chair. "Did you read about all those grade-school kids they found living without an adult in that mobile home park, Dad? Taking care of themselves and getting themselves to school every day for over six months and no one knew?"

My father nodded and launched into his usual spiel about how the structure of society was very fragile. It made him more driven to increase awareness about his podcast, to promote his books more widely. "The basic building block of all societies is the family unit. It's been breaking down for decades, and now we're seeing the results." He sighed. "It's a heavy burden, sometimes."

As he finished outlining thoughts we'd all heard many times before, my mother stood and began clearing the table. My father jumped up to help her, and they disappeared into the kitchen.

I looked around the table. "So we're going to do nothing? We're going to assume the fact that, as far as we know, not a single person on this planet knows where Sunday is or how she's doing is just fine? We're going to accept that she lost her favorite necklace and didn't even bother to ask us to look for it? Is that how it is?"

"You sure are worried about a sister I thought you found as annoying as the rest of us," Collette said. "What's up with that?"

"I love her. She's part of our family. If you don't care about her, you should care about how much Mom and Dad love her."

"They don't seem too worried," Bella said. "Or do you *want* them to be worried?"

Jake laughed in a way that sounded like he was snorting at me. "I guess you think if it turns out something happened, Mom and Dad will know that Annie was the most caring, supportive daughter, who showed the most concern for their fave."

Collette poured coffee into her mug. She splashed in enough cream to turn it into coffee-flavored milk. "It's kind of nice not having her around."

Their lack of concern was so disturbing I couldn't find the words to respond. Had their jealousy become so extreme they didn't care what happened to her?

8

———

I felt like I was losing my mind, watching the placid faces of my family as they dismissed my concerns and went on with their vacation plans as if nothing unusual had happened. No one acknowledged that for most of her adult life, Sunday had been in the habit of texting my parents almost daily.

When Michael said he was thinking of going for a run, I came close to tying his running shoes for him, and shoved him out the door, encouraging him to take an extra-long run. Jake, Bella, and Collette had gone riding again. I had no doubt the horses were getting an earful about my wild imagination. My parents were sequestered in my father's study for a video call with his publisher.

Even though I was essentially alone in the house, I went out to the gazebo. Not only was it private and unused most of the time, I could also see someone approaching from all sides. I scrolled through my contacts and brought up the info for Sunday's ex-husband. They'd separated about a year ago, and their divorce had been finalized a few weeks before Christmas. Despite my siblings' belief that she'd been more impulsive since her divorce, I didn't see it that way. She seemed calmer. She was more focused on her career, more driven. I thought she looked happy, and she'd mentioned a new guy, although I hadn't found any evidence of him on Instagram.

I called Liam and was a little surprised when he answered my call. Maybe the shock of seeing my name come up drove his curiosity to the extreme. Although I had his number, I couldn't remember ever having called him. We might have exchanged text messages once or twice when a family holiday was being planned, but that was it.

"Hi, Annie." His voice was cautious. "What's up?"

"I was wondering if you've heard from Sunday recently."

"I talked to her a few days ago, why?"

"When, exactly?"

"Um … what's this about?"

"We're having our summer family vacation and—"

"Ahh. The legendary Ledger summer holiday." He said this like it was a public event.

"She was here for a few days, and then she disappeared."

"What do you mean by disappeared?"

"Two mornings ago, we woke up, and she was gone. She had a disagreement with my parents, nothing major, but a little unusual—"

"A *little*?" He laughed.

"Yeah. And the next day, she was gone. She didn't tell anyone she was leaving. She isn't answering texts or phone calls. I'm worried about her."

"Yeah. I'm sure you are. Such a loving family. Always so concerned about your beloved sister."

"I am."

"What do you want?"

"I was wondering if you've heard from her. I want to know if … I'm not sure. Was she okay when you talked to her?"

"Have you filed a missing person report?"

"No. My family doesn't want to. They don't think anything's wrong."

"That figures. But it doesn't stop you from doing it. If you're actually worried and not just putting on a show."

"I'm not like that. You know me better than that."

"I know you're not like the older ones. Maybe. Who knows? So why haven't you called the police?"

"I want to, but she packed her things. Her purse and suitcase, everything, is gone. They said if the police come and ask when we saw her and all those routine questions and they tell them she packed, it will look like I made a false report."

Liam was quiet for a moment; then he gave one short laugh. "Okay. That's both an accurate and a brilliant way to keep you from doing what your gut is telling you to do."

"You know how my family is."

"I do. I tried for years to get Sunday to put some distance between herself and that brother and sister of yours, but she wouldn't. She kept going back for more, trying to win their love like she was some kind of addict." He sighed heavily. "What do you want from me?"

"I want to know if you think it sounds like something is off. I don't think she would take off and not say goodbye to my parents, not tell anyone where she's going."

"It's not like you two are best friends."

"I found that diamond necklace she always wears. It broke, and I found it in the mud. I can't believe she left without making us all look for it. She adores that necklace."

"She does." His tone softened, and I no longer felt he might end the call if I said the wrong word at the wrong time. "So you're really concerned? I'm surprised. Usually—"

"Why did she call you? Was she upset? Did she mention plans to meet up with someone? Did she say anything about leaving?"

"The opposite, actually."

"What do you mean?"

"I'm surprised you're so concerned. I've always had the impression none of you gave a shit about Sunday."

"That's not true. It's complicated."

"Loving your sister shouldn't be complicated."

"It is."

"Her heart was broken because of you three. Did you know that?"

"I didn't ... we ... what did she say, exactly?"

"She asked me not to say anything."

"She expected you to talk to us?"

"No. I don't think so. It was more one of those blanket statements—*don't tell anyone*. She really didn't say too much that was specific. She said someone in your family betrayed her. And she wasn't leaving until she settled things."

"What does that mean?"

"I have no idea."

"Do you think she's okay?"

"Again, no idea."

I sighed. He was being so difficult. At the same time, he was still talking to me, and that meant he agreed with me that something wasn't right. He had to, or he would have told me not to worry about it and hung up several minutes earlier. "What else?"

"That's it. But she was extremely upset."

I considered whether I should tell him about what I'd seen. I wasn't sure why I was so reluctant. It wasn't as if he was like Jake and Collette and would immediately accuse me of imagining or embellishing the story. The space between us was silent. I wondered what he was thinking, trying to play out how the conversation might go if I told him about the struggle she'd had with a person I couldn't identify.

"What do you mean by 'extremely upset'?" I asked. "Was she crying? Was she angry?"

"She said something happened that shook her to her core."

"Wow." I realized I was holding my breath, and let it out slowly. "I wonder what that means."

"I think it's pretty obvious."

I couldn't imagine. She already had such a bitter, broken relationship with Jake, if you could even call it a relationship. And not much better with Collette. She and I were coolly friendly with each other. I knew she didn't trust me much, and I always felt torn into ragged strips between my other siblings and Sunday. It was the worst part of going home. I wanted to see everyone, to spend time with my whole family, but I felt this constant ache that things weren't the way I wanted them to be, the way I imagined they were in other families. Even though our family was supposed to be a shining example of strength and affection and love, we were nothing like that.

"Do you think I'm right to be worried?" I asked.

"Do you always ask other people how you should feel? You feel how you feel. *Are* you worried?"

"Yes."

He didn't say anything.

"Can you come to the house and talk to them?"

He laughed. "Are you serious? What would be the point? Plus, it's a four-hour drive."

"They don't believe me when I say that something's wrong."

"They certainly aren't going to believe me. I'm her ex-husband, remember?"

"But you talked to her. You have information. You have proof she was upset. They can't accuse you of imagining things. You need to tell them what she said."

"That would go well."

"They need to realize she wasn't planning to leave. Someone took her. Or hurt her. I saw her wrestling with someone a few nights ago. It looked like they were trying to push her off the cliff."

He was quiet. After a few seconds, he cleared his throat. "Who was it?"

"It was dark. I don't know."

"Someone in your family?"

"I don't even know that. Probably. Maybe? But I don't like to think that ..."

"And now she's missing?"

"I saw her after that, and she was fine, more or less. But I ... please come up here. I know it's a long drive, but it's really important. I won't tell them you're coming. You can just stop by after dinner. I know they don't like you, but they'll be polite if you just show up at the door. They'll listen. Maybe they'll wake up and realize she didn't just decide to casually change vacation plans and not tell anyone. I know it seems normal that she packed her stuff, but it's not normal that she didn't tell my parents she was leaving. It's not normal that she hasn't been in touch with anyone."

Finally, after a long silence, he agreed he would drive up from his apartment in San Francisco. He would stay in one of the B&Bs in Mendocino and stop by the house after dinner the following evening. He would tell them what Sunday had said. They needed to be shaken out of their complacency, and I hoped that Liam, who they thought should no longer have any interest in Sunday's well-being, going to all that trouble, would cause them to realize her disappearance wasn't something we should ignore.

9

The next evening, after the dinner dishes were washed, the teacups were empty, and the fire was robust, I was afraid Liam had let me down. I kept glancing over my shoulder, straining to see even the faintest glimmer of headlights coming up the road to our house. All I saw were the shadows growing darker and thicker as dusk turned to the inky blue just before the light of the sun disappears entirely.

Liam had said he would aim to arrive before eight o'clock. It was ten past when he got there, but I was so anxious about whether they would even allow him inside, so worried they would refuse to listen to him as they had to me, explaining away everything he said, that I magnified those ten minutes ten times that.

Instead of ringing the bell, he knocked. No one else heard him over the conversation and the crackle of the fire.

"Someone's at the door." I stood and headed toward the foyer.

Collette laughed. "You're hearing things. It's not like when we were kids and people were coming and going all the time."

"This was the party house." Jake let out a whooping call that was too loud for the room.

My mother smiled at me. "You know the wind plays strange tricks with sound. Sit down so we can get this game going." She patted my chair.

The knock was louder the second time, and they all looked at me as if I'd had a premonition. I continued to the door and opened it. Knowing they could hear me from the living room, I didn't pretend surprise. It didn't matter to me if my family realized I'd set them up. The important thing was trying to find out where Sunday had gone.

When Liam stepped into the living room, everyone stopped moving, as if they were posing for a tableau. "I called Liam because I was worried about Sunday."

They responded with blank stares.

"He spoke to her a few days ago." I didn't want to say more, didn't want to speak for him or undermine what he had to say before he had a chance to tell them straight up. I wanted them to feel the impact with the same force I had.

"Well, this is surprising." My father stood and crossed the room but didn't try to shake Liam's hand. Instead, he put his hand on my shoulder. "It's a little rude to walk in on a family evening when you weren't invited." He glanced at me. "Not formally invited, but if it makes Annie feel better ..." He squeezed my shoulder.

"It's not to make me feel better. Sunday called him, and she ... I'll let Liam tell you."

"What will you have to drink?" my father asked Liam.

"Nothing. Thanks," Liam said.

No one offered him a chair. Looking for a place to land, he moved toward the fireplace. He glanced at the mantelpiece cluttered with framed photographs of our family. He put his fingertips on the edge of the thick stone as if to keep his balance and looked around at my family one by one. Each of whom returned his gaze with decidedly unwelcoming expressions.

"I can tell you're thrilled to see me, so I'll keep this brief," he said. "I still care about Sunday, although she is a deeply damaged woman, thanks to the bullying of her siblings." He gave a cold stare, meeting Jake's gaze, then turning his attention to Collette. Neither of them faltered under his accusation. "The wounds you inflicted were one reason why our marriage ended."

"Not true," my father said. "Sunday and I had many long talks about what went wrong with you two. Your marriage ended because you refused to follow some very simple principles that are crucial for building strong partnerships and families."

"She's better off without you," Collette said. "I've never seen her so happy."

"Yet she's gone missing," Liam said.

"She's not *missing*," my mother said. "I'm sorry if Annie—"

"If people knew what this family was really like, no one would buy your propaganda. They—"

"Liam," I said, "you were going to tell them what Sunday told you. The reason we think something is wrong."

"My books and seminars have transformed millions of families," my father said, his voice slightly loud for the room. "Do you realize that? They've saved marriages that were spiraling toward divorce. They've helped parents steer troubled kids back into the loving arms of their families, and helped them become productive members of society. They've helped couples who felt isolated and lonely fall in love with each other again."

Liam laughed. "This is the most toxic family I've ever known. And if people knew what I know—"

"And what is that?" my mother asked.

"I know things that could destroy this family and your little empire of books and workshops." He laughed softly.

"You'd better be careful. You're stepping very close to slander," my father said.

I wasn't naïve enough to think this was going to be a friendly conversation, but I didn't think it would go so badly so quickly. I needed them to hear the important part. Liam was trying to upset them more than he was trying to make sure they realized they needed to be concerned about Sunday. I said, "Tell them what she said to you."

He blinked as if he'd just woken from a hypnotic recollection of all my family's flaws. "When Sunday called me, I hadn't spoken to her in a while. The fact she even called me, that there was no one else she could talk to, shocked me. She was extremely upset. She said someone in her family had betrayed her."

I looked around the room as he spoke. Not a single face twitched or changed expression, suggesting they might know how my sister had been betrayed.

Collette smiled with exaggerated patience. "Always the drama queen, isn't she?"

"Isn't that your role?" Liam asked. "She told me she was shaken to her core. I've never heard her like that. Not even when I decided to end our marriage. She would not have left after being so determined to 'set things right,' whatever that means. So what did you do to her?"

My mother's face twisted into something now, but it was more rage than anything resembling fear or grief for her missing daughter. My father must have seen the same thing I did. He moved to her side and put his arm around her, pulling her close. "I think you should leave."

"Annie asked me to come because you're acting like nothing is wrong. A missing person report needs to be filed immediately so the police can start working to find out what happened to her. Or did you do something to her, and you don't want the police involved? Is that the problem?"

"Watch your mouth," my father said. "It's time for you to go."

Jake, Collette, and Bella stood. As a single unit, they walked out of the room. A moment later, I heard them climbing the stairs.

Liam and my father stared at each other.

"What secret do you think you know about our family?" my father asked. "Or are you such a loser you're thinking about dabbling in phony blackmail now?"

"Far from it. I do just fine on my own, as you know. But I think it's very strange you're not showing any concern for your daughter's welfare. Unless you don't want her to be found."

My father took his arm off my mother's shoulders. "I want you to leave." He took my mother's elbow and steered her toward the doorway. Without turning to look back, he said, "Annie, please make sure to escort him out immediately. I don't want any more of this slander. And if you try to make derogatory public statements about me or my family, you'll be having a conversation with my attorneys." My parents left the room.

My husband stared after my family as if he wasn't sure whether he should follow. He looked at me. Concern wrinkled his brow, but I wasn't sure if it was for Sunday or for me. Most likely for me. He seemed frozen to the spot where he stood on the far side of the room, the game table in front of him, game markers and cards and a complicated board spread out before him. He picked up the dice and rolled them around in his hand. I could hear the faint clicking of the hard plastic now that the crackling of the fire had calmed slightly.

Liam picked up one of the photographs off the mantelpiece and gazed at it—a picture of Sunday on her sixteenth birthday, surrounded by sixteen girlfriends. A huge helium balloon shaped like a one and a six hovered above the table, featuring a gorgeous whipped-cream cake and purple candles to match the balloon. He placed it back on the mantel, slightly out of position. I would have to adjust it later. My mother would notice the minute she walked into the room.

His gaze traveled over the rest of the photographs. "She wasn't always so deliriously happy on her birthday, was she?"

"What do you mean?"

"Half the photos are fake." He looked like he might cry. "One of her birthdays was flat-out traumatic. Poor kid." He sighed. "That turned out pretty much as I expected."

"Thanks for coming." I followed him out of the room, leaving Michael still posed like a statue except for the clicking of the dice.

I walked out of the house into the chilly, foggy night air and down the front path toward Liam's black BMW. When we reached the car, he pressed the fob to unlock it and opened the door.

"They act as if they couldn't care less that Sunday might be in a dangerous situation. For all we know, she could be dead, and they really don't care at all. Your brother and sister are two of the coldest human beings I've ever met. Of course, so are your parents. They're the ones who raised them. They just aren't so blatant about it. Maybe they don't care because ..." He shuddered. "I don't know how you can tolerate ever spending time in their presence."

"It's my family."

"Sometimes, it's healthier to find a new family."

"I could never—"

"Jake and Collette were so awful to her. She was absolutely dealing with trauma. She couldn't get into bed at night without first throwing the bedclothes off to check there weren't any earthworms under the sheets. Because of what they did to her. It was sad and exhausting."

I felt tears prick at the backs of my eyes. "What happened at her birthday party that traumatized her?"

"You don't remember?"

"I don't know. I can't remember any birthdays that were terrible. She was always running around like she was having the time of her life. My parents gave her amazing gifts. She always seemed blissfully happy."

"Her ninth birthday. How old would you have been?"

"Seven."

"And you don't remember that party? The party that never happened?"

I shook my head. I closed my eyes, trying to remember something awful, but there was nothing. Just a dark hole inside my head with faint images of all our birthday parties tossed in together, bits of light flickering across my brain, quickly blanketed in shadows.

"The morning of her party, Jake and Collette called the parents of all her friends. They told them Sunday had the stomach flu and the party was cancelled. No one showed up. Sunday was heartbroken. She thought her friends secretly hated her, and they'd all gotten together and chosen her birthday to show her they didn't want to be her friend anymore. She cried all day long. She didn't find out until the following Monday at school what had happened. So she was miserable and upset all weekend."

"My mother didn't call to find out what was going on?"

"Sunday wouldn't let her. They never guessed that Jake

and Collette were involved, so calling seemed like further humiliation."

I felt like someone had taken my heart in their hands and was squeezing it, trying to wring out the blood, twisting it like a towel. I ached for my sister. I wondered why two teenagers would be driven to hurt someone so deeply. I had an overwhelming desire to hurt them back, even now.

"So that's your exemplary family and their principles." He climbed into his car and put his hand on the interior handle to pull the door closed.

"What did you mean that you know something that could ruin our family?" I asked.

He gave me a sympathetic smile. "Nothing. I wanted to get their attention. And I did." He laughed bitterly. "It wasn't a leap. Whatever someone did to betray Sunday, maybe it's something that would destroy them. Who knows? I regret driving all this way."

"Thank you."

"It didn't do any good."

"Maybe after they sleep on it."

"You're very optimistic. Good night."

I moved away from the car, and he closed the door. I stood in the driveway, shivering, as I watched him circle the area in front of the garage and start down the road to the edge of our property. He was out of sight before he reached the turn onto the highway. Even after that, I stood there, turning my face up to look at the moon blurred by a thin covering of fog.

10

The atmosphere when we sat down to breakfast the following morning was stiff. Every member of my family was very deliberately ignoring me, as if I'd committed an unforgivable social breach by inviting Liam to come into our home and accuse them of hurting Sunday. No one made eye contact with me. The conversation sounded staged. I couldn't shake the feeling their gestures looked false, even though I was pretty sure it was simply my heightened awareness making it appear that way.

My father was late to arrive at the table, and we were almost finished with our homemade waffles when he seated himself without saying good morning. My mother jumped up and hurried to his end of the table. She filled his mug with coffee, then reached across Collette to grab the cream pitcher, handing it to him before he had to ask.

I cut a section of waffle and ate it, feeling the crisp batter, damp with syrup and butter, on my tongue.

"I have some news," my father said.

Everyone went on eating.

"Ben Riddell called last night. Late. After midnight. You

remember him. He graduated from high school a year ahead of Sunday. He was with the highway patrol for a few years, then a local officer, now detective. A really good guy."

That ended the eating. Forks tapped against plates as everyone set them down. We looked at my father, and I felt my heart grow so tight with fear I could hardly pull air into my lungs. I wondered why he'd felt compelled to provide Ben's résumé along with the minor personal endorsement.

"There was a car accident. You know that section of Highway 1 where it washed out, and they'd narrowed the road to a single lane?"

"What's the holdup in fixing that?" Jake asked.

"It's a complicated project. A lot of infrastructure support needed along the riverbank. It's not visible from the road."

Jake nodded.

"Why are you talking about road repairs? You said there was an accident," Collette said.

"Liam ran off the road. Right into the Navarro River."

"That's terrible." My mother paused with her mouth open. Everyone waited for her to finish. "I hate to say it, but he drives that car like a bat out of—"

"His car went into the water," my father said. "Completely submerged. He drowned, obviously."

"He's dead?" My whole body was suddenly cold. Michael put his hand on my wrist and held it. His skin also felt cool, although I knew he meant to warm me with his touch.

"That's what drowned means," Bella said.

"Don't be like that," my mother said. "She's trying to process it."

"Yes. Ben said he thought I'd want to know because, of course, he knew Liam used to be married to Sunday. A young woman saw his car sinking into the river—the headlights were pointing right up at her because it had spun around and was going in backwards. But she's a new driver, and it was dark ... she didn't feel safe climbing down to the river herself. Which was good thinking on her part. She might have fallen in the darkness and gotten into trouble herself. She called for help, but by the time paramedics arrived ..." My father sighed, but it wasn't clear whether he was feeling any grief or even sadness. There was a flat acceptance that accidents happen on washed-out roads; what a shame this was.

"But he ... I don't understand how he ..." I wasn't sure what I wanted to say. How could he be dead? He was a good driver. And he must have known it was washed out. Wouldn't he have seen the barriers and warning lights on the drive to our house? It was still light at that time.

"Sadly, you're right, Paula," my father said. "He drove that car much too fast. He thought he was a good driver just because he had an expensive, well-engineered car."

"How is that different from you and your Mercedes, Dad?"

He glared at me. "I drive the speed limit."

"You've never even been in his car. You don't know how Liam drives. It sounds like you're blaming him." My voice trembled, tears at the back of my throat.

"Calm down. I'm not blaming him. I'm just delivering information."

"I ... it's hard to believe," I said. "He was just here. Just talking to us. How can he be dead?"

"Accidents always feel that way." Bella gave me a smile that I think was meant to be comforting, but came across as a look of superiority. "It's the shock. The unexpected nature of it. A sudden death is harder to accept. So the brain processes it as something that isn't real."

"That's a good way of saying it," Collette said. "It sounds almost poetic."

There was nothing poetic about it. I felt sick to my stomach. I couldn't believe he was dead, and it didn't feel at all like an accident. It felt creepy. Liam stood in the living room and told my family he knew something about them that could ruin them, whatever that meant, and now he was dead. It was one thing to skid onto the shoulder, to lose sight of the road, maybe to skid farther off onto the soft slope that started down to the river. But to not slow at all, so that his car traveled that entire distance, and then to end up completely submerged in the river? It didn't feel like an accident at all. It felt like he was conveniently no longer going to say anything uncomfortable to my family, and he wasn't going to tell anyone what Sunday had said to him about the person who had betrayed her.

The waffle and its thick, sweet syrup swam in my stomach. I finished the rest of my milk and wished I also had tea, because I suddenly felt very cold. I needed the soothing warmth of tea. "It's not poetic," I said. "I've known people who died suddenly, people who had accidents. This feels different."

"Probably because it could so easily have been prevented," my father said. "He was overly emotional when we saw him. And we all know that letting your emotions get the best of you never leads to a good outcome. He was probably exhausted from driving all the way from San Francisco, and add to that his tension over showing up uninvited to a gathering where he obviously wasn't wanted. It was a recipe for careless driving. An accident was almost guaranteed."

I wanted to scream at their casual dismissal of a man's death. A man who, until fairly recently, had been part of our family. "That is total victim blaming," I said, my voice slightly shrill.

"Let's not sink into the laziness of pop psychology buzz-words," my mother said.

"I'm not. I just think it's horrible that he died, and I feel slightly responsible. We all should."

"Because you invited him?" Bella said.

"No one is responsible." Michael put his arm around my shoulders, resting it on the back of my chair. "Can I make you some tea?"

I nodded. He moved his arm away, squeezed my thigh, then stood and disappeared into the kitchen.

"I was thinking of a visit to the botanical gardens this afternoon," my mother said. "Who wants to join me?"

Everyone nodded, but no one spoke. My mother didn't follow up with any suggestions for a time they might leave, or who would drive, like she usually did when making plans for the family. Jake turned to Bella and began talking in a low voice about repairs to their deck planned for later that summer. Collette had pulled out her phone and had it on her lap, where she was glancing at it every few minutes. My parents hadn't noticed, and I wanted to laugh that she was behaving like a rebellious teenager, taking advantage of their distraction to flout the dinner table rule.

I felt physically ill, watching them carry on as if a man hadn't taken his last breath and died a painful, terrifying death a few miles from our home, a man who until less than a year ago had been a member of our family.

All but Collette having been deprived of contact with their phones for the past hour, the members of my family disappeared quickly from the table. They drifted up the stairs to their bedrooms, where I guessed they were checking the news for additional details of Liam's death. Unless they cared so little they'd already forgotten, and were turning their thoughts to the botanical gardens or whatever else was occupying their minds. One week into our family vacation, it was turning into a shared nightmare.

Michael and I put away the leftover fruit in plastic containers, loaded the dishwasher, and washed the coffee pot. I thought about Liam, feeling equal parts despair over the loss of his life and my own loss of the only other person who expressed concern that Sunday was missing.

"Liam dying like this makes me even more worried about Sunday," I said.

Michael picked up a linen towel and began drying the coffee pot, polishing the glass so that not a single water spot remained. "The things he said did put the situation in a different light. We could try to file a police report, but as they keep reminding you, the fact she took her luggage doesn't make it seem like she left against her will. I think the police will treat it as an adult woman changing her plans without telling Mommy and Daddy. Nothing unusual."

I knew he was right, but I hated feeling so helpless. My brain refused to stop circling around from sadness over Liam's death to frustration over my family's lack of concern to fear for Sunday. No other thoughts could make their way into the rapidly spinning circle. Was I condemned to the repeating pattern until something came along to knock one of those three pillars off its foundation?

The doorbell rang, as if in answer to my desire for freedom from my circling thoughts. I hurried out of the kitchen, but my father was already in the foyer, opening the door. Ben Riddell stood on our front porch.

"Hi, Mr. Ledger. I just wanted to give you an update on Liam. I know you were upset about the accident."

"That was thoughtful." My father smiled as if the detective were bringing him news that one of our horses had won a blue ribbon in a show. He opened the door wider. "Come in."

"I just have a few minutes. So the bottom line is we checked the side of the road. There were skid marks in the mud and tracks showing the car fishtailed. It appears he braked with too much force, and our guess is he went airborne. Right into that river, and you know what it's been like since this past winter and spring. Way above the usual waterline."

"It's a tragedy," my father said. "I think I mentioned last night I knew he'd been drinking before he got here."

Ben nodded.

I stepped forward. I hadn't smelled any alcohol on Liam at all, and I would know. I'd had nothing to drink since the start of my pregnancy, and I was hyperaware of the odor on anyone's breath. Even a single glass of wine.

"I feel terrible," my father said, "Absolutely awful. I wanted to be the gracious host, and I offered him a drink. I never should have—"

"Don't blame yourself, sir. He's an adult. He knows the law. And he should have known his limit. People from Silicon Valley come up here and think they can drive their hot cars like they do on the freeways down there. They don't bother to familiarize themselves with the conditions. It's tragic." He shook his head.

I found myself shaking my head as well. My father had offered drinks, but Liam declined. "Dad ... Liam—"

My father spoke quickly. " 'Tragic' is truly the only word to describe it. Thanks so much for stopping by to tell me personally. Even though his marriage to Sunday ended so badly, we still cared about him. Obviously."

"Obviously." The detective stepped back. "By the way, thanks again for those seminar tickets. That week away completely transformed my marriage." He laughed. "You promised it would, and I doubted you. I shouldn't have."

"Glad to hear it," my father said. "But you and Jenna are the ones who did the work. All I do is point the way."

When the detective was gone, I stepped in front of my father the moment he turned away from the door. "Liam wasn't drinking before he got here. I would have noticed. And he didn't have a drink when you offered one. Why did you tell him that?"

"He had a shot of whiskey."

"No, he didn't."

He gave me a kind, calm smile. "You were nearly as emotional as he was, Annie. I think you've forgotten."

"He did not have a drink. I was right there. He stood next to the mantel, and he didn't move the whole time."

My father stepped around me. "Don't get so upset, sweetheart." He rubbed my upper arm. "It's a tragic accident, and it plays tricks on the memory when something like that happens. I'm sorry you have to deal with this while you're pregnant. You should go do something life-affirming. Why don't you and Michael go out for lunch?" He rubbed my arm again, then walked to the stairs and started up.

"Dad!"

He continued climbing. I tried telling myself that he was more shaken than he'd let on, and he might have misremembered the events of the evening as easily as he thought I had.

When I called his name again, he still didn't turn to acknowledge me. His back was straight, and his shoulders relaxed as if he'd just spoken to someone about pruning the Monterey cypress that was obstructing the view, not lied to a police detective about the circumstances leading up to a man's death.

11

It seemed as if my father went looking to find strength in numbers when he climbed the stairs, leaving me standing in the foyer wondering which of us had a blank spot in our memory. Within twenty minutes, the entire family had gathered on the stretch of lawn between the garden and the fenced area around the stables, where the horses spent their daytime hours.

"What happened to the trip to the botanical gardens?" I asked.

My mother shrugged. "We can go another time."

She didn't explain why today was no longer an option. Instead, she'd set up the wickets for a game of croquet, even though they regularly reminded us not to play when the lawn was wet from the morning fog. The heavy wood balls and mallets damaged the grass. It was quite damp now, spreading moisture onto my gray canvas shoes the minute I stepped onto the grass.

"It's sopping wet," I said.

"Don't worry about it," Collette said. "The forecast is

eighty today. How often do we get eighty out here? It's crazy."
She laughed. "It will be too hot to play this afternoon."

I lost the game by a significant margin. My ball was
always the one knocking into others and being punished with
a whack out of bounds. I was the last to come through the
final two wickets and hit the stake as the others stood around
watching me try to drive my mallet through thick, wet grass.
But it wasn't the grass that caused my poor performance. My
mind was on Liam and the accident and the things he'd said
to my family.

I couldn't believe the timing of his death, and I felt certain
he hadn't just driven off the road because of a mistake or
recklessness. That left the horrifying realization that
someone in my family might have forced him off the road. It
sickened and terrified me to think that our family had secrets
so dark, and that one of us was capable of pushing a man to
his death, then smiling and chatting, playing croquet and
otherwise behaving in a completely normal way.

The thought made me so cold, my hands and arms shivered when I took my final shot.

Michael came up beside me and pulled me close. "Are
you okay? You look like you're not feeling well. I hope you
aren't overdoing it."

I laughed. "By playing croquet?" But my laugh was forced
and raw, and it made me sound like I was definitely not
feeling well. I straightened my back, letting the mallet fall to
the ground, where Michael picked it up. I looked at my family
standing in a semicircle around me. "I find it really hard to
believe Liam just drove off the road."

They faced me, all of them with half smiles, slightly
indulgent, but no one spoke.

"I can't stop thinking that someone forced him off the
road."

"Who would do that?" Jake asked.

"I don't know."

Their faces were blank, their eyes covered with sunglasses.

"That's ridiculous," my mother said. "Why would someone force him off the road? Besides, that girl saw him go off. She didn't say anything about another car."

"She saw his car in the water. She didn't see him go off."

"You're splitting hairs. And this whole thing is ridiculous," Collette said. "I know you feel awful because you invited him up here, as if you invited him to his death, but you didn't, really. So let it go. He made his own choices and mistakes. It's not your fault."

"That's not what I'm saying."

"What are you saying?" my mother asked. "Are you trying to suggest someone in your family killed your sister's ex-husband?" Her voice was shrill, and her tone offended and deeply hurt.

"I—" There were no words forming in my head. It was a terrible thing to think, much less speak the words. I couldn't do it, but I knew something was wrong. Just as I did with Sunday. To me, it was obvious, and I couldn't understand why no one else recognized it. My eyes filled with tears. I also was wearing dark glasses, so no one noticed. At first.

"Hey." Michael put his arm around me and pulled me against him. I felt the solid line of muscles in his side and the weight and press of his arm that usually made me feel absolutely safe, but now made me feel slightly smothered.

While Michael held me, the rest of my family began pulling wickets out of the ground and putting them on the rack. Jake collected the balls and dropped them into the slot with loud clacking sounds that made my head ache, each one like a gunshot.

Recognizing my gut feeling that Liam had not driven off the road in an accident, I realized another thought had been gnawing at the back of my head, one I'd been trying to keep from taking shape. A thought I hadn't wanted to face that now came rushing forward. Someone in my family, the person Sunday felt had betrayed her, had tried to push her off the cliff, and then they must have done something similar with Liam. But this time, they had been successful.

It hurt to think of my family this way. I didn't want to, and I hated myself. But the thoughts were there, and they refused to go away.

I recalled the way they'd all drawn together when Liam was telling them what he thought of us—that we were toxic, that my father's reputation would be ruined if people knew the truth about us. As we always did, as we'd been taught to do by my father's principles, they'd pulled together and treated Liam as an enemy outsider. Bella, Jake, and Collette walked out of the room without even acknowledging what he'd said. My parents followed. A solid, unbreakable unit. Only I had failed to stand with them.

It was almost pathological, the way they clung to each other. I'd often wondered what would happen if Jake or I, or my sisters when they were in that position, ever chose our spouse over the family.

My father slotted the last mallet into the rack and took the handle to wheel the rack to the shed. Then he let go and turned. "I forgot to mention, Annie. That's what comes of being woken in the middle of the night. You forget things. Important things." He laughed. "When Ben called last night, I mentioned that Sunday had taken off rather suddenly and that we were a little concerned about—"

"A little?" My tears dried suddenly. How could he minimize her disappearance like this? It had been three days now.

"... a little concerned that we hadn't heard from her, although of course she's a free, newly divorced adult woman, and her parents don't keep tabs on her. Right, Collette?"

"I'm not divorced," Collette said. "Why did you say that?"

"But you're single. You like to keep your private life private, am I right?"

She nodded, grinning.

"I told him we worried, as parents do. He said he would put the word out and mention it to a few of his buddies in Humboldt and Sonoma Counties as well."

"That sounds rather casual and slap-on-the-back and do-nothing," I said.

My father's jaw tightened noticeably. "I told him we were concerned, and he said he would put the word out. There's nothing else he can do. She's an adult with her own free will."

Without my noticing she'd moved closer, my mother was suddenly on my opposite side, sliding her arm around my waist, so I was now held up by her and Michael. "You need to stop getting yourself so upset," she said. "It's not good for the baby."

"That's an old wives' tale." I tried to wriggle out of her encircling arm. "You can't hurt the baby by being passionate about something."

"That's right," Bella said. "Paranoid or panicked thoughts create toxins. They move into your bloodstream and cause stress for Baby Girl."

"I'm not paranoid or panicked," I said.

"Well, I thought you could relax, knowing the police are aware," my father said. "If someone is out there trying to hurt her, which I highly doubt, the police are paying attention."

"That doesn't sound like much." I wondered if the police would do anything at all.

He smiled at me, then took off with the rack of croquet pieces. The others drifted away, and I remained, leaning against Michael, devastated by my father's coldness.

Daddy said I was his princess. Whenever he read me a bedtime story, he said that. He closed the book and kissed my nose. "Goodnight, Annie. You're my little princess. Never forget that."

I wasn't sure if he was right.

Collette said Sunday was the princess in our family, and we were her servants. She said I shouldn't let them make me her servant, but I didn't know who she was talking about. I didn't ask who *they* were, because Collette didn't like it when I asked questions. She said, *You ask too many questions. Curiosity killed the cat.* I didn't know what that meant, either.

Even when I was brave enough to ask questions, she usually didn't answer. She smiled and said, *That's for me to know and you to find out.* Or she just smiled and didn't say anything at all.

Once, I asked Daddy if it was true that I was really his princess.

He said, "Why would you ask that?"

"I want to know if it's true."

"Everything I say is true," he said.

I closed my eyes and tried to think if *that* was true. It didn't seem like it was, because no one told the truth all the time. Jake said *Sleeping Beauty* wasn't scary, but it gave me bad dreams. And Collette said black licorice vines were delicious, but I spit it out because it tasted terrible. Even Mommy didn't always tell the truth. She told me Sunshine, our cat, would come home, but she never did.

I tried to think if everything Daddy said was true, and I couldn't think of a single thing he'd said that wasn't. But I didn't really feel like a princess, and Collette kept saying I absolutely was not a princess. All I had to do was look at Sunday's bed to see who the real princess was.

For a long time, I waited to see if what Daddy said was always true.

I reached the top of the staircase after leaving Michael in the kitchen, where he was filling both our water bottles. Bella came swooping out of her room and nearly pinned me against the railing of the landing. She grabbed my hand in her icy-cold ones and pulled it close to her chest. "I'm worried about you, honey."

She'd never called me "honey," or any other term of endearment, in all the time I'd known her, and I couldn't imagine what had caused her to do it now. I tugged, trying to pull my hand out of her grip, but she tightened her fingers around mine.

"Don't be so resistant. I'm trying to give you some calming energy."

"I don't need calming energy."

"I think you do. You are really stressed out."

"Our sister disappeared, and no one has heard from her for three days. I think my feelings are completely appropriate. And now her ex-husband's car crashes into the river and sinks ..." My breath caught, and I couldn't continue speaking.

She rubbed my fingers. "You're overreacting. I'm not sure

why you're having so much trouble seeing that. I'm really worried about you. And Baby Girl." She gazed at my bump. I could tell she wanted to rub it as well, but she wasn't about to loosen her grip on my hands and allow me the chance to pull away. "We love you, sweetie. We really care about you and Baby Girl. You're not thinking clearly. You mock common-sense advice as old wives' tales, but they became accepted beliefs because there's truth in them. Old wives have wisdom." She chortled and dropped my hand, unable to keep hers off my bump, which she began rubbing. "We need to give her positive energy. All this talk of death and missing people is not good for her. You must know that emotional trauma can cause a miscarriage."

"That's ridiculous."

"Even though I'm an RN, I'm not so caught up in the medical-centric view of the human being. There's a mind-body-spirit connection that can't be ignored. I've seen it many times. I've never shared this, but you should know, I've come to see my anxiety caused two of my miscarriages. The third ... well, it most likely played a part there as well." Her eyes filled with tears. She blinked rapidly and increased her pressure on my bump.

"Please don't press on me like that." I grabbed her wrists and lifted her hands away from me.

"Don't deny me the pleasure of giving loving touches to your baby. Hopefully, someday, she and I will be related by blood, when Jake and I are finally blessed with one or two. Maybe more." She gave me a watery smile.

"Then be gentle," I said. "And my emotions are absolutely normal. Liam was our brother-in-law. It's natural we should grieve for him. Sunday may have taken her things, but it's concerning that we haven't heard from her. It's not like her, and everyone knows that. I have no idea why you're all acting as if that's not the case."

"Because you're borderline hysterical. You can't see it. Maybe talk to Michael about it, get some perspective. Your hormones are out of control. I know mine get that way when I'm going through a cycle of extra hormones to help us get pregnant. Those little buggers make you cray-cray. Every woman knows that. Come on, Annie. Have some self-awareness."

"I have plenty of self-awareness."

"Those hormones took over my entire personality. It caused problems between Jake and me. The things I imagined ..." She rubbed my belly. "I'm just telling you to be careful. Pay attention." Finally, she removed her hands slowly and reluctantly. "Of course, it's upsetting that Sunday took off without bothering to tell us anything, and it's sad about Liam. But you can't forget that Sunday is a flake, and he was reckless. So the situation shouldn't be a huge shock."

"That's not true. It's almost the opposite. Sunday is always on time; she always keeps in touch with Mom and Dad—"

"Growing a new life is a responsibility people don't take seriously enough. You belong to your little one now. Everything you do should be for her well-being. Indulging in morbid thoughts that upset your system could cause you to lose her. I suppose if that happened, tragic as it would be, you and I would have more in common." She gave me a sad smile and reached out to take my hand again.

I pulled back, moving to the side and gripping the railing. Her words sank into me like heavy stones dropping to the bottom of a pond. It sounded as if she wanted me to lose our baby! I stared at her, looking for some suggestion that she didn't realize what she'd said. Did she hope for something so awful? Did all of them hope that?

Maybe my siblings hated that Mom and Dad were doting on me because I was pregnant with their first grandchild. It had never occurred to me that all their hatred for Sunday might now be turned on me. Or maybe I didn't matter at all. Maybe my parents only wanted my child, the promise their family would continue into the future. Maybe my siblings recognized this and imagined history repeating itself as my parents favored my child as they had Sunday, pushing Jake and his wife and Collette even farther to the side.

Maybe they were pretending not to believe me about Sunday because they wanted me to think I was crazy. Maybe they wanted me to do something that would cause me to lose my baby. I put my hands on my bump, cradling her, moving farther along the railing, shrinking away from Bella as if contracting my body would keep both of us safe from her disturbing imagination. "I think I'll go lie down for a bit," I said.

"See. You're making yourself sick."

I didn't answer.

Alone in our room, I went to the window and stared out toward the stables and the wooded area beyond that ran all the way to the edge of our property. I knew my thoughts had veered precariously close to paranoid and quite a way off balance, but Bella's comments had taken an equally sharp turn into something I couldn't grasp. Her hands all over my body and her talk of miscarriage and trouble in her marriage to my brother disturbed me. But the same could be said of everything my entire family had said and done over the past few days.

These disturbing thoughts about my family were similar to my dreams—they seemed both real and imagined at the same time. It was disorienting, and I wasn't even sure what I believed or thought myself.

I lay on the bed. All I wanted was sleep. It was only noon, and I felt as if the day had already dragged on for ten or twelve hours. I closed my eyes, longing for my mind to settle, knowing it wouldn't. I slipped into a dreamlike memory of my encounter with Bella, feeling her hands crawling over my body like enormous spiders.

The door opened, making me start.

"Are you okay?" Michael came to the bed and sat on the edge. He placed his hand on my hip.

"I just had a weird conversation with Bella. That, and ... everything." I closed my eyes.

"Stop thinking about it so much."

My eyes flashed open. I laughed sharply. "Is that a joke?"

"You're becoming a little ... obsessed."

"You aren't worried about Sunday at all?"

"I am, but I don't think constantly talking about it and trying to make sure your family is equally concerned is very useful. And it's making you more upset and frustrated."

"They're acting as if nothing's wrong."

"So? Maybe they're trying to be positive."

"Do you really believe that?" I asked.

"It's possible. Anyway, you can't let them get under your skin. We're here to relax and spend time together."

"I can't relax when I'm worried something happened to her. Sorry. I'm not wired that way. And Liam is dead. Remember?"

"I know." He took my feet in his hands and pressed his thumbs into the arches. "It's a lot. Too much, I think. Maybe it would be better if we cut this trip short. We could head home Saturday."

I sat up and moved my feet out of his reach, even though the massage felt so good. "No. I can't leave until we hear from her, or at least hear from the police ... or something."

"It's unlikely the police are actively looking into it."

"But my dad said they would."

"You know you don't believe that."

I sighed. Tears pressed against the backs of my eyes. Why hadn't I tried harder to build a better relationship with my

sister as adults? All that childhood drama and pettiness—
although some of it wasn't so petty—should have been
worked through long before now.

"Let's think about going home. We could do some things
locally, stay up late bingeing a few shows, and take naps
and—"

"No. I'm not leaving until we find Sunday."

"What if you don't hear from her for two months?"

"Don't say that."

He reached across the bed and rubbed my leg. "Okay. But
please try to get your mind on other things, will you?"

"Sure. Okay."

He lay down beside me, and we held each other for a
while. I think Michael felt peaceful, thinking of nothing,
much as he often seems able to do. My brain continued
writhing. I felt it was wrapping me in strands of cotton,
weaving a cocoon around me where I felt insulated from
everyone around me, alone with my fears and dreams and
suspicions.

14

That afternoon, when Michael suggested a long walk alone together, I declined. "Why don't you go riding with the others? I don't mind staying back."

"I don't want to leave you when you're feeling so—"

"Stop. I'm not a child or an invalid. I'm perfectly content and capable of being on my own. It's not like the baby is coming any day. I thought I'd drive to Mendocino and look around some antique shops. Maybe I'll find something for Mom."

"That's a long drive for something she probably doesn't need." He glanced around the empty, darkened dining room where we stood, taking in the silver tea and coffee service, the candlestick holders from the 1800s, the other silver pieces she'd collected and carefully polished, the porcelain horses in their own curio cabinet.

"I like the drive. And it will clear my head to get away from here."

He laughed. He took it to mean I wanted to stop thinking about my missing sister and Liam's sudden, horrible death, but it wasn't that at all.

The moment I saw the last horse tail flick out of sight, I took off the dress I'd been wearing and changed into my oldest pair of leggings. I put on a shirt that I usually wore hiking, and tied up my sturdy shoes over thick socks.

It felt strange driving after not having been behind the wheel since we'd arrived at my childhood home over a week ago. I backed out of the spot beside Collette's car and pulled around to the long, curving road that led from our house to the highway.

After I crossed the bridge over the Navarro River, I slowed to below the speed limit, trying to find the exact spot where the road had washed out. I knew there would be barriers and reflector lights to warn me, but I also remembered that it came up suddenly, which helped explain, partly, why Liam might not have been prepared.

When I saw the first barrier, I slowed further, then pulled off onto the shoulder just as the road narrowed to a single lane. The shoulder at that part of the road seemed solid. I could tell from the ruts and gravel that it had been used to park construction trucks and earth movers while road repairs were underway on weekdays.

I opened the car door and was greeted with the loud rush of water running in the Navarro River, headed toward the Pacific Ocean. I got out, closed the door, locked it, and pocketed the key fob. I walked to the edge of the embankment and was stunned by the relatively tranquil look of the water gliding by, despite the loud noise it was making as it gushed toward its destination.

Liam's black BMW had already been removed, and there was no sign it had ever been there. If the detective hadn't carefully described the spot, and if the fishtailing skid marks hadn't still been visible where I stood, I would have doubted I had the right spot. The water was deep, the embankment not impossible to climb down, but it definitely had a good slope.

For a moment, I wondered if I was completely out of my mind thinking I could climb down there.

Michael and I were regular weekend hikers, and I wasn't even close to the awkward, unstable stage of pregnancy, but neither was I an unencumbered twenty-year-old. Still. I had sturdy shoes. I was in good shape. And I had to know if there was something down there the police hadn't seen. I was confident of that possibility because they clearly hadn't looked very hard, if at all.

They'd studied the skid marks, profiled Liam based on his place of residence—*outsider*—and his performance car —*arrogant show-off*—and made a conclusion as to what had happened. I just had to know if there was anything to suggest another person had gone down there in the dark, checking to see that the car was fully submerged. If his death was what they'd intended. If the suspicions I feared with all my heart might be true were, in fact, true.

I began easing my way down the embankment, thankful for saplings that leaned toward the river, offering solidly rooted handholds. There were a lot of fallen leaves and pine needles, years of detritus slowly decaying, keeping the woods alive and fresh.

Closer to the water, the ground turned muddy. There were a lot of rocks and chunks of hard-packed dirt from small landslides. The leaves and broken branches and a few downed trees were denser closer to the water. I picked my way around carefully, unsure what I was looking for, painfully aware of the futility of my plan.

I stopped a few yards from the edge of the water, not wanting to get too close and lose my footing, sliding on wet, possibly unstable earth into water that I might not be able to fight. I surveyed the ground in every direction, suddenly feeling helpless. It was littered with the dead remnants of nature, but there was nothing beyond the tracks of Liam's car and some footprints and more tracks showing where the car had been dragged up the embankment by heavy-duty winches attached to rescue vehicles. I was in the middle of the woods hoping to find something that suggested a person had committed a crime that's virtually evidence-free— forcing a car off the road.

Moving carefully, I kicked at the leaves and sticks, hoping to uncover something useful. But even if someone had been down here in the darkness, what were the chances they would have dropped something telling, something that gave away their identity? I laughed out loud, imagining my family's reaction to my foolishness. My voice echoed strangely around me.

Still, I continued to walk beside the river, making sure each step was a firm placement of my foot, checking that the ground was stable and level, making sure rocks weren't loose and ready to pitch me sideways into the water. I walked in a straight line for about thirty feet, then turned back, feeling more ridiculous with each step. What did I think I would find? An ID bracelet? An engraved cigarette lighter?

Then, as I kicked at the twigs and sticks, something flew away from the toe of my shoe. A very small stick, but manmade. A pale wood that didn't match the other bits of twigs and broken sticks. I bent down and picked it up. A toothpick. It was stained with moisture, but it wasn't something that had been rotting in the woods for years or even months. It looked almost new.

I held it in the palm of my hand and stared at it.

Michael hated that my family kept that crystal glass full of toothpicks on the dining room table. From the first time he'd eaten dinner with us, he'd expressed disgust. He said it was an invitation to pick your teeth at the table. It was rude, and it turned his stomach that my family all followed this practice. All but me, once he told me how it made him feel.

He was horrified when, after the meal was over, his enjoyment of the food was destroyed as he watched people pick bits of it from between their teeth. "It's like spitting into your mouth and eating it."

I could never forget those words. Since that time, I felt equally queasy when I watched my family after meals.

I closed my hand around the toothpick despite knowing it very well might have been in someone's mouth. It didn't surprise me it was still out here. Even if the police had looked around the area, even if they had seen it, the innocuous item would have meant nothing to them. If I showed it to them now, they would laugh at me.

There are probably billions of toothpicks on the planet. Finding one near the scene of a car accident means absolutely nothing. But I couldn't shake the feeling that someone had forced Liam off the road after he taunted them with his mild threat that he had a secret capable of destroying our family. And if they'd done that, they would have taken the trouble to climb down the embankment to check that the car sank far enough into the water that Liam wasn't going to survive.

15

I put the toothpick in my coat pocket and stared at the steep hill above me. I didn't know if I had the energy to climb, fighting the weight of despair that had washed over me.

Before I could grab hold of the first sapling to start my climb back up to where my car was parked, I heard voices: "Annie!" The sound carried, giving me the feeling it was floating on the river behind me. I looked up and saw Jake and Bella standing at the top of the embankment.

Jake shouted at me, "What are you *doing*?"

I wanted to respond with the same question. How had they suddenly shown up here? Had they followed me? I wasn't aware of another car behind me during the drive to the washed-out section of the road. I knew they hadn't gone riding with Collette and Michael and my parents, but I'd assumed they were in their room, Jake working on lesson plans, Bella flitting around Facebook and Instagram, giving unsolicited advice, one of her favorite pastimes.

Jake started down the hill. "Stay there. We're coming to help."

"I don't need help." I grabbed the nearest sapling and began making my way up.

"Oh, God!" Bella moaned repeatedly from the top of the embankment as if I were in danger of being swept away by ferocious rapids at any moment.

Her obvious panic was making me nervous. I moved more quickly, keeping my attention on Jake to be sure I stayed well out of the area where he was making his way down. I did not need my brother assisting me up the hill. Even if I hadn't been pregnant, I wouldn't have wanted that. I'd come out there on my own because they were treating me like an anxious, hysterical child. Now it looked like that was about to get worse.

By the time I reached the top, Jake had reversed his direction, meeting me there. Bella grabbed my hands, rubbing them as if she thought I might have frostbite. I pulled them away.

"Are you okay?" she asked.

"I'm fine."

"What were you doing down there?" she asked. "Did you not hear a single word I said to you earlier?"

"I needed to see where Liam's car went into the water."

"That's morbid," Jake said.

"Her thoughts are getting very dark." Bella reached for my bump, but I moved out of reach.

"How did you know I was here?" I asked.

"We went out for groceries," Bella said. "I'm just so worried about you. This was so, so dangerous. You could have fallen and lost—"

"Stop with the horror stories," I said. "Michael and I have gone hiking since I first knew I was pregnant. I'm fine."

"This isn't hiking. This is a river swollen past its normal level, prone to flash floods and—"

"Flash flooding happens *during* storms. There hasn't been any rain for three weeks."

Bella lunged toward me before I could move out of her way. She put her arms around me and held me close. "You poor, poor thing. I knew you weren't listening when we had our little talk. You're so stubborn." She laughed softly into my ear, her breath so hot on my skin, I shrank from her.

She tightened her arms around me. "Are you cold? Let's get you into the car." She began walking me slowly toward their SUV.

"I can drive myself." I strained to pull out of her grasp, but I couldn't wriggle free. Years of moving patients in and out of beds had made her a woman who not only had superior physical strength, but had a firm belief in her own right to bodily move others into places she thought were best for their well-being. "I have my car, Bella. Please let go of me. You're going to make me fall, trying to shove me around like this."

She loosened her grip, but didn't let go of me entirely.

When we were beside their car, she finally relaxed her arms enough that I could slip free.

"I think we should drive you home. Jake and Michael can come back later for your car."

"Why? There's nothing wrong with me." I pulled the key out of my pocket, feeling in the other pocket for the sharp stab of the toothpick.

"What on earth were you doing down there, anyway?" she asked. "You could have fallen into the water. You could have gotten hypothermia. You could have hit your head and drowned; you could have been washed out to sea."

I laughed. "I was down there because the police made an extremely fast decision about the cause of his accident. It was less than twenty-four hours. Did they investigate at all?"

"There was nothing to investigate," Jake said. "It was clear cut. He skidded off the road because he didn't realize it was washed out. He was going too fast, didn't see the barriers, and over he went. There was no need to go digging around in the woods looking for clues, if that's what you thought you were doing."

They were both staring at me, waiting for me to speak. I said nothing. I pressed the fob, and my car beeped.

After another brief pause, Jake spoke. "Did you find anything?"

"What would I find? They hauled the car away. You saw how it is down there. Fallen trees and years of leaves and mulch."

"Then what did you think you would find? You knew they already pulled the car out. I don't understand the purpose of climbing down there and digging around in the leaves. As if the police need your help. They're the experts. They said it was an accident. You shouldn't be second-guessing them."

"You're probably right," I said.

"Not worth risking a sprained ankle over, is it?" He nudged me with his elbow. "Always the adventurer, aren't you?"

I gave him a tight smile and opened my car door. I glanced at their SUV. A single grocery bag sat in the cargo area. "I thought you said you went grocery shopping?"

"We need to make sure Baby Girl has her nutrients, right?"

"Mom just went two days ago. And it doesn't look like you got much ..."

She laughed. "Just some fruit."

"There's never any shortage of fruit in that house," I said.

"Some of it spoiled."

I nodded.

"So you already went to the store and were on your way back home when you saw my car?"

"What's your point?" Jake asked.

"Nothing." I slid into my car.

"Are you sure you're okay to drive?" Jake asked. "You look pale."

"I'm fine." I pulled the door closed. I felt in my pocket for the toothpick. I wondered how long they'd stood at the top of the embankment watching me. Had they seen me bend over and pluck the toothpick out of the leaves? Had they seen me studying it and closing my fingers around it? They wouldn't have been able to see what it was from where they were standing. But they might have known I found something.

I wondered what they were thinking, and I wondered if they'd followed me there. It didn't seem possible that they had time to go to the market, buy fruit, and be headed back home in the short time I'd been parked on the shoulder. I recalled how I'd seen Jake watching me when I found Sunday's diamond necklace. Now I felt again that he was paying too much attention to me. Had he always been this way, or was this something new? I couldn't be sure.

16

By the time I arrived home, I wondered if my brother and sister-in-law had been partially correct in worrying that I wasn't fit to drive. My hands were shaking badly, and when I climbed out of the car, my legs felt weak, as if I'd lost control of my muscles. I wasn't about to let anyone, not even Michael, see that I was so upset it was affecting my body. I stood for a moment, leaning on the open car door. I took several long, slow breaths. I desperately wanted a drink of water, but I hadn't thought to bring my water bottle with me, something I rarely forgot.

When my legs felt as if they'd regained control, I went directly to the kitchen, glad that I didn't run into anyone sniffing around for a snack. I was able to stand near the sink, looking out at the garden, and drink a large glass of water. I savored each swallow, as if I could feel it flowing to my muscles, revitalizing the tissues, making them stronger.

I felt in my pocket for the toothpick, wondering what the point of it was. It proved nothing, but it wouldn't stop whispering to me that someone in my family had caused Liam's death.

Upstairs, I found Michael in our bedroom. His hair was wet from his shower after horseback riding. He smelled clean. His smooth skin and perfectly groomed fingernails made me feel grubby from my trek along the riverbank.

"You don't look like you had a very relaxing time antiquing." He kissed my forehead. "You smell like pine trees and ... Where were you?"

"I took a detour."

"Oh?" He sat in the armchair to pull on his socks.

"I didn't go to Mendocino after all."

"I thought you were back awfully fast." He picked up his phone and checked the time. "Where did you go?"

"I went to see where Liam's car crashed into the river."

"Oh, Annie." He stood and crossed the room. He wrapped his arms around me and pulled me close. "Why? And if you felt you had to do that, why didn't you ask me to go with you?"

"I didn't need you."

I felt his muscles tighten against my ribs.

"I didn't mean that the way it sounded, but what I mean is that I don't need you to hold my hand. Everyone's treating me like I'm an invalid or incompetent because I'm pregnant. Sometimes it feels like everyone cares more about the baby than me."

"You're completely misreading things."

"Am I?"

"Yes."

"Jake and Bella saw my car on the side of the road, so they stopped. They—"

"Your car? Where were you?"

"I went down to the river."

He pulled back, still holding me, looking into my eyes. He spoke carefully; I could see he was aware of not treating me like I was incompetent. "Was that ... a good idea?"

"Do you see what I mean?" I saw the look of disappointment cross his face. He hadn't chosen his words carefully enough. But I couldn't help myself. It was irritating and insulting. "We go hiking. I work in the garden. I drive to wholesalers to order plants. I'm pregnant. I don't have a debilitating disease."

"Okay. Fair enough."

"They acted like I was truly insane."

"But why did you go down there? I don't understand. They towed the car away already, didn't they?"

"Because I think someone forced him off the road."

"Come on, Annie. Why? There's no proof."

"That's what I was looking for."

"That's a job for the police, and they didn't find anything."

"Because they just assumed things about him. That he didn't know the roads, that he drove too fast because he was overconfident, that he'd been drinking—which he hadn't. My father—"

"Why would someone force him off the road?"

"Remember? He said he knew something that could destroy our family."

"Like what?"

"I don't know. He ..." I paused. There was no dark secret that Liam was privy to, but someone thought there was. I grabbed my jacket off the bed. "I found this." I pulled out the toothpick and showed it to him.

He laughed.

"It's not funny."

"Okay. I see why you think ... everyone in your family is attached to their public teeth cleaning, but that toothpick could have been there for years. It could belong to anyone. A cop could have dropped it, someone from the towing company. It could have come from absolutely anyone. A hiker. A bird could have picked it up for nesting material."

"That seems unlikely."

"Alright, the bird scenario was a stretch, but it truly could belong to anyone. I can see why it looks strange to you, because you've watched your family use them all your life, so it seems significant, but it doesn't mean anything. It's a coincidence. You're infusing it with meaning because you want to explain his death, because you're disturbed that you haven't heard from Sunday. That's all."

"I think you're wrong."

He sighed. "It was an accident. I wish you could let it go. I know you want to be treated like you're a healthy, competent woman. And you are. But at the same time, you're looking almost haunted the past few days."

I laughed. "I'm not *haunted*. I'm worried. You sound like you've been talking to Jake and Bella. It feels like they're influencing the way you look at me, which is a little insulting. Quite insulting, actually."

"I'm not being influenced by anyone. I love you. I know you're upset, but there's nothing we can do. We have to wait until Sunday decides to get in touch, and we have to accept that Liam had a terrible accident. It's shocking and upsetting, but it happens."

I didn't want to talk to him anymore. I felt like he wasn't listening, and I was tired of trying to explain. When he clumsily changed the subject, suggesting we take a drive to a nearby farm that had put handmade signs along the highway announcing the sale of fresh eggs, I agreed that sounded like a fun way to spend the afternoon.

The next morning, I woke to the aroma of bacon filling our bedroom. Michael stood in the doorway, holding a wood tray with a white ceramic teapot and cup, a plate with an omelet, bacon, and whole grain toast. Beside it was a tiny bowl of jam and another tiny dish with a scoop of butter, and a small plate with sliced strawberries.

"I thought you'd enjoy a nice quiet meal without your family breathing down your neck," he said.

I smiled.

He placed the tray on the dresser, came around the side of the bed, and arranged the pillows so I could sit up with comfortable back support. He turned on the bedside lamp, then placed the tray next to me.

"Are you going to eat with me?"

"I drank a smoothie while I was making this. But I'll run back down and get my coffee."

"That sounds nice." I smiled and wiggled my feet under the warm blankets.

I ate a few strawberries and buttered my toast. I'd eaten a slice of bacon and almost half my omelet by the time he returned. He was carrying two paperback books, two hard-covers, and a coffee mug.

"What are those?"

He sat beside me, leaning against his own pillows. He took a sip of coffee. "I thought you could use a quiet day by yourself. I grabbed these from the family library. Two mysteries, a biography of Marie Curie, and some Greek myths."

"That's quite a collection."

"I know you like choices."

"Maybe I want more choices. And maybe I don't feel like sitting in my room on a beautiful day near the coast, reading books that I can read in the middle of winter or when I'm thirty-eight weeks and don't feel like moving much." I bit a strip of bacon.

"You need to rest."

"What is this, the twenty-first century or the nineteenth?"

He gave me a hurt and confused look.

"Am I a fragile lady in the family way, and I must take to my bed?"

"It's not like that." His voice was clipped and cold. "I was trying to help you relax. We're on vacation. There's nothing wrong with taking it easy."

"I didn't say it was wrong. I just ..." I wasn't sure why I was arguing with him. He was being so sweet, but it was irritating me in a way I couldn't fully explain. I began eating my omelet, wanting to enjoy it before it was cold.

"You've had a shock, and you're upset. This is one of the best times of our life—waiting for our baby's birth. I hate seeing you upset and worried and feeling like your family is attacking you."

"This is delicious. Thank you so much."

He kissed the side of my head.

"Reading and spending some time alone sounds nice," I said.

He smiled with such eagerness it made my heart ache. I finished eating, and when he took the tray out of the room, I picked up the book of Greek myths and opened it.

As it turned out, the myths made me drift off to sleep, which was probably what I needed. When I woke from a strangely dreamless sleep, I took a shower and took my time slowly blowing my hair dry. Then I checked email and scrolled through social media. I pinged Sunday's friends again to see if they'd heard from her. The ones who answered right away said they hadn't. I picked up one of the novels and started reading.

It wasn't even noon, and I was already tired of resting. I heard voices outside and went to the window. Michael and my siblings were playing softball, if you could call it that, with two on each team. My parents sat in lawn chairs, sipping from coffee mugs. Beyond the edge of the lawn area, I could see Quinn repairing part of the corral fencing.

I placed the book on the nightstand, marking my place with a seashell I'd picked up. I slipped into sandals and went to the door. I turned the knob, but the door didn't move. I jiggled the knob and tried again. I squatted slightly and looked at the old-fashioned keyhole below the knob. The key had been pulled out. In their effort to make the remodel of our Victorian house authentic, my parents had installed doorknobs with locks that allowed the keys to be inserted from either side. Usually, the key was kept inside the room so we could lock our doors for privacy, but it could also be locked from the outside.

I hurried to the window and opened it wider. "Hey!" I screamed out. Only Michael looked up at me. "Come unlock the door!"

He called back, his voice faint, since he had no reason to be as upset as I was. At that moment, I wanted to take the books and hurl them out the window at him. "You locked the door! Come open it right now!"

"I didn't lock the door."

I didn't want to have a screaming conversation with him. Jake, Bella, Collette, and my parents were all staring up at me now. I knew I looked as deranged as they imagined I was, screaming out a second-floor window like I was locked in a lunatic asylum. Despite knowing how I appeared, I couldn't stop myself. "Let me out! Now!"

Michael dropped his baseball glove on the grass. Two minutes later, I heard the key in the lock, and the door opened.

"Why did you do that?!"

"I didn't," he said. "The key was right there on the floor. It must have fallen out."

"It didn't fall out. Keys don't fall out."

"I didn't lock you in."

"The key is always on the inside. It did not *fall out* and slide under the door into the hallway."

"I don't know. Maybe it fell out, and I kicked it when I went out and didn't notice?"

I grabbed the key out of his hand and stabbed it into the lock. I walked out of the room and along the landing toward the stairs. I had no idea where I was going. I had no interest in playing softball with my family, but I couldn't stand there and listen to him make up lame explanations. I wanted to cry. Did he think I was so unglued that he needed to lock me in my room? But I was not the one who was disturbed here. It was everyone else.

"Annie." He followed me into the hallway. "Please. Let's talk. I didn't lock you in. I would never, ever do that. Please believe me. You know me better than that." I turned to face him.

"It didn't just fall out." I thought about Jake and Bella following me to the accident, Jake watching me. I thought about the odd behavior I'd witnessed from my family the past few days. I walked back to him and put my arms around his waist, resting my head on his chest. "I'm sorry. It was ... I freaked out."

"Anyone would. But it wasn't me."

"I know. I'm sorry." We stood there holding each other. Maybe I would try talking to Collette. She knew what it was like to be dismissed as *kooky, crazy*. She'd had to listen to that for years. They pretended like it was affectionate and fun, but I knew she hated it.

17

E ver since she left for college, Collette had entertained the family with stories of swashbuckling, magical, suave boyfriends when she came home to visit. Of course, she didn't see it as entertainment. But the rest of us did. Each visit brought a story of the latest guy who had swept her off her feet, and it was always a mysterious, one-of-a-kind guy.

Even as an adult, the Christmas holidays and Thanksgiving weekends and our summer vacation gatherings were not complete without a fantastical story of the latest incredible man Collette was dating. None of them ever came to our house. None of them ever progressed beyond the role of new guy. She never moved in with any of them, never talked about marriage. It was the newness that excited her.

To us, the question was whether the stories about their feats were true, or if they existed at all.

She never blushed when she told us about the latest, never acknowledged that, at this point, there was a cast of easily thirty or forty men who had paraded through her life.

The mystique thrilled her. And that mystique often sounded invented. We could never be sure. After a while, those stories took on the proportion of family legend, and Collette took on the unwanted reputation as slightly unstable.

At the start of our current vacation, she'd told us about Neil. He owned a yacht and boated around the world. He'd already taken her on a trip from San Diego, where she lived, to Acapulco. This was a far cry from yachting around the world, but only Jake was cold enough to point that out. The rest of us waited patiently. I think we hoped to find out more information rather than making comments that would cause her to retreat into her own thoughts, hurt and sulking that we didn't believe her or were making fun of her. If we heard more stories, we might be able to figure out the truth.

Neil was tall, as all her mysterious boyfriends were. He had dark hair and dark eyes and had Middle Eastern ancestry, but he, and maybe his father, had been born in the US. She wasn't positive, though, because he hinted that he had a lot of property in exotic but possibly dangerous locations he couldn't really talk about. He also didn't have a career, but spent all of his time and energy on the yacht. According to Collette, he was extremely well-read—he could quote Shakespeare to fit any situation—and he'd read all of *The Divine Comedy*. He was also an expert on Renaissance philosophers.

"How would you know he's an expert?" Jake asked. "Because you wouldn't recognize a Renaissance philosopher even if he had an Instagram account."

Collette ignored him and continued talking about Neil. She showed us pictures of Neil steering his yacht and pictures of them together, so it seemed he was real. But there was something about the way she talked that made me think of fairy tales.

When I knocked on her bedroom door, she opened it

right away. "Annie, how are you feeling? I was having a glass of wine, and I'd offer you one, but of course, you can't have any. That's so sad. But come in and make yourself comfy. Do you want a sisterly confab?"

I went into her room and settled myself on the pile of large pillows she'd arranged in one corner. Those pillows had been there since Collette was in high school. She used to burrow in there to write in her diary. I wondered if she still kept a diary, but I didn't ask.

She sat on the floor facing me and put her phone beside her. She lifted her chin slightly, letting her waist-long, expertly colored red hair slide away from the sides of her face. It was a strict rule of hers that she never brushed her hair off her face with her fingers, to avoid getting any oil on her beautiful skin. She hugged her knees to her chest and studied her toenails painted midnight blue with a hint of sparkle.

"Were you texting with Neil?"

She smiled.

"Sorry Jake makes fun of you when you talk about Neil. He sounds great."

She rolled her eyes. "I'm used to it."

"Being called crazy?"

She laughed.

I asked her a few questions about Neil. She was happy to tell me more stories. I talked about the nursery and how well it was doing, and she seemed excited and interested. It was so strange with my sisters. Sometimes I felt incredibly close to them, and at other times, I feared we were mortal enemies.

I shifted my position on the pillows, crossing my legs in an attempt to look even more casual because I knew my question would not sound casual at all. "Did Jake or Bella tell you what I did yesterday?"

"Nope." She took a sip of her wine, then set the glass back precariously on the carpet.

"I went to the place where Liam's car crashed."

"That's creepy. Why?"

"I had to see it for myself."

"He was already out of our lives when they got divorced. Knowing he's dead doesn't seem much different."

"I don't think Sunday will feel that way. I wonder if she knows."

She shrugged.

"I was looking around because it still doesn't seem like an accident."

"Think what you want. I believe the cops."

I laughed. "Do you?"

She gave me a slow, wicked smile. "Okay, maybe not always, but it sounds logical. I certainly don't think someone forced him off the road."

"I found a toothpick by the spot where he went into the water. At least I think that's where he went in."

She stared at me. "A toothpick? So what?"

"Our family. It makes me think someone in our family was down there."

"That's ridiculous." She laughed and picked up her wineglass. "Is that why you're here having this cozy chat? Do you think it was me?" She gave me that same wicked smile.

"No ... I ..."

"Listen to how that sounds. You found a toothpick in the middle of the woods, by a river that's carrying all kinds of stuff people toss outside of campsites and picnic areas. A toothpick?" She took a long swallow of wine. "Besides, think about what you're saying. How can you believe someone in our family is a killer? We may have our issues, but what the hell?"

"But Liam almost sounded like he was threatening us.

Saying he knew something that could destroy us ... implying one of us did something to Sunday. If—"

"Can you hear yourself?" Collette moved onto her knees. She stood and put her wineglass on the nightstand, then came toward me, sitting close and wrapping her fingers around my ankle. "You need to stop thinking about all this stuff. And you need to stop worrying so much about Sunday. She's a spoiled brat. She always has been."

"She can't help how Mom and Dad treated her."

"But it made her think she can do whatever she wants. You're forgetting how it was, with her private horseback riding lessons, while we learned from Quinn's dad. Then she gets to go to fancy horse resorts with Mom and Dad because she was a better rider? Of course she was." She laughed, but it was gentle, and she squeezed my ankle. "Her private dance lessons? Claremont College while the rest of us went to state universities?"

"I didn't care about any of that. I liked going to school where my friends were going."

"Maybe, but it made Sunday insufferable. And now she wants to destroy our vacation. It couldn't be all about her because you're pregnant and Mom and Dad are excited about being grandparents. So she disappears and makes it all about her after all."

I sighed. It didn't feel that way. "Don't you ever think about the awful things you and Jake did to her? And maybe I did them too, I guess. It's hard to remember."

"You were little, so not really. And they weren't awful. It was normal kid stuff."

"Some of it was pretty awful. It crossed the line from normal."

"It wasn't that bad."

That didn't sound like how I remembered it. I remembered feeling terrible. But Collette was right: I was a lot younger, and those memories were blurred and difficult to pin down. Mostly, they were bad feelings, yet the events around them were completely lost inside my head. "I feel terrible, that's all."

"She asked for it, parading around like—"

"What about the birthday party?"

"What birthday party?"

"When she was nine. When you and Jake called her friends' parents and said she had the stomach flu. You told them the party was canceled, so no one showed up. She was heartbroken. She thought none of her friends liked her anymore."

"That never happened."

"Liam said she was broken up about it all her life."

"Well, it never happened. She lied to him."

"He said it was her ninth birthday party. Why would she make that up?"

"She's a drama queen. It never happened, I'm telling you. Don't you remember her ninth birthday party? That's when Mom and Dad gave her a damn cell phone. And all the kids were going nuts wanting to play with it. Maybe it's too hard for you to remember. But calling her friends so they wouldn't show up?" She laughed. "Nope."

Before I could say more, she asked me if we'd settled on names for the baby yet. She suggested "Collette" might make a nice middle name. I told her it was still a long list, and I doubted we would use a family name at all. She pouted, but then she laughed. She got up and walked over to her nightstand to pick up her wineglass.

I felt unsettled about the birthday party. I couldn't imagine why Sunday would make up a story like that. Did she want Liam to feel sorry for her? What was the point? If she wanted sympathy, there were a hundred other ways to get it rather than making up a silly, pathetic story from her childhood.

When I went to bed, I didn't tell Michael about talking to Collette or about the birthday party. The memory felt confusing to me—something about the cell phone—but I couldn't figure out what was wrong with it, and trying to explain it to him would make it more confusing.

18

My little sister has a bigger bedroom than mine. I don't think that's fair, but I'm not supposed to complain because complaining is not nice, and no one likes a complainer, and it's not being grateful for what you have.

I'm not supposed to go in her bedroom because we don't go in other people's bedrooms without permission, but I can't help it. My mom took Sunday to horseback riding lessons, and my little sister Annie went with them. Jake is at basketball practice, and Dad is giving seminars in Los Angeles, where he got to go on an airplane.

I have the house all to myself. Conner and his son, Quinn, are at the stables, and they're supposed to keep an eye on me, but I don't think they know what that means. That's what Quinn said. I think it mostly means they have to make sure I don't invite strangers into the house or use the stove or jump off the roof. I never thought about jumping off the roof until Quinn said that's the kind of thing that *keeping their eye on me* must mean. Now I kind of want to jump off the roof.

I open the door to Sunday's bedroom. It isn't like I've

never seen it before, but sometimes I forget how amazing it is. Her room faces the front of the house, and it has a huge, round window with a curving window seat that looks out across the edge of the garden and the front path. She even has her own bathroom. I don't know any girl at my school who has her own bathroom attached to her bedroom. With a shower *and* a bathtub.

I step into her room and feel the pale blue carpet under my bare feet. It feels softer than the rug in my room, softer than any carpet in our house, softer than a cloud. I look at the walls showing huge, framed pictures of Sunday on her horse, jumping over hurdles and posing with blue ribbons after shows. I look at the display case that holds some of her ribbons. The rest of her ribbons and trophies are displayed in a glass cabinet downstairs. It's taller than Jake, and we aren't supposed to touch it because of fingerprints.

Her bed has four white posts and a purple canopy. It matches the bedspread, which has ruffles like a princess skirt. There are ten pillows with big ruffles at the top of her bed because her bed is bigger, like it was made for two people to sleep in, almost as big as Mommy and Daddy's bed.

I go into her bathroom. I sit on the toilet, and when all the pee is out, I dip her toothbrush in it. Then I flush and go out. I lie down on her bed and cuddle her stuffed elephant. I cry my tears into the back of its head. After a while, I get up and open her desk. I look at her diary, but it has a lock, and I don't think I can find a way to get it open without being caught, so I put it back.

I close my eyes, and I can hear my daddy talking while we were eating brownies after dinner.

Jealousy is ugly, he said. Jealousy means wanting things other people have. It means not being happy with all the good things you have. It means always looking at the other person instead of looking at yourself. Other people are none of your business.

A good family can't have jealousy, I hear my daddy say. He went in the kitchen and came back with an orange. There was a fuzzy white spot on the side, and the orange was starting to cave in, like our carved pumpkins did after Halloween was over. He passed the orange around the table and told us to smell it. The smell was awful. He asked if we wanted to eat it. We all said yuck.

He said jealousy rots the foundation of a family. Like the orange, in case we didn't get it.

You can't be jealous. It's bad. Not being jealous is a family principle you have to follow.

Maybe I'm bringing rot into our family because I'm jealous of Sunday. Jake too. He's even more jealous.

But Mommy and Daddy love Sunday more than us. Everything she has is better. It seems like it should be a family principle to love all your children the same. To try to give them the same things. It's not fair this way. I don't know why they love her more. I want them to love me just as much.

Isn't that how it's supposed to be?

I go back into her bathroom and flush the toilet again, just to be sure. Then I go out of her room and close the door.

I wonder if our family is rotting, and no one knows it.

19

Collette was so sure that Sunday had lied about her ninth birthday party. But I couldn't stop thinking about it. Liam was just as certain that Sunday was so hurt by what they did it had damaged her in a way that affected her as an adult. It was such a strange thing to lie about. Which one of them was lying? Collette? Sunday? Liam? Why?

At the same time, there was something about that birthday party, the year she got her cell phone, that was bothering me. I just couldn't remember anything about that part except the cell phone. I hated that feeling of knowing something was in my head, knowing the memory was there, but I couldn't do anything to make it come to the surface. Trying gave me a headache. It made me feel as if my brain was full of junk that had collected for years, and I was digging around, but couldn't find the one thing I was looking for, as if it kept slipping to the bottom the more I dug.

I went out to the gazebo, hoping I could think without anyone trying to talk to me, without someone putting their hand on my bump or, worse, rubbing it as if I were some kind of magic genie. I wanted to feel the cool breeze on my face. I wanted quiet except for the crash of the surf.

I sat inside the tiny building, shivering as the cool wind blew through the open sides. I pulled my coat around me. Feeling cold was worth it, because all I could hear were water and birds and the sound of my own breath. I slid my hand inside my coat and rested it on my bump.

The tips of my fingers were cold, and being inside my coat didn't warm them, but my baby didn't seem to mind. After a few seconds of quiet breathing, I felt the familiar flutter of her hands and feet. I'd seen her gentle movements on the ultrasound, and I'd felt them quite a few times by now, but it still filled me with amazement each time. The idea of another human life inside me, separate from my own, was too incredible to believe. While I went about my regular routine, when I wasn't even thinking about her, she was already living a life of her own. I wondered if she was already having her own thoughts, or would she have to hear human conversation for those to begin taking shape? I had no idea, and I supposed no one really did.

Closing my eyes, I tried to picture what I could of Sunday's birthday party and that cute little cell phone that everyone wanted to hold. Kids didn't have cell phones then. A lot of adults didn't have cell phones. All the kids at Sunday's party wanted to flip the cover open and closed. They wanted to call their brothers and sisters. They thought it was so cool.

My memories of the reaction to that tiny silver phone were sharp and clear, but other than that, there was nothing. I couldn't remember any other kids' faces or their names. I couldn't remember how the cake was decorated. I couldn't remember what games we played or any other gifts she'd received. The backs of my eyes ached from trying to picture it.

As I tried to relax, to stop forcing myself to bring to mind something that wasn't there, the sensation that someone was watching me crept slowly over my shoulders and up my neck. I opened my eyes and turned. No one was there. The front porch was empty, as much as I could see from the gazebo. There was no one in the garden or anywhere around the house. The only sounds were the wind and gulls, as they had been when I'd stepped inside the tiny, isolated building.

I closed my eyes again, wondering why the human memory, certainly mine, was such a devious creature. It spewed memories at me when I didn't want them. It taunted me with the same images over and over, and at other times, when I needed an important piece of information, it folded in on itself like a clam, locking everything tightly inside.

I rubbed my belly, hoping to stir the baby into more activity, but she was content to rest now. Again, I felt the creeping sensation of someone staring at the back of my head. I whipped around, but I saw the same tranquil setting—an empty landscape of beach grass and trees, the lawn and garden, and our beautiful home—pale gray with white trim, a stone around the foundation and stone-framed entrance and porch.

Straining so hard to remember something that refused to take shape in my head was exhausting. I wished the wood benches of the gazebo had cushions so I could lie down and enjoy a nap. I was so sleepy. I shifted a little, considering lying on my side even on the bare wood, but I knew the price would be aches in every bone of my shoulders and hips.

I stood and walked to the front of the gazebo, looking out over the water. It was obvious the memory of Sunday's party was not going to return to me, if it had ever been there to begin with. I leaned on the half wall and tried to resist the desire to look over my shoulder again, still convinced someone was watching me.

Now, it occurred to me that someone might be in the

house, looking out one of the windows with a clear view of me, but impossible to make out from where I was standing. Could it be Sunday? Maybe she was okay after all, and she'd returned. Maybe she was lurking around our property for some reason, waiting to confront the person who had betrayed her.

I whirled around, looking first at the upper floor of the house where my father's study and the guest bedrooms were, squinting as if that might help me see farther, past glass, into darkened rooms. I let my gaze travel to the second floor, which housed all of our bedrooms. If someone was there, they were taking care not to be seen.

Turning slightly, I looked in the direction of the stables. Suddenly, seeming to appear out of nowhere, Jake was standing about twenty feet away from the gazebo. My gaze flicked wildly, trying to figure out where he'd come from. I hadn't seen him cross the open space or emerge from anywhere near the house.

I spun around, looking over my shoulder toward the cliff, feeling utterly disoriented. When I turned back in his direction, he'd moved closer, but he wasn't approaching me. He didn't smile or wave. I couldn't see his eyes, only the set of his face ... yet there was something that I could only describe as pure evil in the way he was looking at me.

I wanted to lift my hand to wave at him, but I couldn't seem to move it. My bones felt too heavy, and my arm was strangely stiff, almost paralyzed. I was filled with fear that I knew was irrational, but was overwhelming all the same.

20

I don't know how long I stood staring at Jake. It seemed like hours but was probably a matter of seconds. Then he turned and walked toward the stables. I pulled out my phone and texted Michael. I asked him to bring me some tea and sit with me in the gazebo. I didn't tell him that I couldn't face going back to the house, couldn't face talking to anyone but him right at that moment. I needed to settle myself down.

Michael brought me tea and his company, more eager than ever during my pregnancy to make sure I was comfortable and content. He'd always gone out of his way to meet my physical needs, and I loved that about him. He gave shoulder rubs and foot massages without me asking. A few times, he'd given me simple manicures when my fingers were grimy and my nails rough from working at the nursery. He brought me coffee in bed every single morning of our marriage. When I took a bath after a long day, he sometimes tossed a large towel in the dryer for a few minutes and brought me a warm towel to wrap in when I climbed out of the tub.

It wasn't as if he ran around like my little servant. He did all these things because he seemed to be constantly looking for ways to make my life comfy. He wanted me to feel cared for. He figured since I loved cooking for him, serving healthy dinners that were fresh and delicious, even on nights when he worked late, he wanted to give something back. But he was also simply a thoughtful person.

He made part of living together about the physical care of another human being, and it made me feel safe and nurtured.

He had brought insulated canisters filled with peppermint tea for both of us. He sat down and pulled me onto his left leg, looping his arm around my hips to hold me in place. I leaned against his shoulder and took a tentative sip of the tea.

"How long have you been hiding out here?" he asked.

"A while."

"Any reason?"

"Just tripping down memory lane. Literally tripping." I laughed. "Liam told me a story about Jake and Collette being really mean at one of Sunday's birthday parties when she was a child, and I was trying to remember the details." I told him about the party and my frustration over my brain's refusal to recall large parts of my childhood.

"I think that's normal," he said. "I can remember about ten things from when I was in early elementary school. And it's strange what those events are. Some of them are so insignificant, it's funny."

I took a sip of tea even though it was still hot enough that it seared my tongue. I needed the warmth of it inside me. "I wanted company because I kept feeling like someone was watching me."

"When?"

"Not when I was little. Sitting here. Before you came out."

"Was there?"

"Actually, yes. The first few times I looked, I didn't see

anyone. But then Jake was standing right over there." I gestured to where he'd been. "It seemed like he appeared out of nowhere, and he was just staring at me. It was almost ... creepy."

Michael laughed. "Pregnancy is playing tricks on your mind. Or being around your family is."

"He didn't wave at me or say a word. He had this look of ..." I laughed, knowing I sounded nervous and self-conscious, but I had to say it because the feeling had been so strong. "He looked like pure evil."

He laughed again, although he sounded uncertain.

"It's not funny."

"How can someone look pure evil? That's such a cliché and so dramatic. He's your brother. He can be a bit of a tool, but evil?"

Sitting so close to him, our faces almost touching, I could see the skepticism in Michael's eyes. I regretted telling him. Of course, it sounded like I was nuts. It sounded like something out of a cartoon or a superhero movie. No one is pure evil, and no one can have a look that suggests that, either. There is no such thing. It's a figment of human imagination. Yet I still felt that was what I saw.

Michael squeezed my hip and put his mug to his mouth. He swallowed some tea and looked away so that I could no longer see into his eyes. I wondered what he was thinking. Why was it suddenly so hard to communicate my feelings to him? No matter what I said, I sounded like I was hysterical or imagining things. But I wasn't. Everything I'd told him was real.

"Have you given any more thought to what I said about cutting our vacation short? Not our time off work, but heading home and spending some time with just the two of us?"

"No."

I wasn't sure if I was angry with him or hurt. I hated that he seemed not to believe anything I told him. He had an explanation for everything that had happened the past few days. I felt like his one desire was to talk me out of believing things that were perfectly logical, as if only he could see the world clearly and accurately. It felt like he believed my perceptions were distorted, while his were assumed to be correct.

Yes, I was definitely angry. The hurt followed along on its heels.

He pulled me closer to him so I still couldn't see his face. "We need to get out of here. If you don't want to go home, let's at least drive to Mendocino for lunch."

I wasn't sure what I'd expected, but it wasn't that. My temper eased slightly. I was still annoyed, but the anger faded quickly. The desire to start a fight. A lunch out sounded very nice. I loved Mendocino. It was filled with cute restaurants, nearly all of them offering fresh seafood. "Sure. Let me change my clothes."

"Me too. A date." He kissed my cheek.

LESS THAN TWO hours later we were seated across from each other on the outdoor deck of a restaurant that had been converted from a home built in the 1920s. Only three tables occupied the deck closest to the main room. A lower section of deck had two tables for two, one of which was placed beside a tiny burbling fountain in the midst of a rock garden. We'd arrived early enough that it was *all ours*, according to our friendly server.

We both ordered fresh crab sandwiches on sourdough bread. It was absolutely heavenly until Michael changed the subject away from his work and mine.

"I have a suggestion, and I hope you won't take this the wrong way," he said.

More of the same. Those were my thoughts, but I said nothing. More assumptions that I was fragile and prone to overreacting.

"Allison Sharma, you remember her, right?"

"The therapist you refer some of your clients to."

It was obvious where this was headed. I felt my face stiffen, and I was sure he saw it since he was looking intently at me, the second half of his sandwich sitting on his plate, untouched. "She has a colleague in Mendocino, who's agreed to meet with you if—"

"You already talked to her?" I glared at him to deliver my outrage without raising my voice.

"Please hear me out. I love you. I'm not suggesting there's anything wrong with you. This isn't an idea from anyone in your family, if that's where you're going next."

"Don't assume you know what I'm thinking."

"I'm not. Please. Just listen. Please."

"I don't need a therapist. So I don't need to hear you out."

"Every time we visit your family, you have these crazy dreams. And with all the stuff that's happened since we got here, I just thought it would be helpful to clear your head."

"My head is perfectly clear. It's other heads, including yours, maybe, that need clearing."

"You could talk to her about your dreams. You could—"

"Why don't you talk to her? It sounds like you have it all worked out, what needs to be discussed."

"I'm trying to help. You're upset about Sunday; you're frustrated. You're angry with your family and don't understand their behavior. You feel like they're not taking your concerns seriously. Isn't that worth bouncing off someone who isn't directly involved? Someone who doesn't know them?"

I stared at him. He had a point, but I didn't want to tell him that because I still felt like he was treating me like a basket case. I shouldn't have been entertaining those thoughts, because Michael had always treated me with respect. Until recently. And maybe I was reading things into some of his behavior, because absolutely everything was distorted by my family. And that dream. And Sunday vanishing into thin air. And Liam. "I don't see how one session with a counselor is going to resolve a dream that plagues me every time I visit here."

"Maybe you can get some insight. And you can talk to her about your concerns. Maybe she'll have some suggestions regarding Sunday."

"That's not what therapists do. They don't give advice. They get you to figure things out yourself."

"Your family can be smothering. I thought a different perspective would help. I thought she would be more helpful than talking to me."

"You're helpful."

"This isn't a plea for sympathy or a pat on the head."

I took a bite of my sandwich. I turned my attention to the musical sound of water trickling from the fountain beside me. It was so soothing. What was it about water that calmed your thoughts? Any kind of water had the same effect—enormous crashing waves or something like this. Maybe it really did remind us of the womb, as some people said. I placed my hand on my bump and wondered what it was like for her inside me. I wondered if she heard the amniotic fluid like a river moving past her ears. I wondered if she was hearing at all yet. I would have to look that up. I couldn't remember at what stage hearing began.

"Okay, fine. Why not? It's a way to spend the afternoon instead of going back to the house right away. But what will you do?"

"I'll stop by the bookstore and pick up a book about fatherhood. Have a cup of coffee and read." He grinned.

"I haven't sent you enough blogs and articles about parenting?"

"Sometimes I need more depth."

We finished our sandwiches, and I found myself looking forward to talking to a woman who wasn't related to me.

21

This was my first time visiting a therapist, but a friend from college who was raised by an alcoholic mother had seen one for several years, so I knew a bit about what to expect. Her waiting room was modern and sparse.

She came out to greet me right away, which I appreciated.

"Hi, Annie. I'm Kate Irving." She ushered me into her office and showed me a floral armchair. She sat across from me on a matching love seat. I also appreciated that she didn't look eager to take notes on what I might say. Instead, she crossed her legs and placed her hands on her lap.

"I understand we'll only be talking this one time," she said. "I'm good friends with Dr. Sharma, and I'm doing this as a favor." She smiled. "It's not my typical policy, but a little talking never hurt anyone." She broadened her smile, then turned serious. "If you decide you want to talk to a therapist when you return home from your vacation, I can give you a referral at the end of the hour."

"I doubt it, but never say never."

"Right. So tell me what brought you here."

The words began pouring out of me, faster than I'd expected. I told her about what I'd seen on the cliff, my dream, the confusion between dreaming and whether I'd actually seen Sunday struggling. I told her about Sunday's abrupt disappearance and her attempt to talk to my father alone and my parents' odd behavior. I told her about the favoritism and the family principles. Before I knew it, I felt like I was explaining my entire family history. As I talked, I saw that her expression remained neutral, yet the sound of my voice and the things I was saying made me realize that my family might have been more unusual than I'd acknowledged.

And then, although it seemed like only a few minutes had passed, she told me we were halfway through the hour. I hadn't even mentioned Liam's death.

"If you have something specific you want to focus on, you should think about what that is to be sure we have enough time. I'm not trying to cut you off; there's obviously a lot going on with you. But I just wanted to make you aware."

"Just one more thing, to explain why I feel anxious about my family's behavior." I told her about Liam's accident and about my father telling the police he'd been drinking, when he had not.

"Your family dynamic sounds very complicated. I'm not referring only to the lie—which I agree, could be forgetfulness, if we want to take a charitable view. How old is your father?"

"Fifty-eight. I don't think he's—"

"No, probably not. But let's assume it was stress or some other factor. As I said, the family dynamic sounds very complicated, based on what you've described. It might be something you want to explore with a therapist on an ongoing basis, because I think it's had more negative impact on you than you might realize. And especially with a baby coming, it might be worth exploring what kind of family you and your husband would like to create. It sounds like your parents were very authoritarian and still are. It doesn't sound like you feel confident expressing your own voice."

"How did you get that?"

"Just an impression, because of their insistence on all of the children adhering to their belief system, even as adults. It does sound like there are some buried issues, some secrets being kept. But it's also your family, so it's important to be really certain before making accusations. Especially if you're going to involve the police. In fact, although I don't usually like to give advice, if there is a crime that's been committed, you probably don't want to get too far ahead of things and allow someone a chance to hide evidence or something like that."

I nodded. She made me feel calmer but also more frightened. I was suddenly curious to know if she'd heard of my father before I showed up, and if she'd read any of his books. I wished I'd asked her that at the beginning. Now, it didn't seem like it mattered. And as she'd reminded me, there wasn't much time left, so I didn't really want to spend it talking about him and his teachings.

"So what do you want to focus on during the time we have left?"

"I think I'd like to understand why I have these disturbing dreams when I sleep at my childhood home. I'd like to understand why I get confused as to whether I'm dreaming or remembering things. It's so disorienting; it makes me feel a little like I'm losing my mind. This never happens to me at home. I hate that I can't remember things. My sister told me a story about one of Sunday's birthday parties that I feel like I should remember, and I do remember a specific incident from it, but Liam told me a completely different story about the same party, and I just can't remember a single thing that tells me which one of them is telling the truth. It ..." I put my hands on the sides of my head. "I don't understand why I can't remember."

"Memories are very elusive because—"

"That's stating the obvious."

She laughed. I was glad she hadn't taken it as an attack. I hadn't intended it that way, but I wanted her to say something helpful. We had a few minutes, and I needed some useful insight to hang onto. This was exactly what my friend had told me about therapy. It could be frustrating—more questions than answers.

"Since we don't have a lot of time, I have a suggestion that will give you something concrete to work on. I think this will make you feel like you're moving forward. And it could possibly address your frustration with your dreams as well as your memories." She uncrossed her legs and leaned forward slightly. "First, I suggest you keep a dream diary. Even though you feel as if you remember this dream, and others, in great detail, I expect it's fading more than you realize. The very act of writing it down will bring out even more details and will help make connections in your mind. Alongside that, I suggest constructing a timeline of your childhood. Just jot down events you remember in chronological order, nothing complicated. You might even note what age you think you might have been in some of your dreams, if you think that's helpful. If not, just stick to the two exercises as separate activities."

"It sounds just as frustrating, maybe more, if I write down memories and there are huge gaps."

"When you're not trying so hard to force things, to make yourself remember a specific incident, it's very likely that small pieces will come to you, and you can fill in other pieces later. That way, a full picture will take shape over time. You won't be forcing it. I think it will be very helpful for you. I think you'll be surprised." She smiled. Her expression was warm, and I felt like she actually believed this would work.

It did sound interesting. And it sounded better than growing tired and frustrated as my mind circled around the same things over and over, driving myself crazy wondering if something was a memory, or I was only remembering thinking about it before, or remembering a dream. Writing it down might get rid of the clutter.

I felt a little foolish for not figuring out something so simple by myself.

She moved to stand, and I did the same. We shook hands. "I know these are simple exercises," she said, "and it might feel like something you should have worked out on your own, but sometimes, just taking the time to focus on a problem, like you've done by coming to talk to me, can clear things up. We have a tendency to create patterns in our brains without stepping back to observe, to take a more deliberately analytical approach."

"Thank you," I said.

She showed me to the door and touched my shoulder gently as she wished me success and told me she would email me the name of a therapist in the Bay Area.

I didn't tell Michael everything she'd said. I did mention the exercises. We went to a stationery store to buy a notebook. I told him I wanted the notebook in case I decided to try what she'd suggested.

"Honestly, I'm kind of tired," I said. "I feel good that you and I got away and had time alone." I kissed his lips. When I moved away, he smiled, looking happier than I'd seen him in several days. "I'll see how I feel tomorrow about the exercises. Maybe talking was enough to clear my head."

"Could be," he said.

We climbed into the car. As he pulled out onto Highway 1 and headed south, I thanked him for arranging the time with

Kate, for urging me to talk to her. He didn't crow about it, and he didn't pry into the details of what we'd talked about.

He did make one comment, so quietly I almost dismissed it as a whisper to himself. "I'm starting to wonder why we spend these long holidays with your family. They're so awful, sometimes. It's hard to—"

"You only get one family," I said. "Maybe we think too much about the bad memories because we keep retelling those stories, and they bury all the happy moments."

During the drive home, I fell asleep, but I didn't dream.

22

When I woke, it was because Michael was slowing to turn into the road leading to our property. The trees cast a shadow over the car, and I looked at my hands on my lap. They appeared limp and chalky white, as if the blood wasn't flowing to them. I rubbed them on my legs, but they weren't cold.

As the car turned, my memory suddenly clicked into a previously hidden slot, proving to me again how much it worked on its own inscrutable timetable. As if it had been there all along, I remembered why I knew Sunday hadn't been given the cell phone at her ninth birthday party. When I watched her open the small box containing the cell phone, I'd been missing my top front teeth. I clearly remembered standing off to the side as the kids played with her phone, sticking my tongue through the gap. I was pretty sure the second tooth had only fallen out a day or two earlier. That entire day, all I remembered was the space at the front of my mouth. It fascinated and consumed me.

I lost my teeth when I was six, so Sunday would have turned eight. It was a small thing, but in all the millions, possibly billions of senses and moments stored inside my brain, most of them never to be found again, this one had stayed close enough to the surface that hearing Collette insist Sunday was nine when she received the extravagant, slightly inappropriate gift of a cell phone had caused a rough spot that wouldn't be smoothed over.

The feeling that washed over me was one of being a child again, triumphantly telling one of my older siblings that I was right, and they were wrong. I could probably count on one hand the times I'd been able to do that as a child. It was a feeling of power, a feeling of trusting my own mind, knowing I could count on myself. Collette had been so sure she was right. She'd tried to convince me that Sunday had made up a self-pitying lie. She'd implied I was foolish for believing a story like that. I was probably meant to infer that I was a terrible person for thinking Collette and Jake would have been so cruel to disinvite her friends, making her think she was hated.

But I was *right*.

Michael couldn't drive the car fast enough for me. I wanted him to race up the drive so I could run into the house and find Collette.

Instead, what we found was an empty house. I went out to the stables and spoke to Quinn, who said they'd all gone riding. He said they'd left an hour earlier, which meant they could be back in fifteen minutes or not for another two hours.

The rest of the afternoon dragged, and dinner seemed to go on forever. It wasn't until after we'd played two hours of the days-long board game we were involved with that I had a chance to get Collette alone, following her up to her room. She was carrying a glass of red wine and a plate with three chocolate candies from a box Jake had given to my mother.

"Do you have a few minutes to talk?" I asked.

"Always, for you." She nodded at her door.

I opened it for her, and she carried her wine and second dessert into her bedroom. We settled into the same places we'd taken the day before, as if this was about to become a nightly routine. She took a sip of wine and held out the plate of chocolates to me. "Would you like one?"

"No, thank you."

She took a bite from one of the chocolates, inspected the filling as if it wasn't what she'd expected, then took another sip of wine. "What's on your mind?"

"That birthday party where Sunday got the cell phone was when she turned eight."

"So?"

"My teeth were missing, which means I was six. So it wasn't when she turned nine."

"So what?"

"You were so sure that wasn't the party where none of her friends came, because it was all about the cell phone."

She laughed. She ate the rest of the chocolate. "You're confusing me. Eight, nine? What's your point?"

"Maybe you and Jake did call all her friends, and now you feel terrible about it, so you didn't want to tell me the truth."

"You must think we're awful if you believe we would do something like that."

"Liam said—"

"You believe Liam and not your own sister? He dumped Sunday."

"I don't think he dumped her. It was more complicated than that."

"Whatever." She took a bite out of the next chocolate. "These aren't as good as I thought they'd be. No wonder no one else is eating them."

"No one else is eating them because they were a gift for Mom."

"It looks like she doesn't want them either. They've been sitting there all week."

"So you never called her friends and told them Sunday was sick?"

"Why are you so obsessed with a party that happened twenty years ago?"

"It sounded so painful for her. It hurts to think about it."

"We all had painful childhoods. She's not special."

"You were so definite it couldn't have happened because of the cell phone at her ninth birthday, but the cell phone wasn't at her ninth birthday. So I just wondered why you were so positive that was the right year."

"Can you please let it go?" She took a long swallow of wine. "I don't know why Sunday made up a story like that to complain about us to her ex, and I don't know why you're so fixated on it. If you're just going to keep worrying about it, then this conversation will get really boring really fast." She ate the rest of the chocolate, keeping her gaze fixed on me while she chewed.

"Liam had no reason to lie about it," I said. "And I can't think of any reason why Sunday would make up a story like that. I'm really confused about what's going on. He said she was unbelievably upset, and now she's missing." I felt myself tearing up. I heard the tremble in my voice, that thin sound that announces tears are coming.

Collette heard it, too. She placed her wineglass on the plate and crept toward me. She nestled herself beside me on the pillows and placed her hand on my bump. "You need to stop getting yourself so upset. It's okay to admit you're feeling hysterical, but you need to let us help you. We're your family. Being with us is the safest place in the world you can be."

I stared at her. I felt the baby flutter under her touch.

"Oh! I felt her move. I think. Was that it?" Collette asked, her voice shrill.

I wanted to point out that she'd called me hysterical, and she sounded far closer to that edge than I did. "Yes."

"How exciting." She moved her hand around slowly. "The family is like your womb. We keep each other safe, right?"

"I don't know if that's the same thing."

"It is. It's okay to admit you're imagining terrible things about Sunday, thinking the worst. It's okay to admit you're having dark thoughts about Liam's accident, but you have to deal with it. You have to get rid of those things. Our family loves each other. We love and protect each other. We don't do bad things to hurt each other. And if we did bad things as kids, we should forgive each other."

"But she told Liam someone betrayed her. She said she wasn't going to leave, so why would she suddenly take off?"

"She changed her mind. She also promised she would love Liam until she died, and she changed her mind about that."

"He wanted the divorce, not her."

"My point is, your family takes care of you. If you're so afraid something happened to Sunday, you need to stick close to your family. Not alienate them by saying terrible things about the people who love you more than anyone else on earth. The people you've loved for your whole life. Your family are the ones who would protect you from something bad happening to you or to Michael or your tiny precious baby. Without your family, something terrible could happen to one of you." She patted my bump.

I nudged her hand off my bump. She didn't object. She sat up and moved away from me. "Do you see what I'm saying?"

I wasn't at all sure what she was saying. It almost sounded like a threat, but I couldn't pinpoint why. I felt a little sick. If it was a threat, what was she threatening? And was it really? Her voice was quiet and low, very calming, but why did it sound so awful?

"I'm worried about Sunday. No one has heard from her, and that's *not* normal," I said.

"Everyone knows you're worried. That's all you talk about. I suggest you stop. Worrying accomplishes nothing, and if Sunday wanted us to know where she is, she would let us know." She stood and went to her bed. She picked up her wineglass and the plate. With her back to me, she took a sip of wine.

I took it as a dismissal. And honestly, I wanted to leave. I didn't understand what had just happened. I heaved myself out of the pile of cushions and started toward the door. I wanted her to admit she'd tried to get me to believe Sunday was lying about the party by making a big deal out of a gift she knew I would remember, trying to reshape my memories. In that moment, I almost hated her for it. And I hated that I'd told her about finding the toothpick, that I thought it meant someone in our family had run Liam off the road. I wondered if she knew more about Sunday than she was saying. She seemed awfully confident that everything was okay.

Trusting her with my thoughts had been a mistake.

I truly loved my family, and I wanted to be close to them, but sometimes they were so awful. It was painful and confusing, as it had been most of my adult life. I found myself wanting to push them away and try harder to make them love me more, all at the same time.

When I returned to our room, Michael was already in bed, reading. I told him I'd been talking to Collette. He didn't seem interested in what we'd discussed, so I didn't say more than that. After he fell asleep, I took out the notebook I'd bought and marked out a rough timeline of my childhood, making notes of the obvious milestones such as high school graduation and getting my first period and my first kiss. I also noted when I'd lost my top front teeth.

23

The next morning, I skipped breakfast with my family. Michael gave me the idea when he said he was going for a long run and didn't want a heavy meal. I made tea and took the insulated container, a hard-boiled egg, and an already peeled orange to the prayer garden behind the house.

The prayer garden had been designed by my mother and brought to life by Quinn and Jake when I was a little girl. Originally, a wooden playhouse and a sandbox had occupied that section of the property, surrounded by a split-rail fence. The playhouse had been dark blue with pink trim and had a real doorknob and windows and carpeted floors. Those were the only things I remembered about it. I was never sure why it had been torn down when I was so young. I suppose because the other kids had outgrown it, and maybe it needed repairs; probably they didn't think it was worth it for one child. I never asked, and no one said, because as best I could remember, I hadn't played there much.

The prayer garden consisted of a Japanese maple tree with an iron bench underneath. Large, smooth stones had been arranged in a rectangle to encompass the tree, a granite birdbath, and a sundial set in a straight line from the tree and the bench.

It was a tranquil spot, but I wasn't aware that anyone used it. My mother had, years ago, but when we came home for family visits, I'd never seen anyone go out there. No one ever talked about it.

I settled on the bench and ate my egg and the orange. I sipped tea and watched a starling splash vigorously in the bath. Every few seconds, it paused and cocked its head as if it was aware of my presence, but it didn't turn to look directly at me. I tried to keep still, not wanting to upset its morning routine.

After the bird flew away, the place took on a desolate atmosphere. I wasn't sure why. The fog had receded early that morning, and sunshine splashed across the stones marking the edges of the prayer garden and fell in a perfect angle on the sundial to give an accurate reading that it was just past eight thirty. It was not a time of day I considered bleak, but I felt very alone and exposed. This was supposed to be a comforting, healing place. Maybe the fact that it was never used had given it an air of abandonment.

I gulped down the rest of my tea and stood. I shoved the container and the napkin containing my eggshells into the cloth bag I'd used to carry my food outside. I walked to the now-empty birdbath and looked at the downy feathers floating on the water. Other than those few feathers, the water was clean. I supposed Quinn must change it every day. I smiled, thinking about him providing fresh water for wild birds when it probably wasn't in his job description.

I felt slightly ridiculous for not feeling comfortable sitting in a very pleasant, contemplative garden, but I needed to get out of there. I walked quickly toward the corral, knowing the horses would be out for the day, already fed and groomed.

Even though I couldn't ride them, just being around them always made me feel grounded.

As I approached the corral, I saw my father's horse, Nobility, standing close to the corner. He always looked like he wanted to escape, to get moving. When my father didn't go riding, Quinn tried to take Nobility out almost every day. He was an active creature, full of energy and adventure. He seemed to crave human interaction and was always eager for a pat on his shoulder or a rub of his cheek, even if there was no treat enticing him to accept affection.

I walked up to him and let him sniff my fingers. He whinnied and lowered his head toward me, taking the briefest sniff, already aware of who I was. I felt sad to be sidelined from riding while I was pregnant, but even with well-trained horses, the risk of a fall was always present. I missed my own horse, Tabitha. As if she knew I was thinking of her, my gorgeous white horse trotted over and stood beside Nobility. I stroked her nose, then ran my fingers through her mane. I was the only one she allowed this intimate contact.

I missed being with her. I missed riding along the cliffs, missed the absolutely mindless pleasure of feeling a large animal carrying me wherever I wanted to go, feeling the sway of her body, the solid muscle and power of her. I couldn't remember a time in my life when I hadn't known the freedom and utter joy of riding our horses.

My father loved our horses to the point of worship. He boasted to anyone who would listen about the care he'd put into choosing the animals we owned, about the purity of their bloodlines, about how important good breeding was to finding creatures that would not only show well, but could be trusted around his family and were properly trained to give a lifetime of enjoyment to their owners.

From the corner of my eye, I saw Quinn at the entrance to the stables, sweeping excess hay off the ground. I called out to him. He propped the broom against the stable door and walked to where I stood. The horses moved out of the way, tired of their pats now.

Quinn had been as much a part of my life as anyone in my family. His love for our horses mirrored my father's. He was friendly and could be quite charming, but much of the time, he didn't talk much. When he went riding with us, he was perfectly content to sit silently on the back of a horse for an hour or more. I liked that about him. Some people feel the need to fill the air with conversation, even if it's meaningless, simply because they think it's expected. He never did.

Despite seeing him almost every day of my life when I lived at home, there was a lot I didn't know about him. I sometimes wondered whether he was content to look after my father's horses until he was an old man, or if he dreamed of other things. I liked him, and I felt he'd always been a steadying presence in our lives. Even though my father instructed us to avoid drama, there was still a fair amount of drama in my family.

"I haven't seen you around much." He took off his baseball cap and ran his fingers through light brown hair that was getting long in the back and starting to curl. He towered over me, taller even than Michael, who was six one.

I cupped my bump. "I'm sitting on the sidelines."

He smiled. "It'll be fun teaching the little one to ride. Only a few years."

"I hope so."

"How are you doing otherwise?" he asked.

"I'm worried about Sunday. It's so strange that she just disappeared. It's been six days."

"Not really disappeared. Just that she left without telling anyone."

"But it's like she vanished."

"Well, she packed her things, so it's not as if something terrible happened to her," he said.

"How did she seem when you went riding with her the day before she disappeared?"

"Fine." He touched his sunglasses, adjusting them to settle more solidly on the bridge of his nose. "Quiet, maybe."

"She didn't seem upset?"

"No. She wasn't crying or anything like that. Like I said, quiet. She hardly spoke ten words, which isn't like her, but otherwise, she was fine."

"I've called her and texted, and she hasn't responded."

He glanced over his shoulder, looking toward the water trough where Tabitha was taking a long drink.

"She didn't say *anything* about being upset? Not even a hint? She was arguing with my parents before she went riding with you. Did she mention that? Remember when she called and asked you to get my father's horse ready?"

He shrugged.

"Did she say anything about that? About want to go riding with him, but my mother didn't want him to go?"

"No."

"I don't understand why she hasn't texted back just to say she's okay. How much does it take to send a thumbs-up?"

"Yeah." He looked at the ground and kicked the toe of his work boot against the fence post. "So I wasn't ... I was going to tell someone, but I didn't know ..." He made a fist and coughed against it. "I found her phone."

"When? Why didn't you—"

"Hold on. I just ... I was nervous. Okay? I was the last one with her before she took off or disappeared or whatever, and I wasn't sure what everyone would think."

"Where is it? Where did you find it? Why didn't you tell anyone?" I glared at him, but it was impossible to make eye contact, his glasses were so dark.

"I'm sorry. It was only this morning. I was going to ... I just ... It was a coincidence."

"So you *do* think something's wrong, don't you? Or you wouldn't have been worried about telling everyone you found it."

He shoved his hands in his pockets and hunched his shoulders slightly. For a moment, I thought he hadn't heard me. Finally, he said, "I do, yeah. I guess."

"Where is it?"

He walked quickly back to the stables, stepped inside, and returned a moment later holding her white phone in its gold silicone case. He handed it to me. Feeling the weight of it in my hand was like holding a part of her. Inside were fragments of her life. I couldn't believe it was in my possession. It was painful to think what that meant.

I pressed the power button. The battery indicator showed a thin red bar. The messages and missed calls from me, and two missed calls from Liam, and a few other messages from other friends cluttered the lock screen. "Can you show me where you found it?"

"Near those rocks just past the gazebo."

"Show me."

"What good will that do? It won't tell you anything."

"I want to see."

He walked to the gate, unlatched it, and stepped out. We walked together past his cottage and along the horse path toward the cliff. The gazebo was to our left, the field of beach grass behind us. When we reached the footpath that ran along the edge of the cliff, he turned right. I followed him for about thirty feet, and then we went around an outcropping of boulders to a small clearing that extended right to the very edge of the cliff, seeming to drop into nothingness. It was the kind of spot that caused vertigo even when I stood several feet back from the edge. At the same time, it was the kind of place where I was tormented by my weird compulsion to look down, to see what was on the shore below. It was the reason we always took the coastal trail south when we rode the horses. It was impossible to navigate them around the boulders and that precipitous drop.

"Right here." Quinn kicked the boulders, then shoved his toe into an opening between two of them.

It looked like a small cave, a place where you expected to see a lizard dart out for a bit of sun, if the ground hadn't been shrouded in the dark of two human shadows.

"It was underneath. It looked like it must have fallen and slid into the rocks."

"Do you think ..." My voice caught, and for a moment, I couldn't get enough breath to make a sound. I swallowed and tried again. "Do you think she fell or jumped or ... and her phone ..."

"Or was pushed? No. This seems too far back."

"But if she was shoved, and she was holding it, and it flew out of her hand?"

He walked to the edge and looked down, causing my knees to feel like pots of jelly. In response, I moved even farther back toward the boulders. He stepped back to where I stood. "I don't think so. It's easy to let yourself think the worst."

"But I can't believe she packed her things and left without her phone, without even asking anyone if they'd seen it. She did the same with her diamond necklace." I told him about finding the broken necklace.

"It does seem hard to believe she would do that, but we can't assume the worst. We really shouldn't."

I wasn't sure why, but I didn't argue. We started back toward the stables. I tapped the screen on Sunday's phone and tried entering her birthdate. The phone remained locked. I tried her wedding anniversary and the date of her divorce. Neither series of numbers worked. I put the phone in my coat pocket.

When we reached the corral, before Quinn unlatched the gate, I said, "Don't tell anyone you found it. I'm not sure why. But they think nothing's wrong, and they'll just make more excuses."

"Fine by me. I was a little worried about telling you I found it. I don't want you, or anyone, to think I had something to do with her going missing."

"No one would think that."

He looked skeptical.

"They wouldn't. Stop thinking that way."

He shrugged and opened the gate. We said goodbye, and I went back to the house. Hoping to avoid running into anyone, I hurried up the stairs. Michael was still on his run. I went into our room and plugged Sunday's phone into my charger, using the outlet behind my nightstand, and hiding the phone under the bed. I made sure the sound was turned off.

Despite his desire to help me settle my thoughts, to understand my dreams, Michael tended to dismiss my concerns or try to explain them away. I wasn't in the mood for hearing that *of course* Sunday might leave without her phone, because of this or that completely illogical reason. There was no way she would go anywhere without that lifeline. I went into the bathroom and washed my face to stop myself from crying, knowing that something had happened to her.

24

After dinner that evening, Michael had a conference call for a case he was working on. The woman he was representing had learned her husband possessed a bank account she hadn't known existed, a bank account with a balance of seventy-four thousand dollars.

I took advantage of this to dodge my family entirely. Because they were missing a player for their game, they were settling in to watch a movie. I bowed out, saying I'd already seen the selection and I didn't want to force others to bow to my wishes. No one objected beyond polite clichéd comments that we should choose something everyone would enjoy. I grabbed my notebook and headed out to the gazebo.

With sunset now coming close to nine at night, it was still daylight. The sun was a hot, glowing ball starting to spread golden light across the surface of the ocean. I settled into the gazebo and opened the notebook. I clipped the pen to the open page and closed my eyes for a moment.

I replayed what I'd seen two nights before Sunday disappeared—my sister struggling with that dark figure. They'd been nowhere near that outcropping of rocks. It wasn't even visible from the gazebo, so there was no way Sunday's phone could have flown out of her hand or from a pocket in her dress during that struggle. That meant she had been out there another time. Unless someone had found her phone and tossed it there, but that seemed unlikely. If someone wanted to get rid of it, they would have done a much better job of hiding it.

The skin on the back of my neck prickled as the breeze blew my hair across my face, a few strands flicking themselves across my eyelids. I brushed my hair away and turned, again touched by the distinct feeling that someone was behind me, watching. No one was there. The sun had moved much closer to the water, and I wondered how long I'd sat with my eyes closed. Had I fallen asleep? Was the prickling sensation just my body waking up from a dream? I picked up the pen and clicked it open. I drew a series of circles on the page.

I closed my eyes again, trying to recall more details from that scene on the edge of the cliff, comparing it to the dreams I'd had, so I could write the details in my notebook. Nothing but the same repeated images came to me. I wondered if this was a futile exercise in writing down random thoughts that had absolutely no connection to each other.

Again, I felt that prickling across the back of my neck and down my spine. My eyelids flashed open, and I whipped my head around. Again, no one was there. I stared hard at the landscape, remembering how Jake had seemed to appear out of nowhere, giving me that evil look.

As I turned my head back, a memory rose from nowhere, shocking me with its clarity. I gasped out loud as I recalled seeing that identical look in Jake's eyes once, possibly many times, before. I felt like I was suddenly a little girl. Long braids hung down my back—the way I'd worn my hair before I'd started kindergarten, at which point my hair was cut to my shoulders, because I'd wanted to look like my best friend. Jake had looked right into my eyes, scaring me to death, his eyes almost black as he'd whispered to me in a low, nearly growling voice, "I'll push Sunday off the cliff. She'll be smashed on the rocks."

Was that the root of my constantly repeating dream? Was it all a dream that night when I'd gone out there and found the gazebo and the surrounding area deserted? Had his threat scared me so badly—a tiny girl, facing her much larger, much older, much more worldly brother—that I'd buried those feelings at a depth I hadn't been able to access? Forced out of sight, they'd emerged in that strange, persistent dream. Maybe.

I opened my notebook to the page where I'd written the ages "four" and "five." I made a note about the dream and also the memory of Jake's threat. What a horrible thing to say, to even think! Why would he say such a thing, especially to his little sister? It was terrifying. I turned to the middle of the notebook, where I'd dog-eared a corner and written a title page for "Dreams." I'd started writing what I dreamt, even when all I had were blurry impressions. I wrote about the dream, with the details I could remember.

After I'd written until my hand ached, I closed the notebook and sat staring out at the breathtaking view, watching the water slowly swallow the sun. It was so beautiful and soothing, I wanted to sit there forever. I wanted to forget about dreams and my older brother and that horrible memory that had erupted out of the depths of my heart.

Soon, the sun appeared to be resting on the water, the light spreading sideways, and then it was a semicircle, quickly disappearing below the horizon. When it was gone and the sky was a light-filled navy blue, I stood. Thankful for the oversized pockets on my jacket, I shoved the notebook and pen into one of them.

I stepped out of the gazebo and started walking south along the footpath. As always, my compulsion to look down overtook me, and I glanced at the rocky shore below. There was nothing but foam-splashed rocks and tangled strands of kelp. I turned away, put my hands in my pockets, and continued walking. It felt good to be moving, and to be alone. I let my thoughts quiet to nothing but appreciation for the endless stretch of water and sky, and the wind on my face.

After another fifty feet or so, I moved closer to the edge and looked down again. This section of the shore had a bit of sand, and I stood for a moment watching waves as they washed lazily across it, then pulled back. Of course, there was no body down there. I had never seen a body down there, and I was sure now it was Jake's threat that had caused me to develop this sick habit that plagued me all my life.

I began walking again, resisting the compulsion, feeling I finally had power over my weird, deeply engrained habit. Then it became too much once again, and I had to look. By now, I was almost half a mile from our house. I looked down at a section that was one large slab of flat rock, and there she was—Sunday.

I screamed, a long howling cry that felt like it was tearing my lungs out of my body.

There was her white dress, half torn off her body. There was her wet hair, plastered across the rock like more strands of kelp, tangled from the ocean floor. I was crying so hard now, her body was a blur. I saw the dress, such a brilliant white, and her body lying so that it seemed as if someone had taken her limbs apart and arranged them differently.

I turned and began running. I veered off the path, even though it was rougher going and I risked stumbling. I was conscious of the baby, not that I shouldn't be running, but aware that I couldn't fall. I needed to be fully aware; at the same time, I couldn't slow myself. I needed to get the others. I needed help. We needed to get down there and help my sister. Maybe we could do something to help her; maybe we could still save her.

Then I was sobbing uncontrollably, knowing that of course we couldn't do anything to help her. She was dead. She'd been dead for days, probably for a week. I was right, I was *so* right … and I hated, more than I'd ever hated anything in my entire life, that I was right.

They'd all tried to tell me that what I knew in my heart was not the truth. Someone in my family had killed my sister. I had no idea why. The family I thought was built on love and respect and strong principles was not just flawed, it was rotten to the core.

25

W hen I reached the edge of the garden, Jake and Collette were on the front porch. Jake was yelling, telling me to stop screaming. I wanted to scream that he was yelling as loudly as I was.

"She's dead. Sunday's dead. I saw her. She washed up onto the beach." I sobbed and doubled over as the grief ripped through me again. He grabbed me and held me, pulling my head close to his chest. "Shh. It's okay. Let's go take a look."

He took one of my arms, and Collette went to my other side. They steered me back to the narrow path through the beach grass and out to the footpath.

"It's faster if we—"

"You can't be cutting across uneven ground like that," Collette said. "What if you'd fallen?"

"We have to get her. It was faster."

Collette stroked my arm. "If she's dead, faster won't—"

"*If?*"

Jake squeezed my arm. "Let's go see."

I heard Michael behind us, calling my name, but Jake and

Collette continued moving quickly, and I didn't want to wait for him. He'd have to catch up.

Finally, we reached the point where I'd seen her. I pointed to the slab of rock, tears pouring out of me again, blurring my eyesight as they had before, until all I could make out was her white dress in the growing darkness.

After a moment Jake spoke softly, but his voice was tight. "Did you push her?"

I wrenched away from him. "No! Why would you say that? No, I didn't push her." I began crying harder, if that was possible.

"How did you know she would be there?" Collette asked.

"What?"

"This is so far from the house. And totally random. Out of the entire coastline, how did you know to look down right at this point and see her? It looks like you pushed her." Jake pulled me to him. "It's okay. We'll—"

I wrestled within his grip, twisting around, going nowhere. "Let go of me! I didn't push her!"

"What's going on? What's wrong?" Now Michael was beside me, pulling me away from Jake, who released me easily into Michael's arms. Jake took a few steps away.

Michael held me close. "What happened? Are you okay?"

"Look. Look down there. She's dead. I knew something had happened to her, but no one would listen."

He let go of me and moved carefully toward the edge of the cliff, looking back at me several times. He looked worried that I might rush up to him without warning, perhaps run too close and fall over myself, in some crazed attempt to reach Sunday. He glanced down at the shore. I saw the shock burn through his body as he quickly looked away. He shuddered and took a step back. He came to me and wrapped his arms around me again.

"Why wouldn't anyone listen?" I wailed. "Maybe we could

have found her. Maybe she didn't die right away. If we'd tried harder to look for her, this wouldn't have happened."

"Okay. Maybe a lot of things can happen. You need to calm down," Collette said.

"She's dead! Do you even care?"

"Of course I care! But we can't go blaming ourselves. We didn't know."

"We did know."

"You're the one who was so sure about it. You're the one out there in the gazebo every day, staring out at the water, moping around. So did you push her over?" Jake asked. "It seems like a huge coincidence that you're walking this far from the house, with miles of coastline, and you just happen to look down right at this spot and see her."

Michael leaned his head on mine. I felt his body tremble. His voice in my ear was low and hoarse, as if he was choking on the words. "Did you?"

I peeled myself away from him, crying so hard my chest was convulsing. I was scared for the baby as my muscles contracted violently, and I gasped for air, heaving sobs as if I'd just come up from being under fifty feet of water myself. "How can you ask that? How can you say something like that to me?" I shoved him.

He stumbled, deliberately throwing himself to the side as he gave a panicked look toward the edge of the cliff, making sure he would fall in the opposite direction. We were well back by now, but its constant presence felt threatening all the same.

"We need to go down there. Where's the nearest access path?" I looked around wildly. I couldn't deal with their horrible accusations right now. We needed to get her body and bring her up before the sea took her away again. High winds and rough surf often came up unexpectedly, and I couldn't bear the thought that her body might be lost forever.

"Absolutely not," Michael said. "It's too dark. And it's not safe for you to go down there."

"Michael's right," Collette said.

"I don't care what any of you think. We need to do what's right for her."

"You need to *calm down*," Collette said. "You need to think about the life inside you that you're responsible for."

Michael began pulling me along the footpath. "Let's get you home and warmed up. Then—"

"I'm not an infant. You don't need to swaddle me and put me in my bassinet."

"You've had a terrible shock," Jake said.

"We've all had a terrible shock."

"Shh," Collette said.

I hadn't realized I was screaming, but I also didn't care if I sounded shrill and hysterical. Their calm acceptance was unbearably disturbing. Where was the guilt that they'd failed to listen to me? Where was the regret that we'd done absolutely nothing to try to find out why our sister had disappeared into thin air?

"We need to get back to the house." Michael was ignoring everything I'd just said. I understood I was coming apart, but the feelings spilling out of me were impossible to control. I was strong, and I knew our baby was strong. We would both be okay. I didn't need to be treated like this.

"You aren't thinking straight," Jake said. "It's not safe to go down there in your condition. It's dark, and the path is steep and difficult in daylight, even for someone who isn't pregnant."

"We need to get to her before she's washed out to sea, and we never find her."

"We'll take care of it. I just don't think you're the one to do it. Climbing down a trail like this when you're upset isn't safe," Jake said. "And I think you know that. Dad and I will get some flashlights and a tarp and some rope and go down there. But you need to go home and rest."

I shivered, thinking about the tarp and what it meant. New tears seeped out of my eyes. My voice wavered when I spoke. "Now. You need to do it now."

"I said we'll take care of it."

"Not it! Her. You'll take care of *her*."

Jake sighed, but didn't make the effort to correct himself.

Michael put his arm around me, his hand under my armpit, and began walking, almost dragging me along the path, back toward the house. My shoes scuffed on the dirt and banged against small rocks embedded in the hard-packed earth. Now that we'd stopped speaking, the sound of the ocean swelled around us, waves crashing like the sound of teeth gnashing and chewing up anything it could get in its maw. The ocean had the strength to pulverize massive redwoods as if they were toothpicks when storms dumped the fallen trees into rivers, carrying them to the ocean. The waves chewed up ships and tore at the rocky cliffs, eroding them year after year. A slender young woman didn't stand a chance against its strength.

26

W hen we were halfway back to the house, my mind began to clear, and I was overcome with certainty that Jake would not go down to retrieve Sunday's body as he'd promised. He hated her. He'd hated her since before I was born. What did he care? He'd never done the right thing for her when she was alive; why would he start now? I tried to pull away from Michael, but he tightened his grip and began moving me more forcefully in the direction of home.

"Stop, Annie. You're going to hurt yourself. And the baby."

"I'm fine. I want to see them bring her up."

"Don't be morbid."

"How do I know they're going to get down there in time?"

He didn't answer. He continued moving me in a homeward direction, and I continued fighting him, trying to pry his arms away from me, scratching at his hands and wrists.

When we finally reached the house, exhausted from wrestling with each other, Bella was standing on the front porch. Her blonde hair was pulled back tight, as if she were an actress playing the head nurse in a psychiatric hospital. To enhance the impression, she wore a stiff white shirt and white pants. Her usually heavy makeup was even more so, with thick black eyeliner and her eyebrows dramatically darkened.

Now I heard Jake and Collette behind us.

"I thought you were getting Dad to help with Sunday?" I cried.

"First we need to get you settled," Jake said.

I continued fighting Michael as we climbed the front steps, his grip strengthening with each placement of his foot. "Please be careful," he said. "You're going to hurt yourself. You're hurting me." His voice was gentle, but I still wanted to claw at him, hating him for seeming to side with my brother and sister. Like them, he was treating me as if I was having a breakdown, when the truth was, all of them were behaving like cold-blooded monsters. They'd seen a dead woman's body smashed on the rocks, and they were treating it like a common occurrence, which had caused only a minor disruption in their evening plans.

Jake grabbed my arm, and Bella came to my other side. Together they pulled me toward the front door. I screamed for my parents, but there was no response. I had no idea where they might have gone. Jake and Bella pulled me into the house, continuing to tell me I needed to calm down; I needed to stop fighting. Their threats and promises that I would hurt myself, that I was hurting my baby, grew stronger and more frightening.

They pulled me up the stairs. I tripped after them, resisting every step, but fighting with less strength now, knowing in my heart they were right. I didn't want to pull away from them and go crashing to the bottom of that long staircase. I realized Michael had disappeared.

They pulled me along with less trouble now, down the

hallway to the back staircase and up to the third floor. "Where are you taking me?"

"We're going to the spare bedroom so you can spend some time alone and think about your hysteria."

"Our sister is dead! My behavior is perfectly normal. You're supposed to be getting Dad to help bring her body up. The tide will start coming in soon. Where *are* Mom and Dad?"

Bella patted my cheek. "It's okay, sweetie. It's okay," she said in a voice like thick, sickly-sweet syrup.

They brought me to the tiny room with its single bed, narrow dresser, wooden chair, and writing table where we'd spent time as children when we needed time out to reflect and *come to our senses.*

"Where's Michael?"

"You hurt him badly," Bella said. "Collette is dressing his wounds."

"No, I didn't."

"You drew blood. There was a lot of blood."

"There wasn't."

"You don't know. You didn't see how you were. You were out of your mind. Stay calm. I'm going to make you some tea."

I started crying again. "Why are you doing this to me? I want Michael. And you need to get Dad. You need to get down to the shore before it's dark. It's already getting so dark. Her body will be gone. The tide—"

"Stop," Jake said. "Stop with the tide and dead bodies. There was no body. You're imagining things."

I laughed. I laughed with confusion and then heard the hysteria tinge the edges. "You saw her. Don't tell me she wasn't there. We all saw her, Jake."

He smoothed my hair back from my forehead. Bella was moving me toward the bed. She pushed me gently but firmly until I was forced to sit on the edge. As Jake held me in place, she knelt and began untying my shoes. She pulled them off, taking my socks off too. She pressed on my shoulders, trying to push me down onto the mattress.

"I'm not getting into bed."

"You have to. It's for your own good," Bella said.

"I want Michael."

"After Collette fixes his injuries. Maybe then. But first you need to calm down and get some rest."

Jake grabbed both my arms and pinned them to my sides. Bella turned away and picked up several long nylon straps with plastic buckles that looked like they belonged to camping equipment. She approached me and looped one around my left arm.

"What the hell are you doing?"

"Don't get upset, sweetie. This is for your own good. And for Baby Girl's. We have to make sure you don't hurt her. You're getting so violent. You're going to risk falling, and that would be terrible. You could lose her."

"You're not tying me to the bed."

"Don't shout at her," Jake said.

"You promised you would get Sunday's body," I said. "If you don't hurry, she's going to wash out to sea again. Please don't do this. I know you hated her, but please, please don't let that happen."

He put his hand on my forehead. "There was no body, Annie. I don't know what you think you saw, but there wasn't a body."

"There was. Ask Michael."

He gave me a sad, pathetic look. "Is this because you feel guilty? When you were a little kid, you were always saying you were going to push her off the cliff. No one understood why, but you said it quite a few times. I think the guilt must have festered, and now ..."

"I never said that! Never. You were the one who said that."

He shook his head. "No."

"I remember you saying it. I'd forgotten all about it and then—"

"You need to stop. There was no body. Sunday left because Sunday does whatever she wants. She's not dead; she didn't fall onto the rocks. She wasn't washed up onto a beach. Your imagination is out of control. I'm not sure what's causing it, but we're here to help you," he said.

I shook my head, letting my hair fly across my face, crying so hard I couldn't see anything except the hair whipping back and forth. "No. No, no, no."

"Lie down," Bella said. "Can you take care of this, Jake? I need to get the tea made. She's still so worked up."

"Sure," he said. "Hurry."

"I can't make water boil faster," she said.

He laughed. She giggled in response.

A moment later, I heard the door close.

Stronger than I was by far, Jake managed to hold me down and tie my legs and arms to the bed. He pulled the blankets from underneath me and covered my legs and feet, warming them, which soothed me despite my burning need to escape. I twisted, pulling at the restraints, crying for him to let me go.

Jake said nothing. He moved close to the door and turned off the overhead light. The only remaining light came from a small lamp on the dresser, making it difficult to see more than the shape of him standing there, his arms folded across his chest in a show of power.

"I remembered you telling me you would push her over," I said. "I remembered you looking me right in the eyes. It's like it happened yesterday."

"I never said that. You need to get some sleep."

I whimpered, still making occasional futile tugs at the straps holding my wrists and ankles. "Why aren't you looking for Dad? You need to get Sunday's body, like you promised."

"Because there is no body. No more talking or I'll leave you all alone. I can just as easily wait for Bella in the hallway."

I started crying and continued weeping softly until Bella returned. She held two capsules in the palm of her hand. "You need to take these."

"No. I can't take anything. You know that. It—"

"I know what's safe. You seem to forget I'm an RN. This is just acetaminophen and diphenhydramine. It's perfectly safe while you're pregnant as long as you don't overdo it."

"I don't care if it's technically safe. I don't take anything that's not necessary. I don't have a headache. I don't have any pain, and I don't need it."

"You need to calm down and get some rest. You're very wound up, and you're having what I would call hallucinations. You keep—"

"I am not. Where's Michael? I want you to untie me. Right now."

"You aren't going anywhere, and you won't be seeing Michael until he's patched up. So you can lie here and cry and thrash around and maybe harm your baby, or you can get some badly needed rest. Those are your choices."

I glanced toward the door. Jake was gone. In a pathetic and dismal hope that he only said there was no body to stop me from worrying and talking about it, and that he'd gone to find my father and recover my sister's remains, I gave in. I swallowed the capsules and sipped the tea. Bella settled in the chair at the foot of the bed, hanging my jacket over the back of it. I let myself sink into the bed and fall asleep.

27

The sun was up when I woke. The restraints and Bella were gone.

The dream I'd had was crisp. It seemed as if it had lasted the entire night. The acetaminophen meant to make me sleep had stirred up my brain, as medications like that usually do, making my dream more vivid and detailed and confusing.

I crawled across the bed and grabbed my coat off the back of the chair. My notebook and pen were still tucked securely in the pocket. I pulled them out. Sitting cross-legged, I began writing as fast as my hand could move, even though my fingers were still slack from the medication and sleep.

In some ways, it was the same dream I'd had before, but it had changed shape.

This time, I clearly saw that it was a man and woman struggling with each other. The woman wore a long white dress, but it was more like a nightgown. The man's face was obscured, not by darkness or any object, but by my own mind. The woman was also unrecognizable, but somehow, in

the certainty of a dreamworld aftermath, I knew it wasn't
Sunday.

They struggled violently, then almost seemed to dance
with each other. When the man disappeared, it wasn't
because he'd dropped off the edge of a cliff, but because he'd
collapsed to the ground, his body becoming part of the dark
earth.

As I wrote, as the images replayed themselves in my
mind, I realized I hadn't dreamt I was near the cliff this time. I
was near the playhouse that used to stand in our backyard.
The vibrant pink trim stood out like a frame behind the two
figures, glowing an almost neon color in the moonlight,
although it hadn't been like that in reality. This was so
different than the earlier versions of my dream, I wondered if
it was even the same. Maybe my entire life was dissolving into
a soup of images and memories.

I wrote every detail, focusing on what I remembered
about the playhouse, about how the figures moved, about
what I was wearing and how I felt. As much as I tried, I
couldn't recall whether I was hot or cold, whether or not my
feet were bare. All I remembered was the white gown on the
woman and the outline of the playhouse.

Sitting in the prayer garden, remembering the playhouse,
must have stirred it up in my memory. So was this dream an
actual memory, or just something created out of thoughts I'd
had the previous day? Had it only been twenty-four hours? I
felt like I'd lived a week since I'd watched that bird splashing
in the bath.

I felt that I must have been five during the dream, because
I no longer had the long, thick braids hanging down to my
waist. I knew the playhouse was gone by the time I was in first
grade.

As I made a note on the timeline, I thought about how
just the day before, I'd believed the dream was reminding me

of Jake's threat to push Sunday off the cliff. Now I thought it was something else entirely. I was younger when he'd said that to me. Besides, the dreams were different. The feelings they evoked were the same, the struggle between two people was so similar it felt the same, but the circumstances very different.

Maybe it wasn't that straightforward. Maybe I was looking at my brain as if it could be explained by pop culture or an app. I was pushing my brain to remember things. Being in my childhood home was doing its own work at exposing memories and prompting dreams. It wasn't as if it were a neatly cut jigsaw puzzle that I could piece together. It was an unknowable mass of impressions and flashing neurons.

Hopefully, if I kept encouraging it, my mind would make sense of the things that troubled me. Eventually.

I closed the notebook and tucked it back into my coat pocket. I lay on my side, pulling the blankets over me. I was drowsy again now that I'd lost the fire of writing about the dream. The effects of the medication were still obvious in my blurred thoughts and a soggy feeling pushing me back toward sleep. My eyelids felt heavy, and I let them fall closed.

The sound of the door opening woke me, whether it was a moment later or an hour, I couldn't say. Michael stepped into the room and closed the door with his foot. He was carrying a tray with a teapot, cup, and a plate of buttered toast and a small bowl of sliced strawberries.

He placed the tray on the writing table and came quickly to the bed. He knelt beside the bed and kissed my cheek. "I'm so sorry. I never should have said what I did. I have no idea why ... I don't even know why I thought it—suggesting you could have pushed Sunday off the cliff. You would never hurt anyone, ever. You won't even uproot a plant." His eyes were glassy as he moved his face close to mine and kissed me softly on the lips. "I'm so sorry," he whispered.

I turned my head away from him. "It's the worst thing you've ever said to me."

"I know."

"I can't understand why."

"I don't know. Maybe because you were so upset. It seemed like you were out of your mind, and I ... I don't know. There's no explanation, no excuse."

"I was upset. I *am* upset. We might have saved her life if everyone hadn't pretended nothing was wrong."

"I know. It was stupid, and they put the idea in my head, and I just ... it was so upsetting. I don't know why I thought it. I don't truly think that. Please believe me."

I wanted to. It sounded true. But he had thought it, even if it was only for half a second. And knowing that left a sharp pain in my chest that wouldn't go away. I wanted it to stop. I wanted him to never have thought something so terrible about me. I didn't know what to say to him. I wasn't going to tell him it was okay, because it wasn't. But I felt sorry that he felt terrible and that he couldn't take it back. Maybe the hurt would fade to nothing after a while. I hoped so.

"I'm sorry you didn't want to be with me. That I—"

"What do you mean?"

"Bella said when they brought you inside, you made them bring you up here."

"No. That's not how it was." I told him what had happened. Ignoring the tea and berries, I moved over in the bed, and he crawled in beside me. We held each other, each thinking about my family, trying to find an explanation for something that was impossible to explain.

After a while, we got up. I drank the lukewarm tea, and we both ate the toast and berries.

"Did they have trouble getting her body up to the top of the cliff?" I shivered, trying not to picture Jake and my father with the tarp carrying Sunday's body. "I feel like I should have been there, even if I couldn't help. I'm so angry at what they did to me."

"There was no body."

"Yes, there was. I saw her. You saw her."

"I thought I did, but ..."

"What do you mean?"

"I just glanced down. And you were freaking out, and I was worried about you. So now I guess I'm not sure. Jake said he and your dad went down there and didn't find her."

"They took too long." My words came out on the edge of tears. I'd known Jake wouldn't care. He wasted time and waited too long, and the tide took her away.

"He said the tide wasn't in."

"I saw her body on the rocks, Michael. And so did you, even if it was only for half a second. Maybe you blocked it out because it was so awful. Maybe you were scared or worried about me, but I saw you look, and I saw you react. You saw her."

"If they found her, your father would be a mess. If his daughter was dead, he would be broken. But he's ..." He shrugged.

"I don't know. I can't explain it." I crept out of bed. "I need a shower."

Michael carried the tray, and we went downstairs to our bedroom. In the shower, as I let hot water pour over my face and run through my hair, I decided not to tell Michael about my dream or the things I was writing in my notebook. I knew he'd seen Sunday's body, even if he was doubting it now. Maybe my father *hadn't* seen her body. I had no idea what had happened on that rocky beach, but nothing was going to make me stop believing what I'd seen with my own eyes.

28

Michael and I walked into the dining room holding hands. I needed the comfort of his hand if I was going to look at the faces of my family and see them returning my look of grief with their blank stares. Their everyday expressions that made me feel like I was in a fun house, seeing distorted reflections all around me.

We took our seats, and Michael filled our glasses with orange juice.

"Did you rest well?" Bella asked.

I looked at Jake, waiting until he caught my eye. "You didn't find Sunday's body?"

"Annie!" Jake said. "There wasn't—"

"I know what I saw with my own eyes. And you saw her too. You accused me of pushing her off the cliff. So I know you saw her! Her body was lying smashed on that rock. She was wearing her white dress that—"

Jake coughed so loudly I couldn't make myself heard over the sound of his barking. "Can we please not start this again? Michael, I thought you and Collette had an understanding?"

I wrenched my hand away from Michael's and glared at him.

"All I said was I agreed it wasn't healthy to talk about it all the time. And it's not."

I turned away from him. "I feel like this entire family is psychotic! You're sitting here eating breakfast as if nothing is wrong. Sunday has been dead for days, and her body washed up on the beach, and you're all pretending it didn't happen. What's wrong with you?" I looked around the table, trying to catch the attention of each one in turn, but all of them avoided my gaze. They didn't look uncomfortable or afraid to meet my eyes, just disinterested.

I felt like the entire inside of me was burning. What had happened to the people I loved and called my family? Had they all lost their minds? "What's *wrong* with you? She's dead! Someone in this family killed her, and no one is concerned about that either. Liam knew something about it, and you're all—"

"That's enough, Annie," my mother said. "Have you stopped to think how it hurts me and your father to have you going on and on about Sunday being dead? Now you're going to start hurling cruel, ugly accusations at the people who love you? I don't understand why you're doing this. You're breaking my heart."

Collette pushed back her chair and stood. "I'm sorry you had to hear that, Mom. I'm sorry for all of this. Having Sunday take off in the middle of our vacation has been hard on all of us, but we need to focus on enjoying the people who are here, not giving all our attention to the one who left."

"Yes," my father said. "That's a great attitude. Thank you, Collette."

"I think Annie didn't get enough rest. She's clearly over-tired," Collette said.

"I'm absolutely fine. I slept like a baby."

"You're having hallucinations. You're obsessed. You were hysterical last evening, and you had to be carried to your room. You clawed at your husband like a wild animal."

"I'm fine." Michael patted my leg. "It wasn't anything. Let's not overdramatize."

"I think more rest would do her good. I'll take her upstairs, if you'll make some tea, Bella. And get some ..."

Bella jumped up from her seat. "I keep telling her she's hurting the baby, but she won't listen. I'm really concerned."

"The baby is fine," I said.

"All the crying and shouting. It's not good," Jake said.

"We're all worried about you," my mother said. "It's not helpful to be in such an emotional state."

"This should be a happy, peaceful time for you and Michael," my father said.

"I had a friend who, sadly, lost two close friends while she was pregnant," Bella said. "The grief tore her apart. Literally. She ended up going into labor at six months. Luckily the baby survived, but you know what a long, hard road that is, with a child born that early."

I felt a cold chill run through me, imagining my baby coming out in just a few short weeks. It was a horrifying, sickening thought. She was so tiny, barely larger than an heirloom tomato right now.

"It almost seems like you don't care about your sweet, little baby," Bella said.

"Hey." Michael's voice was loud and commanding. "That's way out of line. Annie is a fabulous mother. You owe her an apology."

"I'm just saying," Bella said, "that all this trauma is not good. I'll get the tea going." She went into the kitchen and closed the door firmly behind her.

Collette remained standing, watching me, waiting for me to get up, I suppose. Did she think I would obediently trot out of the room after her? I took a sip of orange juice, but on an empty stomach, it didn't go down well. I felt a pain in my stomach, and suddenly their horror stories and elaborated fears felt like they might be real.

Could I be wrong? Was all of this upsetting my body more than I realized, inflicting trauma on my baby? I placed my hands on my bump. Maybe I wasn't thinking clearly about my health. Maybe I wasn't thinking clearly about anything. My thoughts were so twisted around my dreams and memory fragments and the increasingly strange and disturbing behavior of my family. I almost didn't know what was real. If I was wrong about how my feelings were affecting the baby, could I be wrong about Sunday's disappearance and seeing her body?

But I knew I'd seen her body on those rocks. I knew it without a single thread of doubt. Yet, listening to them insist I had not seen her had a strange way of making me think they could possibly be right. How could I hold those two contrary thoughts at the same time? It was a senseless impossibility. One of us was wrong, and I refused to believe it was me.

When I looked down at the shore, I'd known I was right and that I needed to trust my own view of the world instead of allowing my family to tell me what was real, and what I should be thinking, and what was best for me and my family.

After Bella came out with the tea, I let Collette lead me up to our bedroom. I didn't want to fight her. I did want to take care of myself; I did want to rest if that was what the baby needed. Maybe they were all wonderfully concerned for me, and I'd been looking at them through a negative, suspicious lens. No matter what they were, or what their motives, our baby mattered more than anything. I owed her everything I could give, and that meant taking good care of myself.

As I settled into the bed I shared with Michael, the pot of tea and a cup beside me on the nightstand, Collette pulled the armchair closer to the bed. "You need to remember the family principles, Annie."

"How can I ever forget them?" I laughed softly. "We get reminded of them every day of our lives."

"Because they matter. And showing excessive emotion makes a situation spiral out of control. If something happened to Sunday, we can't become hysterical about it. We need to be calm and accepting."

"I don't think that means blandly accepting your sister died a brutal death."

"You're hurting Mom and Dad. Have you thought about that? You're hurting them, and you're becoming a disappointment to them. You aren't following the principles, which always lets them down. And you're hurting them by constantly going on about their favorite child being dead. Just forget about yourself for one tiny minute and think about how that makes them feel." She held out the acetaminophen with diphenhydramine.

Part of me craved that abnormally deep sleep of escape, but another part of me didn't want to be unconscious, plagued by troubling dreams. I was angry at my parents' blank acceptance that everything was fine with Sunday, based on absolutely nothing. At the same time, a tendril of guilt had begun creeping through my gut, taking root, making me feel as if I'd hurt them terribly, when I didn't really have very much to go on except isolated events that could be interpreted differently.

At least that was the case until I'd seen her body. I *had* seen her body. I knew I'd seen her body.

Still, I took the acetaminophen and drank half the tea before burrowing under the covers, hoping for the relief of dreamless sleep.

When I woke, I heard voices. It was still daylight, but the shadows filling the bedroom suggested it was mid to late afternoon. I'd slept through lunch. It was disorienting to know I'd slept all night and been awake only for breakfast. I propped myself up on my elbow and tried to figure out whose voices I heard, and where they were coming from.

As much as I strained, I couldn't make out any words. I couldn't even say for sure who was talking. I heard male and female, and that was it.

I got out of bed and went to the door. I opened it carefully and stepped into the hallway. The people talking weren't on the landing as I'd thought, they were standing in the foyer, but their slightly raised voices, despite one of them—Bella—constantly urging them to shush, had carried up to the second floor.

I took a few steps along the hallway closer to the landing. I still couldn't make out what they were saying, but I heard Bella, Collette, Jake, and Michael. What was Michael talking to my siblings about? Obviously me, but what about me? Why would he be speaking a single word to them without letting me know? I didn't care that I'd been asleep. I felt betrayed.

Before I could make sense of the conversation, like a sharp, cold wind, I felt my mother's breath and heard her speak directly behind me. "Go back to bed. You shouldn't be up." Her voice was crisp. There was no warmth or concern, just a cold statement, almost like an order. Then she walked past me, hardly looking at me. At the landing, she turned toward the hallway leading to the back stairs up to the third floor.

I had no idea where she'd come from, unless it was the large linen closet across from my bedroom. But why ...

I returned to my room to take my second shower for the day, so I could wash the dulling effects of the acetaminophen out of my system. My mother's words ran in a circle inside my head, like a diamond slicing a perfect disk from a sheet of glass, repeating themselves. Her words seemed familiar, but I had no idea why. They just felt like something I'd heard before. Something threatening.

29

THEN: ANNIE

Sunday isn't like us. She thinks she's a queen and we're her royal subjects. I don't know what a subject is. Collette said it means she's in charge of us. I don't know what that means either.

Her bed is a princess bed, and a princess is a baby queen, so maybe she is a real queen. Everyone says that.

Brothers and sisters should be the same as each other. They should be in the same group, like a club. Sunday isn't in our club, because everyone in the club is supposed to look out for the other kids. You should do what's fair for the other kids, and you shouldn't think you're better. Not the queen.

Sunday makes Daddy and Mommy like her better. And that's bad. You aren't supposed to make people like you better. It's mean.

Since Daddy and Mommy like her better, she gets better things. Like her princess bed with lots of ruffles and a canopy over it. And her bedroom is really big. It's almost as big as Mommy and Daddy's bedroom. Just like her bed is almost as big as theirs. She's almost like a grownup, because she has whatever she wants.

She has better stuff than me. And she has more stuff than the older kids, and she doesn't have to do as many chores.

It's not fair, and things are supposed to be fair. Everyone knows things have to be fair.

There are other reasons she isn't like us. But I don't know what the other reasons are. Maybe because she's bad. Maybe she did bad things. Maybe she stole things. I don't know. I don't know what all the bad things are, because I'm little, and some things you can't know when you're little because they're bad.

That's what Jake said.

Collette said I should always listen to Jake, because he knows everything.

Even Mommy and Daddy said I should listen to Jake. I should listen to Collette because they're older.

But Mommy and Daddy don't know that Jake and Collette say I shouldn't love Sunday. I should pretend I can't see her or hear her. I should pretend she isn't even there. They told me to stay away from her because she's bad, and bad things might happen to me. They said she isn't like us.

It's not fair that Daddy and Mommy love her so much more, but Daddy said life is not fair. I don't know what that means.

30

The minute Michael came into our room, I pounced on him. Literally. I acted as if I were a cat, sitting on the foot of our bed, waiting for the door to open. When it did, I said, "Why were you talking about me?"

His arms jerked slightly, and he stared at me, blinking. I think I scared him. He knew I was in there, but he expected me to be asleep, or at least lying down in bed, not sitting there like a gargoyle staring at the door, waiting.

"We're worried about you."

"So I've heard. Why were you talking about me behind my back? Talking about how crazy I am for thinking I saw my sister's body? No one is going to talk me into thinking I'm imagining things. I really hope you aren't listening to them. That you're not going to turn into my enemy."

"You think your brother and sister are your enemies?"

"They tied me to the bed! What do you call it? Someone in this house killed my sister."

"You don't know that. She could have fallen. She might have jumped ... you already know she was upset. Maybe she didn't resolve things with the person she felt betrayed her, and she jumped." When he heard the sound that came out of me without me realizing it, he flinched. "I know it sounds awful, but it's one possibility."

"No matter how it happened, she's dead. So why are they trying to make me think I'm losing my mind?"

He sighed. "I don't know. I believe that you saw her. And just so we're clear, I wasn't talking behind your back. I thought you were asleep, and I was going to tell you what we talked about. I do agree with them that you need to take a step back. You need to consider your health and the baby's."

"I'm sorry if I've lost sight of that. I just don't think pregnant women need to be treated like we have a life-threatening illness." I got up and went into the bathroom. I brushed my hair and put on lip balm and hand cream. I returned to the bedroom.

Michael was still standing by the door, looking slightly dazed.

"Why don't you go for a run?" I said. "Or play croquet with them?" I could hear their voices drifting up from the lawn as they set up another game. I really liked the game, but I couldn't face the surreal atmosphere of normal family life. I had to figure out what I should do next, how I could make them stop living in their disturbing state of absolute denial. Using Michael to keep them away from me seemed like a good idea for now.

He came toward me and put his hand on the side of my head, weaving his fingers through my hair. "Are you sure?"

"Collette gave me more acetaminophen with diphenhydramine, and I'm really groggy. I'll just rest and drink lots of water. I need to flush this stuff out of my system."

Michael brought me a large bottle of cold water and a plate of crackers, sliced cheese, and red grapes. He kissed my nose and left to play croquet. It wasn't his idea of a good time, but maybe he sensed that the best thing he could do was exactly what I wanted—keep them away from me.

Once he was gone, I ate the entire plate of food, took out my notebook, and started writing.

I didn't know if my thoughts came from dreams or memories. I just wrote down everything that had floated to the surface while I slept. I started with my memory of the playhouse being torn down. The suddenness had shocked me. I'd felt as if my childhood was being ripped away. Of course, I didn't put it in those complicated terms at the time, but later, I did see it that way. All the other kids in my family had enjoyed playing in it for years. Then, just as I reached the age when I began developing the ability to engage in imaginary play, the tiny house vanished as if it had never existed. I hadn't seen it dismantled. I hadn't heard the blow of a hammer or the crack of boards ripped from nails. One day it was there; the next it was gone. Quinn had done the work; I remembered it was soon after his father had left.

I wrote about my memories of Quinn's father—Conner Wiley. He was the man who cared for our horses and first taught me to ride. He'd also taught Jake and Collette, as far as I knew. Sunday, of course, had private lessons, one of the many privileges that enraged Collette and Jake.

Conner and his wife, Lori, had lived in the cottage that Quinn now occupied alone. Lori died of cancer when I was so small, I had no memory of her. All I remembered of Conner was that he was tall, almost always wore a cowboy hat, and Collette used to whisper that he was *so* good-looking. When Quinn and Jake were both fifteen, Conner took off. I was only five, but I did remember my father talking about how Conner had abandoned his son. I remembered Quinn joining us for Christmas presents around our tree, looking lost, hardly talking, acting as if he didn't want to be there. I remembered him seated beside Jake for Christmas dinner and our Thanks-giving feast.

After a few years, that ended. I supposed by the time he was in his twenties, he'd found his own friends and no longer wanted to pretend his employers were his family. I'd never talked to him about it. I knew him as someone who loved horses and needed to be outdoors. He'd told me he couldn't imagine living more than a few miles from the coast, so I assumed those desires led him to continue working for my parents for all these years.

I also remembered that my riding lessons stopped suddenly after Quinn's father left, and it was several months, maybe nearly a year, before Quinn started teaching me.

Turning to the front of my notebook, I wrote my memo-ries of Conner and the destruction of playhouse and riding lessons on the timeline. I wrote the date of the last time I remembered Quinn joining us for Christmas dinner. I figured it was better to be complete, and I was starting to realize that the more notes I made, the more memories rose to the surface. Kate must have had a lot of experience suggesting people keep timelines and dream diaries. So far, it seemed to work. Writing things down, even random, disconnected bits of memory, was having the effect of sweeping the constantly repeating memories and dream fragments out of my head, clearing space for the things that had been buried under the clutter.

I put down my notebook and pen. Still groggy, I crawled under the blankets and closed my eyes. I heard voices from the lawn area outside, but they sounded far away, seeming to drift farther as I fell asleep.

I dreamt about Sunday. I was at an equestrian competi-tion, watching her jump Evergreen over hurdles. When she finished, I saw her straddling Evergreen, sitting tall, her shoulders back and her chin lifted, receiving a trophy for her perfect execution of the course.

When I woke, I had a smile on my face. I had always loved my sister from a distance. I had never felt the violent jealousy that tormented Jake and Collette. Maybe because I was younger. Even though I was afraid to be near Sunday for some unknown reason, even though Jake and Collette constantly warned me to stay away from her, they couldn't touch the inside of my heart. They couldn't see how I adored her.

I loved how she looked at her trophies and ribbons and never bragged or acted important. Instead, she laughed that she was so lucky. But Jake couldn't even let that go without anger seeping out of his pores like sweat. When my parents couldn't hear, he grabbed Sunday's wrist. "You aren't *lucky*. You're privileged. It's not the same thing. Don't ever forget that."

Sunday laughed and shook him off. "I feel lucky," she said. "I know I am. Remember, I was born on 7/7 under a lucky star. Lucky sevens."

My heart beat a little faster as I thought about her words. I climbed out of bed and scrambled around on the floor. I pulled her phone from under the bed, where it was still lying next to my charger. I powered it on and entered the number seven six times. The phone unlocked. I felt like I'd hit the jackpot myself.

31

W ith her phone opening before me like Pandora's box, I read through Sunday's recent text messages. There were over fifty; it took several minutes to read them carefully. It turned out my mom had sent her quite a few messages right after she went missing. I wondered why she'd never mentioned it. There were messages from friends telling her to check in, and messages from Liam after he and I had spoken. I suppose he'd wanted to confirm that I was telling the truth. I looked through all her social media to double-check that she hadn't posted anything since the last time I'd seen her. She hadn't, which felt like another stab in my heart.

I'd been so eager to get into her phone, but I wasn't sure what I'd hoped to find. So far, there was nothing that told me a single thing I didn't already know.

The notice for her email account showed she had 150 unread messages. I opened her email and scrolled through quickly to see if anything caught my eye in the midst of promotional offers and newsletters and payment and appointment reminders.

Then it jumped out at me like a snake striking at my ankle on a mountain trail. The sender was one of the well-known DNA testing companies, and the subject line announced that the report on her DNA sample was now available in her account.

My heart thudded as my thoughts rushed back to the previous Christmas. My family had been drinking coffee and eating cookies shaped like reindeer and snowmen. The pie was gone, and my father had just asked who wanted an after-dinner drink. He was standing behind his chair, looking down the table, smiling at his family.

Jake, who always liked to bring up topics unrelated to what was happening, or so it seemed that night, said, "I had my DNA done. It's fascinating to find out there's a lot more nuance to our ancestry than German, Italian, and English."

"Do you want brandy?" my father asked.

"Sure," Jake said. "It looks like there was some Jewish blood about three generations back. We should all do it. The more people in your family who submit their DNA, the more complete the picture becomes."

"We know who we are," my father said.

"History is important."

Collette laughed. "Says the guy who earns his living shoving history down kids' throats."

My father went to the sideboard and brought the brandy bottle to the table. He returned and began placing glasses on the corner of the table, appearing to decide everyone would have a brandy since we were ignoring his inquiry.

"I don't like the frenzy over DNA testing," my mother said. "It's invasive. And it's a fad."

"How is it invasive?" Jake asked.

"It's like having your medical records available to strangers."

"No, it's not. No one can access it without your permission."

My mother laughed. "Credit cards, social security numbers ... everything about us is breached every single day."

"Well, I think we should all do it," Jake said. "It's a good historical record."

No one said they would. No one seemed interested in a historical record. It was never mentioned again over the Christmas holiday. And no one had brought it up when we arrived for our summer vacation. Now, it looked like Sunday was the only one who had been intrigued by the idea. I wondered why she'd waited so long.

I opened the email, clicked the link, and began reading.

The report noted that Sunday was related to Jake Ledger, but it stated they did not share both parents.

I stared at the words. I read them a second time, thinking I hadn't understood the meaning correctly. But the meaning was clear. As if a series of doors had opened simultaneously inside my brain, revealing a long hallway I'd never seen, I knew in the next moment that my father was not Sunday's biological father. I'd seen many photographs of my mother pregnant with Sunday, and if my brother and sister shared one parent, that meant my mother had cheated on my father.

The family principles chattered in the background as I tried to sort out my scrambling thoughts. My mother. I couldn't imagine it. I couldn't believe it was possible. My parents' marriage was idyllic. They were affectionate without ever seeming forced or fake. She supported his work wholeheartedly, and he was enthusiastic about the things that interested her. They enjoyed the same activities. They went out to dinner alone and with other couples; they enjoyed romantic weekend getaways.

I couldn't believe it. I read the words again.

Sunday was my father's favorite child. He doted on her. Sometimes it felt as if he came close to worshiping her. Did he have any idea? Was she his favorite in spite of knowing she wasn't his? Or was he clueless even now?

I wondered if Jake knew. I was pretty sure if Sunday ticked the appropriate permission box, the company would notify Jake she'd had her DNA tested. He'd hated Sunday all his life. He could never shut up about her not being one of us. I'd never understood what he meant by that. When I was little, it simply felt childish and mean. Now I wondered if he'd always known. He was ten years older than I was. He'd experienced things that I might never know. He must have all kinds of knowledge about our family that I was unaware of, that I'd never been told because it had been forgotten or brushed aside as unimportant. But when you put it all together, maybe those things mattered quite a lot.

Jake had been watching me all week, seeming to follow me at times, even to the scene of Liam's accident. Why was he paying such close attention? Was he worried that I was asking too many questions? Had he done what he'd threatened to do since I was a little girl—shoved my sister off the edge of the cliff to her death? Despite knowing how incredibly jealous he was of her, I still couldn't believe that of him. I loved my big brother. Even when I was angry at him, afraid of him, or frustrated by him, I still loved him.

Knowing about the DNA test results made me revisit the last morning Sunday had been in the house. It was clear now why she'd been frantic to be alone with my father. And I was pretty sure my mother must have known why she wanted to speak with him. She'd done everything short of physically restraining Sunday to be sure they didn't go riding together. Had the person I'd seen struggling with Sunday on the cliff been my mother? But did my mother seriously believe she could prevent Sunday speaking to him forever? Sunday always did what she wanted. Eventually, she would have found a way to talk to him. Unless …

My thoughts halted, unable to move any closer to that horrifying conclusion. Instead, I turned them to Collette and Bella. If Jake knew Sunday wasn't my father's biological daughter, Bella knew. Maybe the entire family knew, and I was the last to find out. I tucked her phone into my suitcase and went downstairs. For the first time in my pregnancy, I desperately wanted a glass of wine.

Instead, I made tea. I needed to keep my mind calm and steady, away from the thought that I needed to numb my shock with alcohol.

Was one of my siblings capable of murder?

Knowing Sunday was not our father's biological child would drive Jake and Collette insane with years of pent-up jealousy. They would not want her sharing in his estate. They would want my father to cut her off completely. She didn't share his blood. I could hear them saying it. But he adored Sunday. His star rider, his beautiful dancer, his favorite.

And Bella. She took on all of Jake's grievances and enflamed them with her own bitter feelings. She might have grown to hate Sunday more than he did, brooding over the wrongs that had been done to her husband, listening for years to his complaints and the petty and not-so-petty injustices of his childhood.

It was a terrible thing to think. To believe a person you love and have shared your life with could be capable of the worst thing. I felt like an awful human being for letting these thoughts pass through my mind. To be turning them around and considering the possibilities made me feel like a bona fide monster.

My tea was ready. I took the mug to the front porch. I sat down, looking at the fog that was rolling across the property, creeping toward the garden like a living thing. The croquet game was long over. I wasn't sure where they'd all gone. Somehow, I'd managed to come downstairs without seeing anyone, make my tea, and escape again to the front porch. It was a miracle of logistics. I smiled. And it was the first time I remembered feeling a smile on my face in days.

The sensation disappeared quickly. I took a sip of tea and watched the fog dancing closer.

The front door opened and closed behind me.

"Hey," Michael said. "I was looking for you." He kissed the top of my head.

He sat in the chair beside me. I told him to move closer. Leaning my head toward his and nudging him to do the same, I spoke in a low voice, telling him what I'd found on Sunday's phone.

When I finished, we moved away from each other. The fog had advanced to the steps of the porch. I shivered at the drop in temperature.

"What are you going to do?" he asked.

"I'm going to talk to my mother."

He nodded. He reached across and closed his fingers around my wrist. It helped reduce the chill I felt from the enveloping fog.

32

I found my mother in the gardening shed, sorting through seed packets.

"I need to talk to you."

She sighed. Then she placed the seed packets she was holding back into the divided wooden box where she stored them, and took off her hat and gardening gloves. "I guess I won't be doing this today. What is it?"

"Not here."

"Why not?"

"I want to talk where we can be alone."

"We are alone."

"Where we can be sure no one will walk in. Can we go to your bedroom?"

She laughed. "Seriously?"

"It's really important."

She sighed again.

The door to her bedroom was partially open, as it usually was. Even so, my parents' bedroom was separated from the other bedrooms by a short hallway and then a sort of foyer of its own. It felt like another world, and I couldn't remember the last time I'd stepped inside. I'd probably been a small child.

Something about being in that room struck awe in me—their king-sized four-poster bed, two massive dressers, the eight-foot-wide mirror over my mother's and several of her large glass figurines on display. Off to one side of the room, near glass-paneled doors leading to a small balcony, was a sitting area with a love seat, an armchair and a coffee table. She sat in the armchair, and I sat cross-legged on the love seat. She looked at me as if she wanted to reprimand me for putting my stocking feet on the upholstery, but she said nothing. I decided not to obey the unspoken message.

"I assume this is about Sunday," my mother said.

The calm in her voice unsettled me. "It is, but ... I can't understand why everyone is pretending she isn't dead. It's creepy. It breaks my heart that no one is grieving." Already I found myself crying. I hadn't wanted to, but the tears started flowing before I realized what was happening.

"I don't know how many times we have to say this, but you need to stop upsetting yourself."

"I'm not upsetting myself deliberately. I'm upset that she died. I *saw* her body before it washed back out to sea."

"We can't be sure."

"I'm sure! And Quinn found her phone. You know she wouldn't leave without her phone. Her necklace? Okay, maybe. *Maybe*. Her phone was right by the edge of the cliff."

She sighed. "Why did you need to come in here to talk about the same thing? Again? I really wish you would stop tormenting yourself like this. It's like you're looking for things to be upset about."

"Pretending this isn't real is not healthy. It's some extreme, bizarre form of denial," I said.

"You're not a psychiatrist."

"I don't have to be a psychiatrist to know what denial is."

My mother started to get up. "We're talking in circles here."

"There's something else."

She slid back into the chair and gave me a patient smile. "About the baby? I'd love to give you any advice you need. I've forgotten a lot, but I'm happy to share the experiences I can remember."

I uncrossed my legs and tucked my feet to one side. "It's not that. I told you I have Sunday's phone. I figured out her passcode and looked through her email."

"Oh. That's not right. You shouldn't invade someone's privacy like that. What were you thinking?"

"She's dead, Mom. I'm sorry, but she's gone. I needed to find out if there was anything in her messages or mail that might tell us what happened to her."

My mother let out a piercing laugh. "You think someone emailed a death threat?"

"No. But I have a question for you. It's difficult, a little embarrassing, but I—"

"Get to the point."

"She did a DNA test."

My mother's expression didn't change at all. There was no look of surprise or fear. Nothing but the steady gaze of her soft, blue eyes. I expected her to brush her long bangs off her face, as she so often did when she was trying to compose an appropriate response to an uncomfortable question. Instead, she kept her hands in her lap, loosely folded.

"It shows that Dad wasn't her father."

"Then obviously there's a mistake. Those things aren't infallible, you know."

"If you send the right sample, they can't accidentally get someone else's DNA. It's pretty simple."

"You don't know that. There are mix-ups all the time.

Everyone makes mistakes. No test or system is one hundred percent accurate."

"Mom, that's not the kind of mistake they would make. The results line up with Jake's. It clearly shows she and Jake have the same mother but different fathers. Please don't lie to me. Please."

Tears filled her eyes and ran down her cheeks. She still had a tiny smile on her lips. Her eyes stared directly at mine, but I had the feeling she wasn't seeing me. I wasn't even sure she knew she was crying.

After several minutes, she whispered, "It was a terrible mistake. The worst mistake of my life. But your father was gone all the time. I was lonely. I know I ..." The flow of tears increased, but still there was no sound of sobbing.

I wanted to get up and hug her, but I was still too shocked. And disappointed. It was a terrible thing, but so unjust for Sunday. Couldn't she see that? When that conversation happened at Christmas, hadn't my mother considered it could easily come to this?

She moved to the edge of the chair. She rested her elbows on her knees and clasped her hands in a position of prayer. "Please. Please, Annie. You can't ever tell your father. Or anyone. But your father can't know. Please, please don't tell him. It would destroy him."

"How can you live like this, lying to him every day of your life?"

"I'm not lying. I'm putting our family first, just as the principles advise. You know that. The family comes first, and our marriage has to come first, before any imagined need to unburden myself, or some modern obsession with baring your soul in the name of truth telling."

"But your marriage has a terrible flaw."

"It does not! Our marriage is a beacon for hundreds of

thousands, millions of people. I made a mistake, and I've atoned for it. Your father adores Sunday. He always has. I made up for my mistake by treating Sunday with extra love and care and making sure your father felt connected to her in every way. He *is* her father. He's the one who loved her, who nurtured her, who provided for her physical needs, the strong center of her life."

It explained so much. But it was so distorted. Her view of how she'd *fixed* things didn't fit the principles at all. She'd twisted them all around to protect herself.

"The family is more important than the individual," she said. "That's what makes us strong."

"To a point. But this is wrong. It was a terrible thing to do to Sunday—letting her find out like this."

"Don't get carried away by your feelings. You start over-dramatizing, and it makes the problem bigger than it is. You know that."

"I'm not getting carried away. But secrets like this cause damage. I can't imagine what this did to her ... the shock."

"You can *not* tell your father. Not ever. It's not your right. It's not your place."

"Are you going to tell him?"

"No." Her voice softened. "This is between you and me. It's something the two of us can share, as mother and daughter." She stood and came to sit beside me. "You can't tell Michael. If you tell one person, you might as well tell everyone. It's something you and I will take to our graves. And that pledge will bind us to each other forever." She took my hand.

I was overcome with the most conflicting storm of emotion I'd ever felt in my life. The idea of not letting emotion consume me was impossible to practice. Ever since I could remember, I'd ached to be closer to my mother. I'd longed for her to want to be close to me, to share her thoughts and feelings, the real parts of herself, like other mothers shared with their daughters.

Instead, I heard about the family principles and expectations and my amazing sister.

Since the moment we'd told her about the baby, that changed suddenly. She seemed to want to pull me closer, but after a lifetime of distance, I wasn't sure what to do with that. Now she'd finally confided in me, but instead of sharing something to spark a deeper friendship, she'd asked me to hide a terrible secret. One part of me wanted to forget everything she'd told me. I didn't want to be part of the way she'd betrayed my father, the way she'd hidden the truth from my father and Sunday for over thirty years. I felt like I was turning on them and hurting them as deeply as she had.

At the same time, I felt her need for me in a way that I'd never imagined possible. I wanted to share our secrets. I wanted to feel close to her, and I wanted her to look at me and hold onto my hand like she was right now. The feeling of knowing we were connected to each other was so enormous, it was difficult for me to make room even for my grief over Sunday. I felt as if the one thing that had been missing in my life had suddenly materialized right before my eyes. I wanted to stay in that room with my mother and drink it in for as long as I could.

Tears began spilling out of my eyes. She pulled me to her, and we clung to each other for quite a long time.

Finally, we pulled away, but she kept my right hand between both of hers. Her hands were warm and soft. The comfort of her touch made me, for several seconds, doubt that Sunday was truly dead. How could my tender, compassionate mother maintain such composure if her daughter was dead? Was it possible that all my dreams, and my fixation on the past, had distorted my senses? Was it possible I was hallucinating? I didn't want to believe that, but didn't hallucinations, by their very nature, make you think they were real? I didn't want to return to those tormented feelings of self-doubt, but the two views of reality would not reconcile themselves in my mind.

"What did you say when she talked to you?" I asked.

"What do you mean?"

"I saw you fighting with Sunday that night before she went missing. Out near the gazebo."

Her eyes seemed to glaze over. She said nothing, refusing to confirm my belief that she'd been the figure in the hooded jacket.

"Did you tell her?"

She released my hands. "Tell her what?" She looked down at her legs. She ran her palms across her thighs, smoothing the fabric of her jeans as if they might have wrinkles she didn't want seen.

"Who her father is?" I took a deep breath. "Who is he?"

"That's not important."

"It is to her."

"This is all ancient history. There's nothing to be gained from digging up the past."

"It's not the past. It's her life."

"She has a father. She doesn't need two."

"But ..."

"She has a father who absolutely adores her, and that's all that matters."

"She has ... had ... a right to know. And I just wondered ..."

"Your interest is bordering on salacious, Annie. The relationship is over, and the most important thing—the only thing—is respect for your father."

"I'm not being sal—"

"That's enough." She smiled at me as if I were five years old and didn't know the meaning of the word.

I stood. "Thank you for telling me the truth."

She continued smiling at me, her expression starting to freeze.

"It's time to call the police. They need to start a search and rescue for her body. I'm not sure what's involved, or how they decide—"

"Don't do that."

"I'm not going to let everyone convince me I didn't see what I saw."

"Now that you know why she's so upset, don't you see? Don't you understand why I'm able to let Sunday have some space?"

"What do you mean?"

"She was beyond upset. Like you, she wanted to dig into the past and find out things that don't matter. She was angry and petulant. She couldn't control herself. She was hysterical, and she said she felt like she didn't know who she was. So I know she left because she needed time to come to peace with it. Once she's had time to clear her mind, she'll be back, and we can settle things."

"What about her necklace? Her phone? Why would she go without her phone? And you keep forgetting—I saw her body on the beach!"

"It's not possible, sweetheart." She stood and put her arms around me. "Please believe me. She wanted time alone. I wouldn't lie to you about something so important. She probably didn't care about her phone because she said she needed to think. She needed to disconnect. You can't think when your phone is throwing a hundred distractions a minute at you."

I wasn't sure I believed her, but she sounded so certain.

She took a step away from me and looked down at my

bump. "I think your baby girl has grown since you arrived here. I can see the change. It's so exciting."

"I'm sure she has. Every week she's bigger."

She placed her hand on my belly. "It's such a miracle. I hope you're enjoying every moment. It goes so very quickly. You have no idea. You'll blink and she'll be all grown up. You have to find a way to cherish every breath, every waking moment, every smile."

"I know. That's what everyone says."

"I mean it. You think you know, but you don't. So fast. So very, very fast. It brings tears to your eyes. It crushes you. And then you can hardly remember. You forget what being pregnant feels like; you forget that incredible sensation of another life inside you, moving around, drawing its life from you, needing you so desperately."

I nodded.

"That's why we keep telling you to focus on your baby and your health. The days go so fast. And after she's born, and you're tired and busy, you have to take every second you can to hold her and just look at her little face, enjoy the wonder of her existence."

"I will. I promise."

"I'm so happy for you and Michael. Your father and I both are."

"I know."

"Our family is growing. The roots are spreading out to a new generation."

I nodded.

She hugged me again. Then, without me realizing what was happening, I was at the doorway to her bedroom, and then she was opening the door, and I was stepping into the little entry room, and she was kissing my cheek and rubbing my bump and telling me she needed to lie down, suggesting I should do the same.

When the door closed and I was alone in that small room outside their bedroom, I felt like I'd lived half of my life over in the past hour, and that it had been entirely different from the life I'd thought I had. I felt warmed and loved; I felt broken by grief, confused and shocked. I'd never been more drained in my life.

33

I stepped out of the entry room and into the hallway, closing that door as well, figuring my mother wanted all the privacy she could get while she thought about our conversation. I desperately wanted to know what she and Sunday had talked about, but judging from what I'd seen in their violent struggle with each other, words failed them in the end.

I turned and saw Jake sitting at the end of the short hallway. He was sprawled on the window seat that looked out on the backyard—the prayer garden and the wooded area beyond. He gave me a slow, lazy, wicked smile.

"Were you eavesdropping?" I asked.

He laughed and swung his feet to the floor. "I have no interest in a weepy hormonal conversation between you and Mom."

Clearly, he had been listening, or he wouldn't have known we were crying.

Watching him looking at me, I wondered why he'd never said anything about Sunday's DNA result. Maybe he didn't know. It wasn't like my brother to keep his mouth shut about anything. He liked to make his opinions known. He liked to make sure everyone understood how he was feeling. He liked to persuade others to see the world the way he did. He liked to be in the know, and I couldn't imagine him being able to keep information like this to himself.

"Why are you sitting outside Mom's room? Did you follow me up here?"

He grinned.

"Stop playing games. Every time I turn around for the past few days, you're there. It's giving me the creeps."

"That's not something a big brother likes to hear. I give my baby sister the creeps?"

"You're watching me. I don't like it."

"I'm not watching you, I'm looking out for you."

"I don't need looking out for."

"Our sister vanished from the face of the earth, to hear you tell it. She was shoved off a cliff and smashed to a bloody pulp on the rocks, if we believe what you think you saw. So I was—"

"Stop mocking me."

"I think you definitely need looking out for."

"What do you mean?"

"If someone took her, or worse ... which you seem pretty sure of, aren't you scared that something might happen to you? Even a small thing for you could be deadly for your baby."

"Is that a threat?"

"God, Annie! No! I'm your brother. I've always looked out for you. I love you." His eyes actually grew teary, but I honestly couldn't tell if they were genuine. They seemed to be. Still, something made me feel distrustful of him. "If someone hurt her, that person might want to hurt you or Collette or all of us. Don't you realize that? And you're sitting out in that gazebo alone, walking alone on the footpath when it's getting dark, climbing down the riverbank where someone may have run our former brother-in-law off the road ..." He gave me a look that was both stern and full of worry.

"You're twisting the situation around."

"What situation?"

"That's not what's happening."

"We don't know what's happening. I'm looking out for you."

"That's why you have to hang around outside Mom's bedroom? Because I'm not safe in there?"

"I'm just making sure you're okay." He stood. "I know you're tough, but you're pregnant, so it's not like you're in prime condition."

His words sounded genuine, but his words frightened me, whispering that I wasn't safe, that someone wanted to hurt me. But deep inside, he was the one who scared me.

"As I keep telling you, I'm worried about you. Bella said we're worried, but it seems like you can't hear us, because there's so much noise in your head." He tapped his index finger on the top of my head.

"I can take care of myself."

"Don't get overconfident. Don't be stupid."

"I'm not." I stared at him for a minute, trying to read his expression, but I couldn't figure out what was behind the mild look in his eyes. "Do you think there's a serial killer or something out there? Or someone who wants to hurt our family? What are you saying?"

"I don't know. I don't even know if Sunday's actually missing, and I don't know if she's dead. All I know is that you're freaking out, and you're upsetting everyone. I'm a person who likes to be open to all possibilities until we have all the facts that tell us which ones are not the correct answers. You know that about me already."

"Yeah." What I knew was that Jake liked to think he was open to all possibilities, but he had an inflated view of his intellect.

"I need to make sure no one gets close enough to hurt my little sis."

"Why is this the first time you've mentioned this? If you were so worried about someone targeting our family, why didn't you say anything about it when Liam was here? Why haven't you told the others? Why aren't you watching over Collette? Or Bella?"

"Not everything has to be a family discussion. And I can multitask." He squeezed my shoulder. "Don't worry. I'll watch out for you. Even if it gives you the creeps, which I'm sorry to hear. I learned the family principles better than anyone, and I always put our family first. You mean the world to me, Annie." He ruffled my hair, making me feel like a five-year-old for the second time in less than an hour.

He strode down the hall and turned the corner. I couldn't hear his footsteps on the stairs. It felt as if he'd been absorbed into the walls of the house. That structure—its rooms, its memories—was so much a part of all of us, it was possible that bits of us clung to the wood and tile and brick, becoming part of its own DNA.

I ran my fingers through my hair to smooth it from Jake's rough hand, to get rid of the feeling he was playing games with me, messing with my head, and to rid myself of the absurd thought that this ancient house contained actual physical pieces of the members of my family. It was a creepier thought than the others I'd been entertaining lately.

Even though Jake could have been pretending he'd heard my mother and me talking, it was equally possible he'd already known Sunday was not my father's biological child. If he had heard us, he also knew that my mother refused to say who Sunday's real father was. Either way, Jake had learned nothing new by hanging around outside her bedroom door.

All the things he'd told me about why he was slinking around, watching me, made sense. His constant presence should have made me feel loved and protected. But somehow, his explanation sounded like a lot of excuses designed to make himself look good. I didn't feel safe at all. I felt smothered and scared that someone in my family was not at all who they appeared to be.

34

Collette wasn't listening to me. It was hard to make her listen sometimes. I was two years older, so she should pay attention to me, but she ignored me. Even though she was only six, when I looked in her eyes, she looked like the sixth-grade girls who were taller than me and acted like teenagers.

I grabbed her wrist. "You have to come with me."

"Jake."

All she had to do was say my name. That was what Mom and Dad told her. If she said my name, I was supposed to let go of her. It was annoying. She wouldn't listen. How else was I supposed to make her pay attention to me? "I have something important to tell you."

"What?" She continued opening plastic storage containers in the walk-in pantry, trying to decide what she wanted for a snack.

"I can't tell you here."

"Why not?"

"No one can hear this. It's a secret."

"Who can hear you? We're the only ones."

"Mom could. Dad might come home."

"That's only two people. And we're in a closet. They can't hear."

Still, I made her follow me outside to the playhouse. We went inside and sat on the tiny chairs that were too small for both of us now, but especially for me. She'd brought a bag with four Oreo cookies, a small bag of potato chips, and a plastic cup filled with chocolate chips that were supposed to go in cookies.

"What secret?" she asked.

"I saw Mom doing it."

"Doing what?"

"*It*. Sex. She was naked in her bed, and there was a man with her."

"Oh."

"It wasn't Dad."

She stared at me. She probably didn't know as much about doing it as I thought she did. I told her jokes I heard from kids at school, and she heard jokes when her friends and my friends were together, but she was six. She probably didn't get as much as I thought she did, even though she was pretty smart.

"It's how you make a baby. Remember?"

She nodded. She pulled apart one of the Oreos and started licking the frosting. I didn't think she was really listening, but she was looking right at me. "The man with her wasn't Dad, because Dad was gone at a seminar. When he went to Colorado for a week."

She stared at me.

"The baby in Mom's belly isn't ours. Sex is how you make a baby, and she made that baby with someone who's not Dad."

"Oh." She pulled apart another Oreo. "Should we tell her?"

"No! It's a secret. Just between you and me. But it means the baby isn't our sister or brother, like they keep saying. Making a baby with someone else is bad. She shouldn't have done that."

"Will she get in trouble?"

I shrugged. I had no idea. I didn't think grownups ever got in trouble for very many things. Some grownups went to jail, but that was for really bad stuff like killing people or stealing things. I didn't know if you got in trouble for doing regular bad stuff that would get a kid grounded. They didn't get in trouble for using bad language or cutting in line or anything. It seemed like no one cared. Grownups could do whatever they wanted. They could stay up as late as they wanted and eat candy or drink soda whenever they felt like it. They didn't even go to jail for really bad stuff unless they got caught. My dad complained about that a lot—all the creeps who didn't get caught.

"We're supposed to love our new baby," Collette said.

"We should probably be nice to it. But we shouldn't forget it's not like us. We're different. We belong to Dad, and the baby belongs to a different guy we don't know."

She stared at me. "But it's in Mommy's tummy."

"Yeah. We have to pretend we like it, because families have to stick together. That's what makes us strong. We don't want our family to come apart. Not like Brian and Devon's mom and dad. They have to go stay in their dad's apartment every other weekend."

She shook her head.

Maybe she didn't know that Brian and Devon's parents were divorced, or get what that meant. I added, "They have a pool there, but it's not even heated."

She stared at me.

"The water's really cold. Like the ocean."

"I like the ocean."

"They had to sell their horses."

Her eyelids blinked once; then her eyes filled with tears.

That hit her where it hurt. All of us were stupidly in love with our horses. I wondered if we loved them more than people sometimes. "Don't forget. You can't tell. I told you because it matters to us, because we have to stick together. We're a team. You and me. But we don't want our family to break apart. Okay?"

"I don't want to break."

"Good. Should we lock fingers on it? To promise that it's our secret forever?"

She crooked her pinky finger, and I looped mine through it. "Promise?"

We squeezed our fingers and closed our eyes as if we were wishing for something. Maybe we *were* wishing, we just didn't know what for.

35

After talking to my mother, I had to escape from the house. If I stayed inside for another second, I wouldn't be able to breathe. I couldn't even face Michael yet. I wanted to believe my mother, but it felt like my choice was to believe what she'd said or believe myself. At the same time, it felt wonderful to imagine that Sunday might still be alive.

I tried picturing that for a moment. I told myself I'd seen a sea mammal or just a bunch of fabric or even—unbelievably—another drowned body on the shore. Maybe none of her things that I'd found meant what I thought they did. Maybe Sunday had taken off because my mother had refused to tell her the name of her father. I could imagine Sunday doing that. I could imagine her fired up, *needing* to know, not wanting to wait a moment longer. And if my mother refused ... it might even explain leaving her phone behind.

It might explain not caring anymore about her diamond necklace, because it came from parents who had lied to her about who she was from the moment she took her first breath. She might have gone back to her home and used her laptop to begin a search for the man who shared her blood. But wouldn't those emails have shown up in the account I'd scrolled through? I supposed she might have other accounts that weren't linked to her phone.

It was a slightly comforting thought. It meant distrusting myself, and I didn't like that feeling, but I didn't want to be blind to the truth because I refused to consider all possibilities.

In reality, I felt like I'd been punched in the stomach. Everything I'd known about our family was a lie. Sunday would have felt that a hundred times more than I. How could my mother hide this for all these years? She'd treated Sunday like a queen. Was that why my father considered Sunday his favorite? Had my mother encouraged and pushed that as a way to hide the truth, hoping that if he was overly devoted to Sunday, he would never once take a step back, never look at the timing of her birth or her physical characteristics from a colder vantage point?

From the window seat where Jake had been spinning his story of caring for my well-being, I'd looked out and seen my father headed toward the stables. I went directly there now, hoping to catch him before he rode out on Nobility. It was unlikely he would go riding this close to the end of the day, but not impossible for him to take a short ride. Otherwise, he would have gone over there just to look around and check out the horses, to give them treats, to talk to Quinn about their care. It was an almost daily habit, getting an update on how they were feeling, as if the horses were members of his family.

I found him inside the stables, talking to Quinn as I'd hoped. I waited for nearly fifteen minutes while they discussed new shoes for my mother's horse, the next vet visit, and feed deliveries. Finally, Quinn left.

"You look like something's on your mind," my father said.

"I wanted to know more about what happened when you went down to the shore to look for Sunday's body the other night."

He gave me a look that was tender and slightly annoyed at the same time. "Nothing happened."

"Did you actually go down there?"

He grabbed the post on Nobility's stall and rubbed his thumb on the wood. He sighed. "No, we didn't go down there. We brought the handheld spotlights out and searched the entire area from the top of the cliff. There was nothing but bare rock."

"You waited too long! The tide took her out."

"The tide was still low. There was nothing on the shore. Why can't you let this go? It's extremely upsetting. For everyone, but especially your mother."

"Because I saw her down there, and no one believes me."

"It's difficult to believe you when no one else saw what you did."

"Jake and Collette did. They asked me if I pushed her."

"I'm sorry you had to hear that. They know better than to make wild accusations like that. But it doesn't mean they saw anything. They said they didn't see anything when you took them out there. And Jake was with me when we used the lights. I'm sorry." He laughed, with an anxious, nervous edge to it. "I'm sorry to laugh, it's not at all funny, but also, I'm not sorry. Sunday is fine. She obviously recognized her need for time alone, and until she wants to talk, we won't know why."

"Doesn't that seem strange? She tells you everything."

"Not always. I don't delude myself that I'm Sunday's only confidant." He took his hand off the post and rested it on my shoulder. "You've always kept most things to yourself."

"I guess I'm a little like you. I wish I weren't, in that way. I wish we were closer."

"Me too." He gave me a hopeful smile. I did the same.

"Liam said she was so upset. And I just ... I don't know. What do you think she told him?"

He sighed. "As I said, we won't know until we see her."

The way he said it, he really seemed to believe he would be seeing her in a few days. "Why did you tell the police he was drinking?"

"Did I? I guess so. I'm sure I smelled it on him. I offered him a drink; I thought I recalled making him one. Maybe not." He laughed. "It doesn't matter now. Liam shouldn't have come here. He had an agenda. I think he simply wanted to hurt our family because he regretted the divorce. Should we go outside? It's not the most pleasant-smelling place in here, is it?" He laughed.

I followed him out, but his nervous laughter was making me wonder what was going on with him. I walked beside him across the yard and out the gate. We headed toward the cliff, neither of us saying anything, gazing out at the thin strands of cloud near the horizon that would make for a spectacular sunset if they remained in that formation.

"What agenda did Liam have?" I asked.

"Who knows, but you could see he wanted to destroy us. It never goes well for someone whose mission in life is to hurt someone else."

"No." I looked at him, but he didn't turn to catch my eye. "Why do you think we haven't been closer to each other, Daddy?"

"I don't know. And I regret that. I wasn't perfect when you kids were small. No parent is. We do our best, but we make mistakes. You'll find out. But it's okay, that's why forgiveness is important. You do the best you can and—"

"I didn't come looking for advice on parenting."

"Sorry if I overstepped. I forget sometimes how well educated you are. That you're all grown up."

"I just wish we were closer. To be honest, I've always been a little jealous of your closeness with Sunday."

He stopped abruptly. "I'm sorry to hear that. I never realized ..."

"I think there are too many secrets in this family, don't you?"

"Secrets?"

"Maybe that's the wrong way to put it. What I mean is, you should be able to tell me what's on your mind, now that I'm an adult. And I want to do the same. To have father-daughter conversations that are between two adults, not child to parent."

"That sounds nice. I'd like that." He smiled and put his arm around my shoulders. It felt good to have him paying attention to me without my siblings in the way. I still wasn't any closer to finding out if he knew Sunday wasn't his daughter. I was trying to open that door for him to tell me, but I was being too subtle. I couldn't seem to think of a way to make my invitation more direct without breaking the promise my mother had strong-armed me into.

Was it possible my father had never suspected? He was so busy traveling. And people were always talking about how babies and children looked like this parent or that, this aunt or the second cousin. Sometimes it was a smile or the color of their hair, and in the end, it was so subjective. People could never see their own resemblance to another, so it was possible he'd never paid attention.

He trusted my mother. It was unlikely it had ever entered his mind that she cheated on him. I couldn't comprehend how that might hurt him. When he taught seminars now, my mother traveled with him. But when we were small, she'd stayed home to care for us.

"Was it hard when we were kids, being separated from Mom so much with all your traveling?"

He laughed. "That's a strange question. What brought that up?"

"Just thinking about work-life balance, I guess."

"You'll keep running the nursery after the baby comes?"

"Yes. But I'm hiring a general manager, so I'll only be there a few days a week. And I hope that some of the time I can take her with me. I guess you couldn't take three or four kids traveling to hotels and weeklong conferences."

"No. But we managed. You all turned out wonderfully."

"Was it lonely?"

"Is there a point to this conversation?"

"I'm just realizing there's so much I don't know about your life. Like I said, I wish we were closer. I want—"

"Well, we can't fix all that in a single conversation, can we? But we'll definitely work on that. Once the baby comes, you and I should go riding together when you come for visits. Grandma can watch the little one, right?"

"Sure."

We walked a bit farther, then stopped to look out at the ocean. The water was a deep blue, tinged with black, the sky pale in comparison.

"How long are we going to wait before we talk to the police more seriously about searching for Sunday?" I asked.

"Let's give it some time."

"You're absolutely sure you didn't see anything the other night? You're not worried at all?"

"We need to have faith. We need to think in a positive way, not fill our heads with doomsday scenarios."

"We don't want to ignore the obvious, either. *No one* has heard from her. And I'm just sure I saw—"

"We know. But the drop is sharp, and it can be disorienting looking down. Vertigo plays tricks on you, and the light when the sun is gone ... there are all kinds of explanations. And you're worried about her. It's very beautiful to see you expressing so much concern." He put his arm around me again and pulled me close. "She'll turn up. Just have faith."

"I just keep thinking about what Liam said—"

His arm fell away from my shoulders. "That's enough, Annie. Liam and Sunday are divorced. He has nothing to do with this family."

It chilled me to hear him completely ignore the fact that Liam was also dead.

"If Liam had followed the family principles, their marriage would have survived, and Sunday wouldn't have been so deeply wounded. She has not healed from that, and we should not be trying to find her. I have pretty keen insight into human behavior, as you know. You need to trust me on this."

Listening to him, so full of his own beliefs, I realized he had no insight into human behavior whatsoever. He'd forced us all to live according to principles that had broken us rather than making us stronger. His wife had cheated on him and raised another man's child right under his nose, and as far as I could tell, he didn't have the slightest idea. He loved and doted on a daughter who was not connected to him in the way he thought she was.

We walked back to the house. As we climbed the porch steps, my feet seemed made of brick. I felt I could barely make it to the top, I was so filled with regret that I'd bowed to my mother's demand to keep her secret.

36

I n bed that night, lying in his arms, inhaling the scent of his skin, I told Michael about my conversations with my parents and Jake. My words were a jumble of things recalled out of order and feelings that rose while I was talking to him, and constant changes in my interpretations as I tried to dig my way through the confusion.

When I finally wound down and let my head relax into him, my breath and heart rate slowing to a more restful state, he said, "You need to leave it. That's what they want. Even if your father does know, I expect he doesn't want to discuss it with you. Think about it for a minute. Most people find it difficult to talk about their partner's infidelity with a close friend. They certainly don't want to share it with their child."

"You're right, but I want to know if he knows. How can he not know?"

"It would be easy. Very easy. You need to stay out of it."

"It's really hard to leave it alone. It feels like half our family is built on a lie."

"That's not true."

"It feels that way."

"Try not to keep thinking about it. Maybe you're blowing it out of proportion."

"You sound like you're quoting the family principles."

He laughed. "They aren't *all* wrong."

"Sunday wouldn't want to bury it."

"That's different. It's about her, but it has nothing to do with you. So leave it alone."

"It has to do with me in that she's not here to fight for herself. And we still don't know what really happened. I don't believe she's just hiding out, working through her feelings. At the same time, I want to believe that. I really do. I want to believe she went to try to find her father."

"I suppose it's possible." He reached over and turned off the light.

"It would make me so happy if she was okay. I just don't ..."

"So you aren't completely certain you saw her body?"

"I don't know anymore. When I ask myself that question, I absolutely know I saw her. But my dreams and my memories are so tangled and confused. And my parents are absolutely certain she's fine. It almost sounds as if they've spoken to her, they're so calm about it. But I saw on Sunday's phone that my mom texted her after she disappeared and never got an answer." I groaned softly, my neck and forehead aching from my racing thoughts. "I hate that they make me doubt what I saw. And Jake ... I don't know."

"Well, either you saw her, or you didn't."

"It's bad enough they make me doubt myself; now you're doing it."

"I'm just trying to help you be sure about what you remember."

I moved away from him, feeling isolated and confused. I wanted my thoughts to stop spinning like wild spirals that made even the backs of my eyes hurt.

Michael moved toward me and pulled me close again. "If her body washed out to sea, it will come to shore again."

I didn't want to think about how wrong he could be. I didn't want to think about the over twelve hundred miles of coastline from Southern California to Canada. I didn't want to think about sharks. And I didn't want to think about currents that might carry her to shores far away from us, too damaged for anyone to make an identification.

I fell asleep with tears swimming in my eyes.

As I sat at the breakfast table the next morning, looking at the untroubled faces of my family, the baskets of bread, the freshly squeezed orange juice, and the platter of sausage and bacon, I couldn't take it. I felt like I was sitting on the stage, an actor in a farce. We were a huge hit, because the audience was laughing hysterically at us.

If nothing else, my mother was making a fool of my father. She'd done so for over thirty years. She'd sat at the opposite end of the table and mimicked his family principles. I'd never attended one of his seminars, and I hadn't read all of his books, but I was confident he taught that fidelity was critical to a strong marriage. It's kind of a no-brainer.

There was no doubt her betrayal and deceit had cut Sunday to the core. It had very likely led to her death, in some way or another. My mother had made a frantic attempt to fill a hole in me that had existed since I was a little girl, pulling me close to her when it was far too late. And the secret she chose to seal our relationship with was not one I wanted to keep. It was one I wished I didn't even know.

I took a deep breath. "I have something to say."

"Here we go," Jake said.

"Oh dear," Bella murmured.

Colette rolled her eyes. She dropped her knife on her plate, causing a clatter that echoed through the dining room.

"I know why Sunday took off, I know why she was upset,

and I think we need to clear the air. I'm sorry, Dad. I hate telling you like this, and I'm sorry for hurting you, but you deserve the truth. And I think everyone here knows but you."

"Annie!" My mother was pushing her chair back, shouting at me. "You promised! Don't!"

"Sunday submitted her DNA to the same company Jake used last year. And because he was already in the database, the report told her that she and Jake don't have the same biological father."

As soon as I was finished speaking, I wished I'd said it more clearly. It was hard enough, after all these years, to grasp the truth of who Sunday was. It might take a moment or two for my father to get his mind to process the meaning of what I'd said.

"Way to throw a grenade." Collette picked up the knife she'd dropped and began buttering the sourdough roll.

"You broke your vow," my mother said. "What kind of daughter breaks her mother's confidence?"

"You broke Sunday's trust by lying to her every day of her life," I said.

The look my mother gave me was one of extreme disappointment. I knew that whatever fragile threads might have been woven between us were now broken beyond repair. At the same time, it was jarring that her feelings were directed at me. She seemed almost unaware of my father. His expression was unreadable, although that was often the case with him. I supposed that was one of many reasons I didn't feel close to him. He wasn't crying, but he never did. The strangest part was, he didn't look shocked. Had he known after all?

Maybe Sunday had spoken to him despite her failure to convince him to go riding with her. Maybe he'd known since the day she was born, since the day my mother told him she was pregnant, or from some other life-changing moment in time. Maybe he really did know a lot about human nature, and he had figured out a way to live with my mother's unilateral decision. It was even possible that she'd told him about her affair, and they'd decided together to raise Sunday as their favorite child.

It was possible his overindulgence of Sunday came from the same place as my mother's—some kind of overcompensation for something that wasn't right. He wanted to make her feel loved and welcomed into a family that wasn't entirely hers, so he went to the extreme in trying to demonstrate his love. As a result, he alienated the rest of his children.

"Why do you have to make everything into a Shakespearean drama?" Jake asked. "No one needed to get into this at breakfast. And the one person it affects isn't here, so why are you bringing it up? Are you trying to make Dad feel like a fool? Do you want to punish Mom? Are you trying to destroy all of us? What are you after? I don't get it."

"I keep saying her hormones are causing some mental instability," Bella said. "I think it's more than even I realized."

"That's absurd," Michael said. He placed his hand on my leg.

His touch felt slightly hesitant, and I'm sure he thought the timing of my announcement was a terrible choice, but in that moment, I hadn't been able to hold it in for another second. It was bad enough pretending Sunday was off clearing her mind when she was dead. The pretense made me feel like I was losing my grip on reality. You can only live a lie for so long before it messes up your perception of everything.

"You *promised*." My mother's voice was damp with tears, but still firm and harsh. "I thought we had an understanding. I thought we agreed we were going to ..." Her voice trailed off.

"Are you okay, Dad?" Collette abandoned her roll and got up. She walked to my father's chair and positioned herself behind him. She put her hands on his shoulders and massaged them gently.

He didn't push her away. He seemed to hardly notice she was there. "I'm fine," he said.

"We should eat before all this great food gets cold," Jake said.

"How are you, Mom?" Bella asked. "Can I get you anything?"

My mother stared blankly at the center of the table, not making eye contact with anyone. Bella stood and walked to my mother's end of the table. She knelt beside her and leaned her head against her shoulder. My mother continued staring at the center of the table. I wondered what she was thinking. It was difficult to tell if she was even aware of Bella's presence leaning into her. Bella reached up and stroked my mother's cheek. It seemed as if she was feeling for tears, but apparently there was no moisture, because she just gently ran her fingers across my mother's skin.

After a few minutes listening to Jake talk about how we needed to eat and murmuring that I really had a stellar way of messing up a perfect family vacation, my father placed his hand on Collette's to stop her massage. He kept his hand over hers. "This doesn't change anything. Our family is strong. We've remained solid because we place the family over the individual. That's why your mother and I have an airtight marriage. Airtight. Let's try to enjoy this delicious meal she's made for us. We won't allow our emotions to carry us to a dark place. It's the only way to face the difficulties in life and remain centered."

"I absolutely agree," Bella said.

Jake and Collette echoed her words.

The meal continued, but I couldn't eat. I knew I needed food in my stomach, but I felt there was a solid wall in my esophagus. Even the tea cooling in the mug beside my plate looked unappetizing. It had the potential to soothe me, but the thought of swallowing anything felt impossible. "Why wouldn't you tell Sunday who her father is?" I asked my mother.

"She knows who her father is." My mother's voice was robotic.

"That's a disgusting question," Bella said. "Why would you ask that?"

"It's not disgusting. It would have mattered a lot to Sunday."

"Well, Sunday's not here, so there's no point in bringing it up," Collette said.

"I thought a family principle was telling the truth," I said. "If this has been hidden for all these years, it's better to get everything out in the open."

"No," my mother said. "It's not better."

"Your interest is sordid," Jake said.

"It's ancient history," my father said.

They continued eating. Michael put food on my plate and tried to urge me to eat, as if I were a small child. He even went so far to cut up a piece of sausage for me, stabbing a section with my fork and holding it for me to take the fork from him. I refused. I couldn't imagine tasting and chewing and swallowing.

I felt like I was living inside one of my dreams, unclear whether the things happening around me were real or imagined, because I couldn't believe these people were flesh and blood human beings.

After breakfast, alone in our bedroom, Michael told me either we needed to return home, or I needed to stop pushing it. His preference was to leave, and he thought that was the healthy choice for me. I told him again, I wasn't leaving until Sunday's body washed ashore. I asked him what he thought was involved in getting a search and rescue team to look for her. He said it was doubtful they would be willing to search at least twenty to thirty miles of coastline for a possible missing person. The police already had her on their radar; that was all we could do.

Maybe out of desperation, I turned my thoughts to the nearly hopeless idea that I'd hallucinated seeing her body, and Sunday had gone looking for her father. Maybe I could find a way to find out who he was without my mother's help.

37

Although he was trying not to argue about it, Michael desperately wanted to leave. I could feel it in every taut muscle of his body and, most of all, in the pleading look in his eyes. But I was rooted to this place. If I left, I would feel as if I were abandoning Sunday. She would disappear as if she'd never existed. And there was a growing sense that I'd already abandoned her once before.

Michael said he was going for a run. I assured him I would keep myself busy, although I didn't specify how I would do that. I already had something in mind.

After the rest of my family had left the breakfast table, their bellies full, mine still repulsed by food, I'd finally managed a few sips of tea. I'd carried my mug into the living room, hoping it would stir my appetite if I continued sipping it slowly. I needed to eat for the baby, and if my stomach didn't settle soon, I would have to force myself to eat.

As I'd stood by the fireplace and looked at the framed photographs on the mantel, I recalled Liam noticing the picture of Sunday's sixteenth birthday and the memory it had evoked. I thought about our family photo albums filled with so many more moments than what was on display in the living room. After we'd left home, my mother had packed the albums away in the basement. Once technology took over, no one had looked at them much. We kept the photos we liked on our phones. My mother had vowed repeatedly that she wanted to scan all of our family photos and put them into a shared digital album for all of us, but so far, she hadn't even begun that monumental task.

I finished the rest of my tea and went into the now-empty kitchen. I stood by the window and slowly ate a cup of yogurt, followed by half a pear. The food agreed with me, and I was glad I'd made the effort.

I went to the door at the back of the pantry, which led to the basement. Leaving the pantry light on, I opened the basement door and turned on the light in the stairwell. I walked down holding the railing.

The basement had a concrete floor and walls. It was rare to have a basement in earthquake-prone California, but they existed, especially in homes this old.

The space was small, only extending the length and width of the kitchen and the foyer. My parents used it to store holiday decorations and a few toys and boxes of memorabilia from our childhoods. I went to the shelves at the back, grateful for my mother's precise labeling of every box. The holiday boxes didn't simply note the contents were for Christmas or Easter, they specified—glass ornaments, tree lights, winter scene with train, blown eggs, ceramic rabbits.

The photo albums were in plastic bins to protect them from moisture. They were on a shelf several feet off the ground, but not too high that I couldn't easily lift them. I removed the box labeled *1990–2000* and placed it on the floor a few feet from the stairs. It held four albums. I opened a large bin labeled *sleeping bags* and pulled out a child's bag. Overcome for a moment with nostalgia at seeing my pink sleeping bag imprinted with fluffy gray kittens, I unrolled it, folded it in half and sat on the concrete floor. I opened the box and pulled out the first album.

Flickering at the edge of my mind had been the idea that maybe the man my mother had her affair with was a friend of the family. When we were children, the house was always full of other kids and their parents. Family friends whom my parents had become close to through my dad's seminars, and others who worked as support staff—the editorial team for his books, the group of technical experts who recorded and produced his CDs, before he and that same team transitioned to podcasting. Neighbors, of course.

My parents loved to host holiday parties and summer barbecues that also included friends from the equestrian competitions my siblings and I were involved with. Maybe that was one reason I hadn't always been aware of the bullying from Jake and Collette, or seen how oppressive the family principles were. Our life was filled with so many people, there wasn't a lot of time for reflection or for zeroing in on how any individual members of our family were behaving. Life was overflowing. Busyness and activity cover up a lot with a numbing hum that keeps your mind occupied with the surface of life.

I'd thought that looking through the pictures, someone might stand out—a man who was around more often than others, a man who was too often standing close to my mother, or always at her side in group photographs. Putting that into a coherent thought, as the cold concrete crept through the sleeping bag into my bones, made it seem unlikely—but it was clear I was not going to find out from my mother. This was my only thread of hope in a vaporous thread of hope that Sunday could still be alive. And right now, I needed any delicate threads I could find.

After pages of baby pictures of myself, and the accompa-

nying family portraits, I slowed in turning the pages. I
lingered over every photograph of parties and equestrian
events. I pulled a few photos out from behind the plastic,
studying the slightly faded images, looking for something
that I couldn't truly identify in my own mind. I lingered over
photographs of myself and Sunday. My heart became heavier
in my chest as I saw images of myself as a toddler, the two of
us holding hands, running along sandy beaches, sitting on
the living room floor with our heads close together, building
blocks spread out around us.

We were obviously close. What happened? Did all those
other people get in the way? As I grew older, did the jealousy
that consumed Jake and Collette infect me? I didn't recall
feeling a lot of jealousy toward Sunday as a teenager. I was
happy with my friends and my life. I wasn't interested in
becoming an expert at show jumping, so I didn't care about
her private lessons. I liked my small bedroom because it got a
lot of light, and it was quiet. I didn't envy her magnificent
bed, because I thought the canopy hovering over her seemed
a little claustrophobic and possibly scary.

So what *happened*? By the time we were in elementary
school, we never showed up in photographs together unless it
was a posed family shot. By that time, Jake was out of the
house, and Collette was a teenager, almost ready to leave for
college herself.

I reached the end of the book without seeing anything
that suggested one of my parents' friends was particularly
close to my mother.

I pulled out another album. This one wasn't dated and
didn't flow in chronological order like the others. It was all
about the horses. The pages were filled with images of all
four of us learning to ride, performing in shows, the entire
second half of it devoted to Sunday because the rest of us had
given up on the competition aspect earlier than she did. We

simply enjoyed riding the horses without wanting to jump and push them to perform and achieve scores that impressed a panel of judges.

Frustrated, I flipped back to the front of the book and studied a photograph that might have been my first time on a horse. I looked like I was barely four years old. The man by my side was wearing a cowboy hat, so it was difficult to see his face, but it had to be Conner, Quinn's father, because he'd taught us to ride.

In the background, Quinn was sitting on the fence, watching. He was about fourteen years old. His hair was long, almost to his shoulders. Having just seen so many photographs of Sunday performing on horseback, I was suddenly struck by the fact that Quinn looked very much like her when she was fourteen. I felt a sudden coldness through my whole body, a coldness that gripped my head and neck.

As I continued staring at the photo, I realized Conner did not have his attention on four-year-old me astride a pony. His head was turned to the side. He was staring intensely at my mother, who was watching from outside the corral fencing.

I peeled back the corner of the plastic to remove the picture so I could get a closer look. As I did, I heard a loud creak. Without any other accompanying sound, the lights blinked out, and the room was bathed in total darkness. I cried out. In response, I heard nothing but my own voice, the sound deadened by the solid earth surrounding me.

38

K nowing there was nothing to fear, but my hands shaking violently nevertheless, the plastic I was trying to peel back slipped from my fingers. I struggled to my feet, anxious that there was nothing to hold onto, frightened that my legs might give out, because my joints had become slightly numb from sitting on the ground for quite a while.

"Is anyone up there?" My voice had the same deadened sound, making me feel I was in a tomb. There was no response. I called louder, but still heard nothing. Unless someone was in the kitchen, it was unlikely they would hear me. But who had turned off the light?

The door must have closed somehow while I'd been sitting there because there wasn't a whisper of light. I couldn't even make out the shadows of the shelving or figure out where the stairs were in relationship to where I stood. I took a cautious step, moving my feet carefully to be sure I didn't trip on the bunched-up sleeping bag.

I inched my way in the direction of where I thought the stairs must be, since I'd sat down with my back to them. The rubber soles of my Ugg boots made an awful scraping sound on the concrete, the sound of something scratching at the walls. It sent chills down my arms and legs; I couldn't escape the thought that there must be spiders and possibly mice or rats hiding in the rarely used basement. The darkness would entice them out of their hiding places where they'd scurried when I turned on the overhead light.

Still calling out every few steps, even though I knew it was futile, I moved my arms in a circular motion in front of me. I didn't want to swing them wildly and risk slamming my arm into the wall. Finally, the back of my hand bumped the end of the railing for the stairs. I grabbed hold of it and slid my foot forward until I found the step. Planting both feet on each step, I made my way carefully to the top, then ran one hand across the wall until I found the light switch. I turned it on, opened the door and fell into the kitchen, whimpering with relief.

Collette and Bella stood facing me.

"Are you okay?" Collette asked.

Bella grabbed my hand. "What were you *doing* down there?"

"Why are the lights off?" Collette asked.

"I was looking at photo albums. The lights went off for no reason." I glared at them, taking in their wide-eyed innocence. "How did you know I was down there?"

"We heard you screaming."

"Were you in the kitchen?"

Neither of them answered. Bella took my other hand and started leading me toward the kitchen.

"Let go of me." I pulled my hands from hers and started back toward the basement door.

"Where are you going?" Bella asked.

"I need the album."

"You should get some rest," Collette said.

"How many times do we have to tell you to calm down and start taking better care of yourself? You didn't eat a bite of food at breakfast, and now you're creeping around in the basement," Bella said.

"Why did the lights go out?"

They both shrugged.

"I need the photo album."

"Not now." Collette took a firm grip of my upper arm. "You're breaking Michael's heart. It's all over his face when you do crazy things, like that upsetting announcement you felt you had to make at breakfast. An announcement that helped nobody."

"Let go of me."

"You *need* to rest." Bella took my other arm, and they began leading me through the kitchen toward the foyer and the front stairs.

"I don't."

"After we get you settled, I'll make you some toast and tea," Bella said. "You have to eat."

"I ate something."

"What did you eat?" Bella asked.

"It's none of your business."

We'd reached the stairs. "Please do this for Michael if not for yourself. If not for your baby."

"If Michael is concerned, he'll speak to me about it."

Collette's voice was shrill, the volume increasing. "No one can get through to you because you're out of control. You embarrassed Mom, you hurt Dad, you—"

"It needed to be said."

"Enough about that," Bella said. "Let's go."

I couldn't fight them. As much as they claimed concern for my baby, the way they were tugging me forward, if I tried to pull away, I risked falling and truly hurting my child. I yielded and allowed them to lead me upstairs. I would get the

photograph later. I wanted time to think about it. If I got it
now, I would be forced to show it to them before I was ready.
That would be a mistake.

Once we reached my bedroom, Bella left to make toast
and tea. Collette threw back the covers. She ordered me to
take off my shoes and slide into bed. I followed her directions, tired of fighting, for the moment.

"Is Michael back from his run?" I asked.

"I haven't seen him. You had a scare. Focus on getting
some rest."

"I will."

She settled in the armchair across from the bed.

"I'm fine by myself."

"I'll wait until Bella brings the toast."

"I don't need a caretaker."

She smiled and folded her hands on her lap. I closed my
eyes. The room was silent, and I kept my eyes closed, not
wanting to look at her strange smile. When Bella arrived with
the tea and toast, they finally left, closing the door behind
them. I got out of bed and checked that they hadn't locked
the door.

While I waited for the tea to cool, I pulled my notebook
out of the nightstand. Finding a few blank pages between the
timeline and the dream section, and without attempting to
follow a chronological timeline, I wrote down every single
memory I could think of from the time I was four and five
years old. It didn't matter how trivial, and I didn't worry about
whether or not I knew for certain I was either of those two
ages. If I thought I recalled something, I made a note of it. I
wrote as many details as I could remember. I wrote about toys
I'd liked, and friends who had come over for playdates. I
wrote what I remembered about our horses and my siblings
and stories my mother read to me. I wrote what I remembered of Conner Wiley, which wasn't much. Just his calm

instruction on the nature of horses. Then I wrote about how Quinn looked like Sunday, the shape of their faces and eyes and the way their smiles tipped up slightly on the left side. I wrote about how their hair hung in loose waves, the kind of waves that women spend hours in salons, with hot irons, trying to achieve a casually tousled appearance. Aside from all that, it was a feeling. A way they held their bodies, maybe. Their posture. Impressions like that seem like they're imprinted from mimicking a parent, but maybe not. It's hard to say what comes from genetic programming and what comes of watching the people who raise you. Impossible, really.

Half my tea was still in the mug, and it was bone cold. The same for the toast, although I'd managed a few bites. I was exhausted, and my hand ached.

I pulled my pillow to the side and curled up like a kitten. I tugged the blankets over my shoulder and closed my eyes. Sleep came quickly and so did my dream, although I felt partially awake—aware of the weak sunlight coming in through the window and conscious of the fact that I was wearing leggings and one of my favorite tops and that my hair was getting mussed on the pillow.

The dream was far more detailed than usual. I felt like I was standing closer to my mother and the man than I had in previous dreams, as if my mind was zooming in on the scene.

As I watched them struggle, I couldn't tell if they were fighting to get away from one another or if they were desperate with passion, each trying to pull off the other's clothes, or if one was trying to hold on while the other tried to escape. There was no sound, just the tense struggle that seemed to go on endlessly.

Then, instead of looking from any distance at all, I felt as if I was right beside them. I saw that my mother had a large knife in her hand. She pulled her arm back and shoved the knife into the man's stomach, so deep that it seemed as if her hand and wrist might follow it inside, her entire arm being swallowed.

As the man collapsed to the ground, I whimpered softly.

My mother turned. Her face glowed like the moon. It wasn't just white with reflected light, but seemed to have light emanating from beneath her skin. Her eyes were like globes of ice; her voice equally cold. "Go back to bed. You shouldn't be up."

The words woke me as if someone had slapped my face. I sat up, knocking my notebook and pen to the floor. I felt as if my mother's voice echoed in my head, from the dream, from the day before when she'd spoken the same words to me in the hallway as I'd listened to my siblings and Michael talk about me.

Had my subconscious woven those words from the other day into my dream? Did my mother say that to me frequently when I was a child? Or had the event in my dream actually happened, and she'd spoken those words to me once a long time ago? I felt like a thousand bees were screaming inside my skull. I pressed my hands to the sides of my head, trying to quiet the noise, but the effort was useless.

Unable to figure out what had just happened, whether I'd had a dream or remembered something very real, I climbed out of bed. I picked up my notebook and pen and shoved them into the drawer. I tugged up the sheet and blanket and tucked them in, pulling the comforter over them and arranging the pillows.

As I started toward the bathroom, intending to brush my hair, the bedroom door opened, and Michael stepped into the room. I rushed toward him and wrapped my arms around his waist, pressing myself against him.

He held onto me. "Hey. What's wrong?"

"I wasn't sure where you'd gone."

"Your mom asked me to run to the market for some sliced meat and tomatoes and avocado for sandwiches."

"Oh." I clung to him.

"Are you okay?"

I nodded, my head rubbing against his shirt. I couldn't put the images from the dream into words. He stroked my hair for a few minutes; then I pulled away. I told him about the photograph.

"It's possible," he said. "Conner is as likely a candidate as anyone. It would definitely explain why he took off like he did."

"But Sunday was six or seven when he left. So that doesn't make sense."

"I don't know. I can't explain it. And the only one who can, won't."

"I can't be around them right now," I said. "Let's go to Mendocino. We can walk around the botanical gardens, eat dinner there, and come home after everyone's in bed. I need to think. Or not think."

"Or we could go home."

"I told you, I can't. Not yet."

He sighed. "Mendocino sounds nice."

"Will you make sandwiches for us? I want to take a shower, and I just—"

"Sure." He kissed me and left.

I stood in the shower for a long time, not thinking, still feeling like a thousand bees were swarming inside my skull.

39

A s I'd hoped and expected, the house was dark when Michael and I returned from Mendocino at quarter to twelve that night. Tired from the drive, Michael collapsed into bed and was asleep before I'd finished brushing my teeth. I'd dozed off on the drive home and was looking forward to sinking into the comfortable bed and a hopefully dreamless sleep. Instead, the moment I had myself settled under the covers, my mind sprang into action.

I moved from side to side, cuddling against Michael, then twisting onto my back, stretching out, curling up. Nothing felt comfortable. My mind grew more and more agitated. I realized I had to have that photograph. It had been a mistake not going back for it right after my forced bed rest that morning.

I got out of bed, threw a hoodie on over my nightgown and slipped quietly out of our room. I went downstairs and into the pantry, where I flicked on the light and opened the basement door. This time, I had my phone with me. If there were any unexplained *power outages*, I had a flashlight. I walked down the stairs and saw that the sleeping bag and the box of albums had been put away.

The box labeled *1990–2000* was in its place on the shelf. I pulled it out, but the album I'd been looking at was missing. I stared at the empty space, disbelieving. Had Collette and Bella told my mother I was looking at photographs, and she'd come to remove any suggestion of evidence? But how would she know what photograph had caught my eye? Or had my sister and sister-in-law removed it themselves, assuming that whatever I was interested in, it couldn't be good?

Unable to accept that someone had hidden it from me, I pulled out all the other boxes, checking to see if they'd put the album in the wrong box. But of course, that wasn't possible because they were all neatly fitted, four to a box, so there was no room in any of the others.

I returned to the kitchen and filled the kettle with water. I put tea leaves into the infuser and leaned against the counter, waiting for the water to boil. When the water was ready, I poured it slowly over the waiting leaves and set the timer on my phone.

"Is there enough for me to have a cup?"

At the sound of my mother's voice, I turned, shocked out of my hopelessly circling thoughts. "Sure."

"Can't sleep?" Her pleasant smile and the kindness in her voice were disarming. Just that morning, she'd been furious at me for exposing her secret. Now she seemed to have forgotten all about my betrayal.

My phone chimed that the tea was done steeping. I began pouring it into two mugs.

"I always know when my children are unsettled."

"Do you?"

I couldn't see her face, and she didn't respond. I placed the mugs on the table and sat across from her.

"I was looking through our photo albums earlier," I said.

"Why is that?"

"I noticed Sunday and Quinn looked a lot alike when they were teenagers."

She laughed. "Well, Quinn was in his twenties when Sunday was a teenager, so I don't know how you would come to that conclusion."

"Looking at a photo of Quinn when he was fourteen or fifteen, he looked almost identical to Sunday when she was fifteen."

My mother stared at me, but I could tell her attention was fixed on a point beyond my shoulder. She took a sip of tea.

"Is Conner her father?"

"I don't understand what's happened to you. It's not healthy to pick at wounds that are healed. It causes scarring."

"This wound is far from healed. Certainly not for Sunday."

"Exactly. It has nothing to do with you. So why are you picking at it? Your interest is sordid, as Jake pointed out. It seems as if you want to smear filth all over me and our family."

"Can't you just answer with a simple yes or no?"

"Your father nurtured and raised Sunday. He's the only man who matters. He provided for all her physical needs, and he made her into the strong, vibrant woman she is." She took another sip of tea, put down her mug, and stood.

"Was."

"Why do you persist in trying to hurt me?" Her eyes filled with tears.

"I keep remembering you having a violent fight with someone. I've finally realized it was with Conner. I'm not sure if it's—"

"You can't trust childhood memories." Her voice was sharp and full of its usual authority. "Young children don't know what they're seeing. And they make up stories to explain what they don't understand. You'll learn that soon enough. So whatever you think you saw, you're wrong."

She moved closer to me and placed her hands on my head, gently pressing on my scalp. The firm pressure of her fingers was soothing even though her words made me angry. "Why are you doing this to yourself? We are all so very worried about you. It's not good for you or the baby. You have to find a way to put the past to rest. You have to find a way to let go. You must know that. It's one of the principles we've lived by. Let go of the past and move on."

I began crying, my shoulders shaking, while she continued her firm downward pressure on my head. "I can't. I can't let go until I find out what happened to Sunday."

"You already know what happened. She was upset about the DNA test. She was angry with me and couldn't have a rational conversation. She took off in a fit. Eventually, she'll settle down."

I pushed my tea mug away from me. I took hold of her wrists and lifted her hands off my head. Her diamond ring caught in my hair. I winced as I worked the strands free from the prongs. When I could see her face, I continued holding onto her wrists. "Mom ... I *saw* her body on the shore. I'm absolutely sure. Everyone keeps telling me I didn't see her, but I know I did." Even as I said it, I felt the doubt flooding my body again. My mother didn't have to speak a single word for me to feel her certainty pulsing through the veins in her wrists, and I yielded to the doubt in my own hands, which were already loosening their grasp.

"*If* you saw a body, which is debatable, because it was dusk and the shadows and the glare are tricky at that time of day, and you were far away at the top of the cliff, it could have been anyone or anything."

"How often has a body washed up on the shore in the years you've lived here?"

"It could have been anyone. You continue to ignore the fact that Sunday packed her things and took her suitcase. If she fell or, God forbid, jumped or ... if something happened to her, she wouldn't pack up her shoes and makeup. It's almost funny, if you stop to think about it for a minute."

I didn't see anything funny about it. I stared at her. I let go of her wrists, and she took a few steps away from me.

"This is hurting me deeply, Annie. I need it to stop." She walked out of the room.

I remained seated at the table, sipping my tea. I pushed aside my mother's attempt, once again, to be sure I doubted what I'd seen, and turned my thoughts to what she'd said before that. It had shocked me so deeply, I hadn't fully absorbed the meaning while she was speaking. It had almost felt like she'd believed she could shove that memory out of my head by pressing her fingers into my skull. She'd never done anything like that before, and although it felt soothing, it also felt like she wanted to make me feel like there was something wrong with me.

She'd insisted that I couldn't trust childhood memories. Whatever I thought I'd seen, I was wrong. She tried to tell me that whatever I remembered taking place between her and Conner, I had made up because I didn't understand. But she'd interrupted me. She hadn't given me a chance to tell her I wasn't sure if it was a memory or a dream. Because of that, she'd assumed it was a memory. She'd assumed I'd seen something.

And that must mean she had a similar memory. I had seen her struggling with Conner. She'd told me to go back to bed, hoping I would think it was a dream, hoping I would forget. Now she was trying to make me believe that I'd made up the knife in her hand, made up the shock of her plunging it into his body, because I didn't understand what I was seeing. But I knew enough about young children to know that was not the most likely story a child who had never witnessed violence, even on a TV show, would invent.

My hands were so cold, I could no longer lift the mug to my lips. My bones were cold; my lungs and heart felt icy cold as I absorbed the realization that I'd witnessed my mother stabbing Conner Wiley to death.

40

Not caring that my feet were bare, I shoved my phone into the pocket of my hoodie and zipped it up. I went into the living room, took the picture of Sunday at her sixteenth birthday off the mantel, and went out the front door. I hurried along the path through the garden and then across rougher ground to Quinn's cottage. It was nearly one thirty in the morning, but I couldn't wait another minute.

I knocked on the door several times, pausing briefly in between. After several rounds of this with no response, I walked to the side of the cottage to his bedroom window. I knocked on the glass. I felt bad waking him like this, knowing it would scare him, but the longer I knocked, the more my anxiety grew.

Finally, the blinds shot up, and the window opened. His voice was loud, but strangely calm. "What's wrong? Did something happen to one of the horses?" His head disappeared from view, and I heard thumping as he tugged on jeans.

"Nothing's wrong, but I really need to talk to you."

His voice came from below the window. "Did you find Sunday's—"

"No. I just have some questions to ask you."

"It's almost two in the morning."

"I know. I'm sorry. But it's really important."

I walked back to the front door, and a moment later, he opened it. He wore jeans, but his chest and feet were bare. His hair was snarled on the left side. He squinted at me from the porch light shining into his eyes. "What's the emergency?"

"Do you have a picture of you and your father when you were about fifteen or sixteen?"

He laughed. "It's one thirty."

I held up the picture of Sunday. "I think your father is Sunday's father."

He stared at me. "You're crazy."

"Look at this." I held the picture directly under the light.

He glanced at the photograph. "I'm going back to bed."

"Go get a picture of yourself. If you don't have one with your father, at least get a picture of yourself when you were—"

"Come on, Annie. I'm tired. It's the middle of the night. You're acting crazy. Are you walking in your sleep or something? You can't be high."

"No. Please. Just get a picture."

"I wouldn't even know where to start."

"Your yearbook. Do you have any high school yearbooks?"

"Senior year, I think."

"Get it."

"You sound like your mother."

"Please."

"I'm really tired. I—"

"Please, Quinn. This is really important."

"I don't think it's important to do it right this minute, in the middle of the night. And there's no chance my father was, or that he—"

"You could have gotten the picture by now."

He sighed and left me standing at the door. He returned several minutes later, holding a high school yearbook. He flipped to the page with his senior portrait and held it out to me.

I placed the framed photograph of Sunday on the opposite page and held the book so he could see both side by side. "Don't you see it?"

"No."

"I think it's hard to see in yourself. People are always going on about how I look like my mother, and I can't see it at all. But with you and Sunday, it's completely obvious to me. Look at your eyes ... look how your smiles are almost identical."

"I think you're really upset about what's going on with her, and you're going a little bit nuts. I need to get some sleep, so I'll say good night now."

I closed the book with the framed photograph inside and handed it back to him as he started to shut the door. "Wait." I put my hand against the door. "Can you tell me about when your dad left? I was so little, I don't remember very much about it."

"There's nothing to remember."

"What happened."

"He left. End of story."

"And you have no idea why?"

"Yeah, I know exactly why. Because he was a loser and a sorry excuse for a father and a human being."

"But before. He wasn't always like that. Why would he suddenly—"

"I have no idea. I don't talk about him. I don't think about him. And I definitely don't like being woken in the middle of the night to talk about him."

"You have no idea why he left? Doesn't that seem strange? You were fifteen. He didn't leave a note or give any hint in the days before? Nothing about him changed?"

He leaned against the doorframe and placed his hand over his eyes. "Why are you doing this?"

"Because it makes no sense ... the story you believed all your life. But it does make sense that he and my mother had an affair. I think she got pregnant and pretended Sunday was my father's child. Then something happened. I don't know what. But you and Sunday look so much alike, it's impossible not to notice when you see the two of you at the same age. There were so many years between you, I don't think anyone noticed at the time."

"I'm going to bed." He turned and tossed the yearbook onto a chair near the door. It hit the chair and crashed onto the floor. The picture slid out, showing Sunday with a triumphant smile on her face. He left it there.

"I wonder if Sunday realized it was him and tried to find him, or ..." I realized as I said this that unless she'd also gone looking at photo albums, it was unlikely she would have come to that conclusion. Without looking at old photos, there was no reason to make that connection between Sunday and Quinn. Still, it was my final hope, and I was finding it impossible to let go of it. "Maybe that's why no one has heard from her. If she tried to find him ..." I knew it sounded far-fetched. Why couldn't I stop conjuring up stories to make myself feel better? Maybe my mother had been right about children making up stories to explain things they didn't understand. Except I was an adult.

"He can't be found," Quinn said.

"You tried?"

"My aunt tried to find him. About ten years ago. She even

hired a private detective. They did all kinds of internet searches, contacted credit card companies. The detective had a friend with the Sacramento police department who was able to get a DMV search. Nothing. The man does not want to be found."

Quinn's face had transformed to that of a little boy whose father had just now walked out the door, saying he was never coming back. Quinn had been fifteen when his father disappeared, but that was one thing I did remember. Quinn was strong and competent from taking care of the horses, did well in school, and played on the high school baseball team. After his father disappeared, it felt like Quinn was closer to my age. Vulnerable and uncertain. He seemed like a young child again. He never cried, but he always looked deeply and utterly sad. When I looked at him and our eyes met, I felt like crying for him.

"That's one thing I guess your father has right with all his principles. When you put yourself first, everything breaks. And my father only cared about his own feelings. He didn't give a shit about me. So he took off and didn't look back." His eyes were glassy, but he didn't cry.

I spoke, almost in a whisper, afraid of the words coming out of my mouth. "Maybe he never left."

"What?"

I raised my voice. "Maybe he never left."

"What are you talking about?"

"Everyone was shocked that he just took off without saying anything. Did you have any hint that something changed with him?"

He shrugged. "Can't remember. Like I said, I don't like talking about it."

"Why would he do that? It was so sudden. Your mom had been dead for over a year by then, right?"

He nodded.

"I've had this recurring dream. It's changed over the years, but recently, I realized it's a memory that has seeped into my dreams. And when I talked to my mother about seeing her with a man, that I saw her ... I saw her struggling with a man. And then she stabbed him." I gasped slightly, realizing I'd spoken so fast I was out of breath. "When I was a little girl, I saw her kill a man."

Quinn took a step back from the door. "I need to get back to sleep. It sounds like you need some sleep too." He closed the door.

41

I should have been exhausted, and maybe I was, physically, but I slept for only a few hours. I woke as the darkness was fading and the outlines of trees were becoming visible through our uncovered bedroom window. I ran my fingers gently down Michael's spine several times until he stirred.

He turned toward me and opened his eyes. "You look wired."

I told him about not being able to find the photograph of Conner gazing at my mother, of Quinn sitting on the fence looking like a twin to Sunday. I told him about talking to my mother and how she'd unwittingly cleared away the confusion about whether my dream was simply that or a genuine memory. That I now realized I'd seen her murder Conner Wiley.

He groaned and closed his eyes. He let his head fall back onto the pillow. He put his hand on his forehead, covering his eyes at the same time.

"Don't start giving me a list of reasons why I'm wrong," I said.

"Just the opposite." He sighed. "I'm trying to absorb it. And I'm starting to see why you've been tormented by these dreams and memories."

I told him about my conversation with Quinn. I sat up, waiting for his reaction. When he didn't speak, I got out of bed.

"Where are you going?"

"I can't sleep any more."

"Come back so we can talk. We need to figure this out."

"I need to know what Quinn is thinking."

"Not right now. I'm sure he's sleeping, since your news probably kept him awake for quite a while."

I climbed back into bed. "I feel like she's a stranger."

"Your mother?"

"Yes. She *killed* him. I feel like I don't even know who she is. How could she do something like that? It's so awful. It's ... how can you kill a human being? I don't know how you can even think about it. I've never hated anyone that much."

"*If* she stabbed him, maybe it's not about hate. It isn't always."

"Then what? And she did. She absolutely did. She admitted I saw her with him. All she did was try to lie to me and tell me I didn't see what I did, that I made up parts of it. I know that's not true. I know what I saw; I just wasn't clear if it was a dream or something I remembered."

"Maybe Conner was going to tell your father about their affair. If Sunday is his daughter—"

"Wait 'til you see the pictures. There's no doubt. They could be twins. Their smiles are identical."

"What if Conner wanted Sunday to live with him and Quinn? Or at least wanted to share custody?"

I thought about Sunday, their favored child, the focus of my parents' passionate interest in horses, their raptured attention to her. It was a good way to describe how they behaved toward her—they would kill for her.

"But what are you going to do with all this knowledge?" Michael asked. "You can't prove anything. Do you really have the stomach to accuse your mother of murder? And if that's what she's truly capable of, we should be concerned for our own safety."

I tried to think about what we were saying. Part of my mind could hardly accept the words as something real. It was the most awful thing imaginable, and I felt like I was talking about a stranger. It didn't seem possible. Had she really done it? But I couldn't forget how I'd felt sitting at the kitchen table. I could forget the eagerness with which she'd interrupted me to tell me I'd misunderstood and fabricated parts of what I'd seen, but that I had indeed seen her struggling with a man. Her mistake was in thinking I still trusted her wisdom enough to believe her view of my childish mind more than my own.

We lay on our backs, staring at the ceiling, not talking, until the sun was fully up. We showered and went downstairs. Everyone was already seated for breakfast, a full meal spread across the table. Each time I stepped into the dining room and saw my family sitting at the table, their placid faces and eager interest in the meal and whatever trivia was on their lips felt more surreal than the last.

Michael and I sat down. I listened to the conversation humming around me. I wondered if every single member of my family had slipped into insanity and needed to be locked in a psych ward, treated with medication and therapy. Michael and I remained silent throughout the meal. No one asked why we weren't talking. I suspected they were glad we weren't disrupting their illusion of normality.

As the meal was winding down, my father commanded

our attention. "Don't forget, today is the photo shoot. I need everyone looking stunning in the living room at one sharp."

"Photo shoot?" I asked.

"Ah, she speaks." My father chuckled.

"Baby brain," my mother said. "It makes you forget everything. It's the shoot for the cover of Dad's new book. You and Dad will be on the inside flap—his first grandchild." My mother beamed at me.

I felt sick to my stomach. Without looking at Jake or Collette, I felt their animosity that, once again, they were being robbed of their rightful place in my father's affection and pride.

"The back cover will feature the entire family gathered on the front porch," my father said.

"Won't that be awkward now that Sunday bailed on us? You'll get thousands of emails asking where she is," Bella said.

"It was already a problem ... with the divorce," my mother said.

Bella nodded, a look of concern creating a frown that looked almost comical.

I felt sicker with every word. The book cover? That was what they were concerned about? I wanted to hurl dishes at the wall, at their faces. What was wrong with them? Had they always been this way?

My mother held up her hand. "I had a brilliant idea about this. I realized we can do a series of photos like a collection of snapshots. Dad and me. Dad with Jake and Collette—his older two—Dad with Jake and Bella, and then we'll find a recent picture, maybe from Christmas, of Dad and Sunday."

I noticed that Michael would not be included, and I absolutely did not care. I was sure he felt the same. I wished I could escape them entirely, which made me wonder why I was so tangled up with them that I felt I couldn't.

That afternoon, while we waited for the photographer to set up his lights and screens on the porch, I stood alone in the foyer. Michael was in the kitchen, listening through the open window in case I might need support, but not wanting to be part of the *circus*.

The air in the spacious foyer shifted, and I felt someone behind me. I turned and saw Jake grinning like he was about to reel in a fish. "Ready for your big moment as the first to produce a new heir?"

"I'm not thinking that at all. I'm sick about all this pretense. I don't understand. It's a little scary."

"Ooh." He wiggled his fingers at me and made ghost sounds.

I wanted to smack him. "Sunday's world was turned upside down by that DNA test. I wonder if she wanted to find out who her father was, and they wouldn't tell her, so maybe she killed herself."

"You make up a different story every time you open your mouth."

"I'm not making up stories. I'm trying to figure out what happened. I'm trying to find an explanation."

"Whatever."

"Did you pressure her to take that test?"

He shrugged.

"Did you always know Dad wasn't her father?"

"Why do you ask that?"

"Answer the question."

"You first."

"You were always whispering that she wasn't *one of us*."

"Dad needed to know the truth. There's a lot of wealth that this family has all contributed to building in one way or another, and you know how he feels about the solidarity that comes from a shared bloodline, about purity in breeding the horses. It matters. It keeps a family unified. It connects you on a visceral level. Mom made a fool out of him and his belief system for thirty years. Thirty *years*! He needed to know which of his children deserve to inherit what he's created, and which do not. He deserved to know the truth."

"You're a vulture. And he's not even dead yet."

"Not at all. I'm protecting what he built from a vulture."

"Sunday is Mom's flesh and blood."

"Mom betrayed him. She flouted the principles right in front of him. Every minute of every day. She lied to him and forced him to raise a child who wasn't his responsibility. He had no say at all."

"So you decided it was your place to interfere?"

"Someone had to."

"Are you trying to destroy their marriage too?"

"Their marriage is fine. Dad is fine. But Sunday does not deserve to inherit any of this. You should be thanking me. More for you." He poked his finger at my cheek.

I batted his hand away. "So you killed her?"

He laughed. "No. I have no idea what happened to her. I just wanted the truth to be told. You and I are exactly the same. Isn't that what you want?"

We weren't the same at all, but I couldn't put the difference into words. It was too vast. This wasn't about inheriting my parents' estate. Besides, they were only in their late fifties. Why was Jake even thinking about their estate? It was disgusting. It was sleazy at any age, really. Michael and I were focused on creating our own financial security, not trying to grab what we could from my parents or his.

"You shattered Sunday's world."

He shrugged. "The truth hurts." He walked away to the front door and out to the porch. I heard him talking with exaggerated enthusiasm to my father, as if Jake were the savior of the family. His enthusiasm didn't even sound forced. It sounded as if he believed he was some sort of hero.

42

Since I wasn't involved with the pictures being taken on the front porch, I waited in the garden for my father to be finished. The photographer had suggested he would move to the gazebo for our father-daughter portrait, taking advantage of the ocean as a backdrop. It seemed like an unnecessary movement of equipment to me. Since he was planning to focus closely on our faces, only a blurred glimpse of water and sky would be visible. But he was insistent it was the ideal location.

When the other photographs were finally completed, we strolled out to the gazebo. We started with my father standing close to the interior wall, framed by one of the openings. I stood in front of him, slightly off-center at a three-quarter angle to ensure my bump was prominently displayed. I'd chosen a light blue fitted top that complemented my father's navy-blue shirt. Bella had forced me to sit in the bathroom adjoining her bedroom while she applied heavier-than-usual makeup to my skin and eyes to be sure my face *popped* for the photograph. I wasn't thrilled with how I looked—somewhat monstrous, but maybe that was fitting. Maybe I was allowing myself to become as freakish as the rest of my family by putting up with this charade.

My father seemed tired from the endless array of photographs that had been taken on the porch. They'd spent over two hours there. I think he'd assumed it would be a quick twenty or thirty minutes. He'd done many photo shoots before, so he should have been used to how long it could take, trying to capture the illusion of natural. Now he was impatient and edgy.

"Please relax, Dave."

"I'm relaxed."

Ed, the photographer, laughed. "Your shoulders look like two-by-fours. Should I get your wife out here to give you a massage?"

"Not necessary," my father said. "I'm relaxed."

"Talk to me about your book." Ed snapped several photographs as he said this.

I felt my father's fingers clench more tightly on my shoulder with each click of the shutter. What was going on with him? Had something happened when the rest of the family was milling around on the porch, everyone preening to look their best?

"Not sure where to start," my father said. "It's a complex topic."

"Anywhere. Annie, can you lift your chin a bit and look over here?" Ed raised his hand up and to the right, indicating where I should focus my attention.

"The title is *The Long Game*," my father said.

"Yup." Ed adjusted the enormous lens on his camera, but didn't appear to take any photos.

"I guess you know that." My father laughed, his voice taking on a high-pitched squeal toward the end, which made him laugh again. "Sorry."

"No worries. Just re-*lax*."

"Stop telling me to relax. It's not relaxing."

"Sure. Okay. Talk about your ideas; don't worry about my reaction. Focus on what you want to communicate to your fans."

"They aren't fans," my father said, his tone sharp and reprimanding. "These are people who want to live their best lives. They're good, decent men and women who want to build loving, lasting families. They aren't worshiping me. This isn't a cult."

"I didn't mean to imply that at all. I misspoke. You don't need to persuade me. Just talk. As if you were giving one of your seminars. I'm on your team."

"Good to know."

I felt my father wriggle behind me, as if he were trying to escape, as if he felt crowded by my presence. I took a step forward.

Ed took a step away from the camera. "Please move back where you were, Annie."

I moved back, lifted my chin, and turned my attention in the general direction he'd indicated earlier.

"The book is about the secrets for a satisfying long-term marriage. Paula and I just celebrated thirty-nine years of marriage, and I have a deep and broad perspective now of what it takes to nurture enduring love. It's about how to make your marriage last, not just last, but, uh ... how to keep it ... uh ..."

Ed snapped several pictures, then removed the camera lens and put it into a case and took out another. He asked his assistant to adjust one of the lights. "Keep talking. I want you to forget I'm here."

"Not possible," my father said.

"You did fine earlier. I know this gets tiring, but we're almost there."

"Are you okay, Annie?" my father asked.

"I'm okay."

"Make sure you smile. You have a beautiful smile," my father said.

"I'm fine. Let Ed give us directions, okay?"

Ed was behind the camera again. "The book, Dave. You need to talk about the book, or even your horses, anything to get your mind off what we're doing here. Your tension is written all over your face."

"Yeah. So my wife and I have a very romantic, intimate relationship. We understand ... we *know* each other. A lot of couples get bored. They get familiar with the other's bad habits and flaws, and they think they'll find someone more exciting, and they don't realize you can find excitement with the same partner for a lifetime."

"Good." Ed snapped several pictures.

"The book is about the inherent weakness of blended families. It's a trend that has fundamentally weakened our society ... and, uh ... sharing the same blood is, um ... well, I love my horses, and I let the love of what they, uh, the horses, good breeding is ... uh ... you need to know the stock and lineage ... so blended families can fracture more easily, and all these families with step-this and that and ... it introduces weakness and, um ..."

I'd never heard my father like this. He'd spent his entire career speaking in public. Sometimes his seminars had over five hundred people in the audience, and his voice was always smooth, self-assured, his words flowing like cream. He never hesitated, was never uncertain about what he wanted to say.

"You're too much in your head. You gotta relax, man." Ed laughed. "Listen to the birds, the wind. Chill out."

"I'm chilled out," my father snapped. "It's an important book, and I don't want to mischaracterize what I'm trying to say."

"You're not selling to me."

"I'm aware of that," my father said. "Annie, you're standing too close. I feel suffocated."

I took a step forward.

"No." Ed moved from behind the camera and approached us. He repositioned me. "Just tell me about the book. Don't think about the camera. Think about the miracle of life in your daughter's womb. Think about your gorgeous family, the ocean, those stunning animals over there." He gestured toward the corral. "You have it all. You must be doing something right." He returned to the camera. "Okay. Fresh start." The shutter clicked.

"Blended families have created all kinds of difficult relationships in families that shouldn't exist. There's something about a shared bloodline that connects us ... it's nature's, and dare I say *God's*, design and ..." He coughed.

The sound was ferocious in my ear, and I cringed.

Ed moved away from the camera. "I wonder if we should do this another time. The magic is gone, and I don't think—"

"There's no *magic*. It's a photograph," my father said. "It's your job to get good pictures, so get them. I don't need to give you a book report."

I'd never heard him so upset. This ridiculous exercise was bothering him more than Sunday's death or the revelation of my mother's affair. Maybe it was all just sinking in now. Or maybe he'd suddenly realized that what he'd written in his book was going to be a lie because he no longer had a family that was connected by blood. His choices were to disown his favorite child or change his philosophy. Both seemed impossible. I should have felt empathy for him, but instead, I wanted him to feel something himself. I wanted him to be devastated that Sunday was dead. I wanted him to *admit* she was dead.

"I know my field as well as you do yours." Ed removed the

lens from his camera and slid it into the case. "We've lost something here. And now the light is changing. We need to do this another time."

"My daughter doesn't live in the area. She won't be here another time," my father said.

"I'll be here for a few more days," I said.

Ed nodded. "I can come back Monday morning. Ten?"

My father moved away from me and walked to the doorway of the gazebo. I followed him, unwilling to let him run away from me when he was obviously in a vulnerable state. Maybe I could finally get him to talk. He started toward the house, and I hurried after him. I grabbed the back of his sport coat. I heard a few threads rip before he stopped.

"Careful. What are you doing?"

"Jake always knew Sunday wasn't your child."

"I don't want to talk about this."

"He knew, because when we were kids, he was always saying she wasn't one of us."

"Kids say all kinds of ridiculous things."

"It wasn't like that. He meant it. He threatened to push her off the cliff. I guess he made good on it."

I'd never seen my father angry. I'd seen him upset or frustrated, but I'd never thought of him as a man with a temper. I'd always considered myself lucky for that fact, especially when I heard friends talk about fathers who yelled, who had tirades ... worse, those who became violent.

His voice rose. "Don't you ever say anything like that again!"

"He said he would push her off the cliff and tell you I had done it. He scared me to death. I was terrified to even look at Sunday when we were kids, I was so afraid he would hurt her."

"Stop it. Don't talk about your brother like that. We're a family."

"I don't even know what that means anymore."

"Why is your heart so dark? I don't know what's happened to you. Are there problems in your marriage that you haven't mentioned? You can confide in your mother and me. We can help. We can—"

"My marriage is great. My heart isn't dark. This isn't about me."

"You keep assuming the worst about her, and now you're accusing your brother of the most horrific crime imaginable. I don't understand what's wrong with you. Jake did not kill Sunday. Don't ever say anything like that again."

"Are you sure? He's hated her all his life."

"*If* she's dead—and I want to remind you that no one saw her body but you—she jumped. She was out of her mind over that test. She just had to know the truth. Like you. What is this obsession with the truth? You act as if the truth is one thing. Truth isn't always one, simple, uncomplicated thing. And it's not always pure."

"So you *did* talk to Sunday about the test? I thought you said—"

"Your mother told me. Now let's get you inside. The wind is picking up." He put his arm around my shoulders and pulled me close. He began taking long strides toward the house.

My mother had not told him about the test. My mother had cried and begged me not to tell him. Until I'd forced the news down his throat at breakfast, he hadn't had a clue. Knowing that someone in my family had possibly murdered my sister, that my mother had killed her lover years earlier, made me feel so ill I thought I might throw up, a constantly recurring sensation the past few days. But there was nothing I could do. I had nothing I could take to the police except a lot of disturbing behavior and childhood memories.

My family wasn't built on the principles my father taught.

It was built upon the foundation of protecting the lucrative family income and the superficial appearance of a family that exemplified what my father preached.

I struggled to keep up with him, but he didn't seem concerned that I was stumbling and forced to cling to his jacket to prevent myself from falling. In the space of a few short minutes, I'd learned that my father had a fierce temper, hidden from all of us for decades, that he had the will to lie to my face, and that he wasn't all that concerned about keeping me safe for the baby's sake after all.

I wondered if he believed that Jake had pushed Sunday off the cliff. I also wondered if he had seen her body on the shore that night. Had they allowed the waves to take her away again, or had he and Jake carried her up to our property and buried her somewhere? With every thought passing through my mind, a chilling shiver followed it.

43

W hen we reached the house, the rest of the family was sitting in the living room. Bella had made tea for everyone, and they were enjoying a snack of cookies and roasted almonds.

"That was a stressful event," my father said.

No one disagreed, making me wonder what had happened when they'd been photographed on the front porch. Or was he only referring to our part of the shoot, and no one was inclined to disagree with him, ever? I expected it had been the latter, and that it might have always been that way. I just hadn't noticed. There were so many things about my family I'd never questioned and never noticed as being slightly to frighteningly abnormal. But they hadn't changed. The proverbial scales were falling off my eyes, allowing me to see them clearly for the first time.

"I think we should go for a ride," he said.

He glanced at me. "Sorry, Annie. I know that cuts you out of the family gathering, but we need this. It's always a bonding time, right? A centering time. Nothing clears my mind like riding along the cliffs on Nobility."

My father pulled his phone from his pocket and tapped the screen. "Quinn, will you get Nobility, Grace, Atlantis, Mystic, and Princess ready? We're going for a ride." He paused. "I know it's getting late, but plenty of daylight left."

He pocketed the phone and looked directly at me. "Michael will have to stay and look after you."

Michael appeared shocked at the tone of my father's voice, offended both that my father felt he needed to order my husband to care for me, and that he was dictating how he should spend his time. I went to Michael and sat beside him on the sofa. At the same time, Jake, Collette, and my mother stood and began moving toward the doorway.

Bella was on the other side of me. Before she stood, she patted my knee. "Sorry if you feel excluded."

"I'm fine."

I was pretty sure my father wanted me to feel excluded. I'd been disloyal, and that was contrary to the family principles. Excluding me wasn't about my pregnancy. It was about leaving me alone to think about what I'd done wrong, and to come to the *right* conclusion about how I could be a stronger part of the whole. About how I could repent and return to the fold.

But their leaving was what I wanted. The moment they disappeared from sight, I kicked off the high heels I'd worn for the photo session. I put on my walking boots and headed toward the corral. Michael followed after me, reaching for my hand, but missing because I was a few steps ahead. "Let's not do this now," he said.

I ignored him.

We found Quinn putting fresh water in the trough.

I leaned on the fence a few feet from where he stood, Michael beside me. Quinn saw us and turned off the hose. "What took you so long? I expected to hear you knocking on my door at sunrise."

"I'm glad you can laugh about it," I said.

"Am I laughing?"

I smiled.

He moved closer to where I was standing. "Look, I don't really see anything in myself and Sunday, but I do think she looks a little bit like my father. Maybe. A little. It's the first time I've looked at a photo of him in twenty-three years. That's how long I've hated him."

"For good reason," I said. "As far as you knew."

"Thinking about it now, it does seem ... it seems not quite right that he would be able to disappear so completely my aunt couldn't find anything about him. And I didn't know ... he never made me think he was pissed with me before he left. I guess I thought he secretly hated me. And he hid that from me? But now, if I think about it, that sounds like teenage paranoia. Maybe. I don't know ..."

I nodded.

"So it could be what you said. It's possible. Anything's possible. And your dad was away from home all the time. Your mom was here alone ... my mom had just died ... so yeah, maybe. And it sounds like you remember something bad. You seem pretty sure about it. But what are we going to do about it? There's no proof. And what does it matter after all this time?"

"Don't you care? That you hated your father your whole life? And you thought he hated you? And it wasn't that way at all? You didn't deserve that!"

"No. But there's no proof. There's nothing I can do about it."

"She must have buried him herself," I said.

He shuddered.

"Here. He must be here. Somewhere."

He looked ill. He began wrapping the hose around his arm, backing away from the fence.

"Wait. I know it sounds awful. But he must be ... here. She killed him by the playhouse, and then it was torn down. It was torn down right around the same time. I've been writing about my childhood and trying to put the dates of when things happened in order. Maybe she designed that prayer garden as a memorial to him. She was the only one who ever used it. Then after a while, even she stopped going there."

Quinn stared at me.

Michael put his hand on my forearm. "Don't."

"I think I'm right. I think she wanted it as a shrine."

Michael started to pull me away from the fence. "You're upsetting him."

"I can take it," Quinn said. "He's been gone a long time. He's been dead to me anyway."

"Still," Michael said. "We need to leave. This is all too much for you, Annie. And I've had it. Your family is not only toxic, they're dangerous. We need to get out of here."

"No. She had to bury him somewhere. We need to dig up the prayer garden, at least."

"You were five years old," Michael said. "It was the middle of the night. You can't be sure ..."

"I remember certain pieces of it like it happened yesterday. I remember the playhouse. I remember my mother telling me to go back to bed, and I remember the knife. We need to dig up the prayer garden. I'm sorry, Quinn. I know it's awful, but we have to."

The three of us argued in circles for several minutes. Finally, I left them standing there. I went to the shed, which had doors on both sides—one that opened into the corral, and one accessible from outside. I got two shovels and brought them to Michael and Quinn.

They followed slowly behind me as I walked to the prayer garden. They leaned the shovels against the tree and dragged the bench out of the way. Neither one spoke, but I could feel

Michael's irritation in his deliberate refusal to meet my gaze. While they were moving the bench, to steady my own nerves, I began picking up rocks and putting them into a pile several yards to the side of where they'd formed a rectangular border around the bench, plants, and birdbath.

Michael and Quinn left the birdbath in place and started digging in the space between it and the Japanese maple tree.

I was too wound up to sit on the bench and watch, but straining my core muscles with an unfamiliar activity, such as shoveling heavy loads of dirt, wasn't the best thing for the baby. I thought about women who worked harvesting food during their entire pregnancies until the time they gave birth, and wondered at my pampered existence, but still I watched, feeling the tension with each overturned shovelful of dirt thrumming through my bones.

After digging for a while, Quinn dropped the shovel and went back to the shed. He returned with a pick and began breaking up the dirt to make their task easier. It seemed like a small area when I'd sat on the bench watching the starling bathe, but now I realized the monumental task I'd asked of them. Still, they dug without complaint, and I recognized in the vigor of their movements that each shovelful further convinced them that I was right, and they needed to keep going, because not knowing would torment them forever.

After a while, my lower back started to ache. I yielded to my condition and went to the bench that now sat at an awkward angle on the other side of the tree. I settled on the bench. For the first time, my attention was drawn to the opposite side of the yard. Next to the prayer garden was an area that was untended, filled with wildflowers in spring, most of which had died out now that it was nearing the end of June. Beyond that was a small grove of trees that marked the edge of the woods, this one cluster encroaching onto the yard area, which continued beyond that to the far side of the house.

As I gazed into the distance and the sun shifted lower in the sky, I saw something that looked like the frame for a vegetable garden. I stood and walked across the flowerless stalks, past the trees, to the wood frame.

It wasn't the frame for a new garden after all, but the foundation of a small building. There were three rudimentary steps at the front. The layout suggested a large main room and a doorway to a smaller room, then an area that might contain a spiral staircase to a second floor. It was exactly what I remembered of the playhouse that used to stand at the opposite side of the yard when we were children. I stared at the freshly sawed and nailed wood. Someone was building a new playhouse.

I glanced at Quinn. He and Michael continued their methodical digging, paying no attention to me. If he'd been asked to build a new playhouse, wouldn't he have mentioned it? I stepped over the frame and noticed the dirt in the center of the frame had been freshly dug.

Staring at the ground, I felt the edges of my vision grow black. I reached out for something to grab onto, but nothing was there. I lowered myself carefully to one of the boards, perching like a bird on the narrow edge, my gaze fixed on the freshly turned soil.

With sickening certainty, I knew I was looking at my sister's grave.

44

They *had* found her body on the shore. They'd carried her up to the top of the cliff. While I'd been literally tied to the bed, they'd lugged her sodden corpse all the way to the backyard and dug her grave. They'd buried her here and begun building a playhouse to cover her grave forever. I was too horrified to cry. I put my head in my hands, trying to get the blood back into my head, to make the blackness and the spinning fade.

When my head cleared, I stood and stepped carefully out of the frame.

I heard a groan from Quinn and glanced in their direction. He was holding something in his hand that I could only assume was a human bone. Torn, but desperate to know if I was right about what I'd just seen, I left him alone with his gruesome discovery. I jogged to the shed. I put on a pair of safety glasses and lugged the chain saw out of the shed and carried it to the playhouse foundation. I pulled the cord and started it up.

The machine vibrated in my hands like a living beast, but I knew to keep my grip tight, and I knew how to hold it and operate the brake. I'd watched Quinn use it a hundred times. He'd even let me try using it a few times when I was a teenager, fascinated by its power. Putting the blade to the wood, I began cutting the frame.

The noise blotted out everything. All I felt was the power of its metal teeth cutting the wood, the angry buzz of it so loud it filled my entire body, making my bones rattle as it chewed through the wood. I'd cut through three boards when I heard the faint sound of someone calling my name, felt someone standing slightly to my left, shouting at me to turn it off. I continued cutting.

Sawdust and bits of wood flew around me. From the corner of my eye, I could see Michael and Quinn hurrying toward me, shovels still in their hands. The rest of my family, returned from riding the horses, surrounded me.

"Annie!" my mother shouted. "Please. You're going to kill yourself."

I continued cutting, driven by an urgency that suggested Sunday was lying beneath the ground still alive, and I had to get to her before she suffocated.

"Annie, please." My mother took a few hesitant steps forward, coming dangerously close to the chain saw blade. "I don't know what has got you so upset, but we need to talk. Please turn that off before you cut off a limb. Please."

Despite the roar of the chain saw, I heard them continue shouting my name, pleading with me to be careful, to turn it off, to tell them what I was doing. Finally, my shoulders aching and my arms growing numb from the vibration, I turned it off.

"What on earth are you doing?" my mother asked. "You could have killed yourself."

"Sunday's here! There's fresh dirt." I was choking, finding it hard to speak. I coughed from the particles of wood still floating in the air around me. I began sobbing. The chain saw was heavy in my hands, but I didn't want to let go of it. I wanted to splinter the wood into a million fragments. I wanted to ... the horror of what lay under my feet overcame me, and I let out a cry that sounded like the shriek of an animal caught in a metal trap.

"Shh. Calm down. Shh." My father was suddenly beside me, his arms around me. He pulled me close, resting his head on top of mine, pinning my head in place so my gaze was forced toward the ground. "It's okay. It's not what you think. You're so wrong. It's a playhouse. I wanted to surprise you, sweetheart. It's a playhouse for your little girl. You loved the one you had when you were small, and I wanted your little one to have something brand new."

As my father was filling my ears with his lies, Quinn placed his shovel against one of the standing sections of the wood frame. He stepped over the board the separated the two of us and placed his hands on the handle of the chain saw. I let him take it away from me. He moved to the center of the foundation and yanked the pull cord.

For a moment, no one spoke as the sound of the saw cutting through wood filled the air.

My father let go of me. He shouted at Quinn, "Stop! You're destroying all my work. What the hell is wrong with you?" He started toward Quinn, but hesitated, not wanting to get too close.

After several minutes, Quinn turned off the chain saw. He placed it on the ground and began ripping apart boards where he'd cut them enough to weaken them significantly. Wood clattered as he tossed boards to the side. He picked up his shovel and began digging.

"No!" My mother rushed at him, slapping at his arms and chest. She grabbed at the shovel, trying to pull it out of his hands. "Please don't do this."

Quinn held the shovel firmly. He drove the blade into the

ground and leaned on the top of the handle. "Is she buried here?"

"Yes!" My mother was crying softly. "Don't dig her up. Please." She let out a gulping sob. "Please." She stood there for several minutes, trying to compose herself. "I begged her not to tell Dave. I told her everything would unravel. I begged her, but she wouldn't listen. She came at me like a wild animal. I couldn't control her. I grabbed her, the necklace broke, and she fell. She ran away from me. She wouldn't let it rest, couldn't let things be, just like Conner ... wanting to tear everything apart for the *truth*. When he realized Sunday was his, when he saw how she suddenly looked like Quinn, as if she'd changed her skin overnight, he wanted her to live with them! I couldn't ... that wouldn't ... Then Sunday had to tell your father. She couldn't let it go. She had to have it her way."

"That's because you let her do whatever she wanted," Jake said.

My mother ignored him, tears continuing to spill out of her eyes. "You're a visionary, Dave. A shared bloodline is everything, and I ruined it by bringing bad blood into ours."

Quinn had moved away, and now I knelt on the freshly turned dirt, letting my tears fall on Sunday's grave. My father tried to pull me up. "I'm so sorry. She ... I couldn't believe what she was telling me, and for a moment, just one fraction of a second, it was so fast, for one heartbeat, I felt I was looking at the face of a stranger. I shoved her away from me. And she just ... she just went over. It was ..." He began weeping, his tears falling into my hair as mine fell into the dirt.

Michael came over and gently lifted me to my feet.

"We need to call the police," I said. I reached into my pocket and pulled out my phone.

Suddenly, Jake was beside me, grabbing my phone from my trembling fingers. "And what will you tell them? That Sunday lost her mind when she found out she wasn't daddy's girl after all? She jumped off the cliff? A private burial is a misdemeanor, easily solved with a permit after the fact."

"Conner is buried here, too," Michael said. "Quinn and I found ..." His voice caught in his throat. "Parts of him. I think the police will also be interested in that. Which might cast Sunday's death and haphazard grave in a different light."

"They can't prove anything," my mother said. "A little girl, walking in her sleep, decades ago? It doesn't mean anything."

"And Liam." My voice sounded limp, knowing they would quickly find excuses and explanations for his death as well. They already had.

"They ruled it an accident," my father said. "End of story."

I looked at the slowly hardening set of his lips, his eyes hidden by his sunglasses. The hint of grief a few minutes earlier had disappeared entirely. I remembered how easily and eagerly he'd lied about serving Liam a drink. I thought about him terrorizing Liam, forcing his car off the road, then climbing down the embankment to be sure he was dead, dropping his toothpick. He might even have noticed he'd dropped it and didn't bother to pick it up, knowing the police revered every word out of his mouth.

Slowly, my parents, Jake and Bella, and finally Collette moved toward each other. Dressed in their classic riding clothes, they stared at me through dark glasses, barely perceptible smirks on my siblings' faces. They were already composing their logical, well-coordinated stories for the police.

I was defeated before I started. Sunday would lie restless in an undignified grave forever.

45

In silence, my family returned to the house. Michael and I ate dinner at Quinn's place. We had time to calm ourselves over large plates of spaghetti and sourdough bread. We talked in low voices about finding Sunday's body and Conner's bones. We talked about my parents' crimes and my siblings' latent desire to remove Sunday as if she were a cancer. I cried freely and often. Quinn also grew teary. After hours of talking, I knew that despite the odds against them believing me, I needed to tell my story to the police.

My parents deserved to be punished for their crimes, even if they'd taken place in moments of panic. What kind of world is it if we never bother to put effort into anything that appears unlikely? If life is only about the sure thing, there would never be justice or glorious victories. There would be no more breathtaking love stories or lifelong friendships or any of the things that make life a thrilling and satisfying experience.

"Annie and I are leaving tonight," Michael said. "We're checking into the B&B near the Estuary. We'll go to the Mendocino police station in the morning."

"Should I meet you there?" Quinn asked.

"Yes. I think that's important," I said.

"Do you have somewhere you can go tonight?" Michael asked.

"Here is good."

"Now that you know all their secrets," Michael said, "you need to get out of here, too."

"I can't leave the horses."

"My family isn't incapable," I said. "They know how to feed them. The basic stuff."

"I would feel terrible leaving them. It's not right. Who knows if your father would even think to look after them?"

"They're a pretty dangerous group," Michael said.

Quinn stood and began clearing plates off the table. "I can take care of myself. No worries. Really."

We stayed longer, not wanting to return to the house until everyone had retreated to their bedrooms. Quinn made coffee and tea, and we talked more, as if repeating the horrors of what we'd lived through in the past few hours, and decades ago, would make it easier to absorb. Finally, Michael and I went back to our bedroom, packed our suitcases, and drove to the B&B where he'd already made a reservation for a late arrival check-in.

The bed was heavenly. I don't know if it was exhaustion or grief or good-quality bedding, but it felt like I was curling up on clouds. We were asleep before we could kiss each other goodnight.

At two fifteen, we were woken by the scream and wail of sirens. Red lights flashed through the curtains. Both of us were instantly alert as we heard two or three fire trucks race by on Highway 1, not far from our window.

I turned from the window in time to see my phone screen light up with a message from Quinn.

Fire. You might want to get over here if you can. It's bad.

Michael and I threw on our clothes and drove as fast as was safe back toward the house. We saw the flames from a quarter of a mile away. When we neared the end of the driveway, a firefighter blocked our way and told us to turn around.

"It's my parents' home! My family is inside." I found myself crying, shocked by the ferocious blend of rage and disgust and fear for their lives. The love and the grief all battling for control.

The firefighter asked us how many people. He handed me a card and asked me to sketch the layout of the second floor, showing the bedrooms and access points. He ordered us not to get out of the car under any circumstances. After he walked away, I saw from a distance that Quinn was moving the horses out of the corral, taking them to an area inland, for safety.

Michael and I sat in the car for hours, our bodies and minds numb. We didn't talk. We stared out the windshield at flames and smoke and listened to shouted commands and the incredibly loud streams of water coming from reserve tanks on our property. It seemed like we sat there for a lifetime. I saw firefighters enter the house, but I never saw one come out with anything resembling a human being.

When the flames were out, the firefighters spoke to Quinn, Michael, and me. They were gentle and looked in pain when they told us that five people had died of smoke inhalation, all asleep in their beds, so likely not suffering.

"The smoke detectors didn't go off," the lead firefighter said. "The three we've checked so far had the batteries removed."

We stared at him in shock.

"Why would they do that?" Michael asked.

The firefighter shrugged. "I've seen it before. But usually, it's only one or two where it was too sensitive to kitchen smoke and people grew tired of the alarm. But I'm guessing we'll find that none of them were functioning."

"Dave was always leaving that damn fire going all night," Quinn said, his voice strained with despair. "I told him it wasn't safe in that old fireplace. But he liked coming down to a fire ready to blaze to life in the morning."

I swallowed and felt a tightness spread across my chest. My father never left the fire going all night. What was Quinn saying?

As the firefighter asked about the fireplace screen, I sneaked a glance at Quinn. He looked calm, eager to provide a detailed answer to every question. We waited while Quinn explained what had alerted him to the fire—the sound of something crashing, which was probably a beam falling—and other details about the property and the condition of the house. He didn't know much about the house, he said, because he wasn't the caretaker. His job was the horses.

When morning came, Quinn began making calls to look for places to board the horses. After Michael made some phone calls, a van from the mortuary came to remove the bodies of my family.

They wouldn't let me walk around the property alone, but a firefighter accompanied me in a walk around the perimeter of the house at a good distance. It was shocking to see the damage. Our stately, hundred-year-old home was gutted. In the back—which was really why I wanted to walk around—I saw that the bench was back in its proper place in the prayer garden, and the rocks once again lined the area. The dirt had been raked, and other, larger rocks from the shed had been placed to create a Zen garden effect.

The spot where the playhouse had been torn apart was gone. The statue of the angel that used to sit in my mother's front garden had been moved to the area and decorative pebbles from my mother's supplies had been spread over the entire area.

Seeing it all, I knew that Quinn had avenged his father and his sister.

EPILOGUE
ONE YEAR LATER

Michael and I sat on the front porch, two glasses of chilled white wine on the table between us. We looked out at the Pacific Ocean, our view unobstructed by the gazebo that used to stand on the cliff. The house behind us was one that Michael had envisioned, and I'd fallen in love with—all straight lines and glass, the curves and softness coming from our artwork and furnishings.

Seeing the new home we'd built, Quinn was thinking about knocking down his cottage and replacing it with something more contemporary.

Michael had relocated his law practice to Mendocino. Because of the reduction in clients that came with a smaller community, he was also doing online family law consulting. Since we'd completed the house, I'd been preparing a section of our property to be a nursery I planned to open the following spring.

Inside, our infant daughter, Celeste, was sleeping in her crib while we watched her on the baby monitor. Outside, the sun appeared to be settling into the water with the same air of tranquility.

My feelings about my family had come to a strange kind of peace over the past few months, but it was a slow peace. Despite everything, my life still felt slightly distorted without them. I kept expecting to pick up my phone and see messages from my parents and siblings. The holidays had been beautiful with our little family, but so very different from anything I'd experienced before. There was a sadness at the edges, because the celebrations weren't what I'd known every year of my life. It was the shock of the unfamiliar, and the sadness of losing what felt safe simply because of its longevity.

When Celeste was born, I'd reached for my phone to call my mother. When our daughter began giggling for the first time and I took a two-minute video, I was getting ready to text it to my parents before I remembered.

How could I miss these people who spoke so much about love and forgiveness and selflessness, but were monstrous beneath the surface? Although it continued to confuse me, I was learning to live with it. Slowly.

The family principles had become knives they'd used to destroy each other.

I picked up my glass, took a sip of wine, and placed it on the table beside my phone. I closed my eyes for a moment, although I hated to miss even half a second of the flaming orange and red sunset.

My phone buzzed. I picked it up and saw I had a new email from an account I'd favorited.

"It's here." My voice sounded disembodied. I unlocked my phone without looking at Michael, but I could feel him watching me. The email was from the same DNA testing company my sister and brother had used. It confirmed what I'd begun to suspect after hours of scrutinizing the photo album I'd taken with me when I first moved out of my parents' home—the only one that remained, because everything else was destroyed in the fire. Looking at the pictures, recalling my childhood, I'd considered how close Sunday and I were in age. I'd begun to wonder how long my mother's affair had lasted. Long enough that she'd built a memorial garden for her lover.

The test results informed me that Sunday Ledger was a one hundred percent match as my sister. And therefore, I knew that Quinn was also my brother. I wondered if that was why I'd felt close to Sunday, loving her despite Jake's Herculean efforts to divide us.

My thoughts drifted to my father's final book. The photographer had found a picture of my father and me that was deemed acceptable. Now the book was out there, selling very well, my proud father embracing his bloodline, standing with his hand on the shoulder of a daughter who wasn't his, carrying a grandchild who didn't have a drop of his blood in her body. The irony almost made me sad for my father. But after one look at the book jacket, I'd given away the copies of the book the publisher sent to us, and we'd donated the proceeds to charity.

Knowing I had a brother that I respected and loved without reservation gave me a feeling I'd never experienced, a feeling I hadn't known was possible. It made me realize how painful it had been growing up under the weight of Jake's bitter envy.

I was about to find out for the first time—with Michael and Celeste, and now with Quinn—what it felt like to be part of a loving family. I smiled, picturing Quinn at our dinner table as I gave him the news.

We were going to build something new—a family built on truth and love, the only principles we needed.

A NOTE FROM THE AUTHOR

Thank you so much for choosing to read *The Favorite Child*. I hope you enjoyed reading the book as much as I loved writing it.

The idea for this novel grew out of watching several families close to me excitedly dig into the details of their ancestors through the insights offered via DNA testing. Shortly after this, I was told about a family that was damaged when previously unknown, but troubled siblings entered their lives. I was consumed by the thought of all the disruptions that might happen in a family when secret relationships are exposed through a DNA test. It's a fascinating topic, and I think I've barely scratched the surface.

I want to take a moment to give an enormous thank you to Brian Lynch and Garret Ryan at Inkubator Books. Their belief in my writing, their unique, passionate approach to developing and shaping a story, as well as their investment in getting the word out to readers has changed my writing career in amazing ways.

A special thank you to my editor, Line Langebek. She sees characters through a lens that's very much like mine. Sometimes, brainstorming and revising my outline with her feels like talking to my alter ego.

I also owe a huge thank you to Jodi Compton for her exquisite and insightful editing and Pauline Nolet for her careful attention to all the little things. I also want to thank Claire Milto and Stephen Ryan for their incredible support in preparing my books for publication and getting the word out with creativity and style.

Reviews are so important to us authors. If you could spend a moment to write an honest review on Amazon, no matter how short, I would be extremely grateful. They really do help get the word out.

Best wishes,

Cathryn

www.cathryngrant.com

ALSO BY CATHRYN GRANT

INKUBATOR TITLES

THE GUEST

(A Psychological Thriller)

THE GOOD NEIGHBOR

(A Psychological Thriller)

THE GOOD MOTHER

(A Psychological Thriller)

ONLY YOU

(A Psychological Thriller)

THE ASSISTANT

(A Psychological Thriller)

THE OTHER COUPLE

(A Psychological Thriller)

ALWAYS REMEMBER

(A Psychological Thriller)

BEST FRIENDS FOREVER

(A Psychological Thriller)

THE FAVORITE CHILD

(A Psychological Thriller)

CATHRYN'S OTHER TITLES

She's Listening

(A Psychological Thriller)

THE ALEXANDRA MALLORY PSYCHOLOGICAL SUSPENSE
SERIES

The Woman In the Mirror ◆ *The Woman In the Water*

The Woman In the Painting ◆ *The Woman In the Window*

The Woman In the Bar ◆ *The Woman In the Bedroom*

The Woman In the Dark ◆ *The Woman In the Cellar*

The Woman In the Photograph ◆ *The Woman In the Storm*

The Woman In the Taxi ◆ *The Woman In the Church*

SUBURBAN NOIR NOVELS

Buried by Debt

The Suburban Abyss ◆ *The Hallelujah Horror Show*

Faceless ◆ *An Affair With God*

THE HAUNTED SHIP TRILOGY

Alone On the Beach ◆ *Slipping Away From the Beach*

Haunting the Beach

NOVELLAS

Madison Keith Ghost Story Series ◆ *Chances Are*

SHORT FICTION

Reduction in Force ◆ *Maternal Instinct*

Flash Fiction For the Cocktail Hour

The 12 Days of Xmas

NONFICTION

Writing is Murder: Motive, Means, and Opportunity

Made in the USA
Las Vegas, NV
16 August 2022